FALLING FOR ZOE

FALLING FOR ZOE

SKYE TAYLOR

THORNDIKE PRESS

A part of Gale, Cengage Learning

GALE
CENGAGE Learning·

Farmington Hills, Mich • San Francisco • New York • Waterville, Maine
Meriden, Conn • Mason, Ohio • Chicago

Copyright © 2014 by Skye Taylor.
Thorndike Press, a part of Gale, Cengage Learning.

Thorndike Press® Large Print Clean Reads.
The text of this Large Print edition is unabridged.
Other aspects of the book may vary from the original edition.
Set in 16 pt. Plantin.

LIBRARY OF CONGRESS CATALOGING-IN-PUBLICATION DATA

Taylor, Skye.
    Falling for Zoe / by Skye Taylor. — Large print edition.
      pages cm. — (The Camerons of Tide's Way series ; book 1)—(Thorndike press large print clear reads)
    ISBN 978-1-4104-7804-7 (hardcover) — ISBN 1-4104-7804-1 (hardcover)
    1. Single parents—Fiction. 2. Man-woman relationships—Fiction. 3. Large type books. I. Title.
PS3620.A974F36 2015
813'.6—dc23
                                           2014049803

Published in 2015 by arrangement with BelleBooks, Inc.

Printed in Mexico
1 2 3 4 5 6 7 19 18 17 16 15

For Evelyn

Mom, you were the wind beneath my
wings, and I miss you.

TO MY READERS

The Camerons are a big, close-knit, often noisy, sometimes pesky, but always loving family. Descendants of hard-working folk who came from Scotland with little more than the clothes on their back and a steadfast faith in God, the Camerons are a patriotic, enterprising clan more apt to spend their spare time volunteering in the service of others than playing golf or checking their investment accounts. They've settled in Tide's Way, a little town that grew up around the old Jolee Plantation in Coastal North Carolina, and planted their roots deep.

An orphan at eighteen, Sandy Marshall Cameron always dreamed of having a big family. Then she married Cam, and her dream came true. She loves every moment of it, especially worrying about her grown children when they let her and fussing over a growing brood of grandchildren. Jake is her baby, and he's made a few mistakes in his life, but she's proud of the man he's become. She can't kiss away his hurts as she did when he was little, but her love and encouragement are always there when he needs it most. So come on down to Tide's Way and meet Jake and his family, and the new neighbor, Zoe, who challenges everything Jake thought he knew about himself. I hope you enjoy *Falling for Zoe* as much as I enjoyed writing it.

CHAPTER 1

Jake Cameron sorted through the stack of mail as he walked back up his driveway from the mailbox. With the afternoon sun of a perfect North Carolina spring day glaring off the white envelope, Jake shaded his eyes with one hand. As his eyes adjusted, he focused on the official court seal and hesitated, struck with a sudden sinking sensation. Then he flipped quickly past it, past two bills and a grocery store flyer, to a small pink envelope.

He plucked the pink envelope from the bundle and sniffed it. He studied the neat, unfamiliar handwriting. The return address was unfamiliar. A faint hint of perfume intrigued, yet puzzled. Jake had a houseful of females, but no one special who might send him scented notes. He gave up trying to figure it out and opened it.

Dear Mr. Cameron, the note began in the same neat feminine hand. *You insisted you*

9

were just doing your job, but I had to write to tell you thank you again. Your courage, going back into that house when all appeared lost to bring my little dog out, means everything to me. Buttons is all I have left in this world and I would have been so lost without him. It's re-assuring to me to know there are men like you in the Tide's Way Fire Department watching out for our safety. Thank you again, from the bottom of my heart. Dorothy Ostringer

Jake slid the note back into the little envelope. Suddenly the name Ostringer flashed in his brain like a warning light on the dashboard of his car. His heart lurched as if he'd been punched in the solar plexus. Were they related? Couldn't be. In spite of the uncommon name. It had to be a co-incidence.

Karen Ostringer and her little boy lingered in his memories, the what-ifs playing out in his imagination far too often. Logically, he knew his accidental presence at the birth of that baby had not in any way been respon-sible for the frail little preemie's failure to survive, but Jake couldn't help wishing things had been different, and it haunted him. He felt honored to be part of the volunteer fire crew and found it satisfying and rewarding. But back then he'd been a raw recruit, off-duty and alone, and he wasn't a trained EMT even now.

He shoved the pink envelope back into the pile. Then he glanced again the court seal on the large white envelope. He closed his eyes and tried to regain the sense of contentment he'd had before going out to retrieve the mail. He listened to the soft snap of his flag fluttering in the breeze and the cheerful chatter of his twins up in their tree house where they were engaged in some intense project involving beach shells and copious amounts of glue. Ava was in the kitchen fixing something new for dinner, and at least so far today, Celia hadn't done anything dumb. It might not have been what he'd once dreamed of for himself, but it was a life he'd become comfortable with.

The rumble of a diesel engine and the grinding of gears caught his attention. He opened his eyes to see a red and white van with the familiar logo of a well-known Wilmington moving company. Thankful for any diversion to replace the unwanted melancholy, Jake tossed the stack of mail onto the bench inside the garage door and stepped back outside to watch the movers.

The big van negotiated the sharp turn between the crumbling old brick gateposts guarding their little cul-de-sac and eased around the grassy little island in the center.

Jake whistled in mild astonishment as it pulled to a stop in front of the once elegant Jolee homestead that squatted firmly on the rise between the road and the tidal marsh beyond. The real estate market was still agonizingly sluggish, and the neglected building had been vacant ever since the former owner had passed away. The nineteenth century homes with antiquated everything just seemed to sit forever waiting for buyers with an interest in the unique and historic, or for investors on the lookout for cheap properties they could fix and flip.

A battered Toyota pickup truck swung around the van and pulled onto the crushed shell drive. Jake started across his lawn, intending to be neighborly and welcome the new guy on the block, whatever his plan for the place.

The person who slid out of the driver's seat took him by surprise. She had a wild mane of reddish-gold curls and a figure to grab any man's instant attention. Jake hesitated, waiting for a husband to appear from the passenger seat, but none did. The woman turned, saw Jake, and flashed him a friendly smile.

"Hi!" the woman called in an engagingly musical voice. "Are you my new neighbor?"

Jake yanked himself out of his momentary

confusion and finished covering the distance to the drive. He held out his hand. "If you're moving into this place, then that would be a yes. Name's Jake Cameron."

"Nice to meet you, Jake." Her eyes traveled down over his paint-stained T-shirt and frayed khaki shorts and came back to his face with a curious sparkle in their greenish-brown depths that made him wonder if he'd left his fly down. "I'm Zoe Callahan."

"Sorry, I'm kind of a mess. Been painting." He forced himself not to check the status of his zipper as he shook her hand briefly before jamming his hands into his pockets.

She wasn't as young as he'd first thought. Late twenties maybe, or early thirties. She was attractive in a fresh-faced, girl-next-door sort of way. What, he wondered, could have induced this engaging young woman to buy a house that was going to need an army to put it to rights?

"This time next week, I'll be the one apologizing." Zoe jerked her head in the direction of the house. "Everything will need painting inside and out, I'm afraid."

"It'll take a lot more than a coat of paint to get this place ready to put back on the market." Jake studied the peeling paint and derelict railings more closely, reflecting on how really bad it had gotten over the months the house had been vacant.

"Oh, I don't plan to sell it." Zoe's hazel eyes widened in exaggerated enthusiasm. "I'm here to stay."

"Is . . . is there a Mr. Callahan?"

"Nope! Just me and the menagerie."

"The menagerie?" Jake felt buffeted by the level of cheerful energy radiating off the woman.

Zoe waved her hand in the direction of the pickup truck. "Yup. Three dogs, two cats, and Polly. And the fish, of course. The dogs are mine. I inherited the rest when my siblings moved out and left them behind. All except Polly. She was Michael's, but his wife refused to have her around after they were married."

Jake felt like taking a step backwards. "Wow!" he said weakly, trying to imagine the chaotic atmosphere her *menagerie* brought with them. Was Polly what it sounded like? He gestured vaguely in the direction of the run-down mansion. "So, you made of money, or what?"

Zoe frowned. "Made of money?"

Jake belatedly realized that his comment was both rude and intrusive, although he hadn't meant it that way. "Just . . . it's going to take a ton of money to fix this place up. If there's no Mr. Callahan . . ."

Zoe's finely arched brows peaked into a challenge.

Now he was being politically incorrect. *Nice way to impress the new neighbor, Cameron!*

"You think just because I'm a woman, I can't handle it?"

"Well, no, ma'am. I . . ." Jake fumbled. If he was honest, that was exactly what he'd been thinking. It was a beautiful place. Old, rambling, and unique, but it had been left untended for far too long. "It's just that it needs a lot of work."

"You sound like my father." Zoe flipped her hand dismissively.

Sounding like Zoe's father was clearly not a compliment.

"Sorry," Jake muttered, mentally chastising himself. The woman definitely had spunk. "It's really a grand old place. Lots of history. Solidly built. Back when houses were built to last for generations. Here —" He reached for his wallet and dug out a business card. "Maybe you're already in the business, but if not, I'm in construction. I'd be glad to check it out for you. Give you some estimates. Make sure there aren't any serious problems you'll need to address right off. I can steer you in the direction of

15

some good craftsmen. Might even be able help out myself on some of the stuff."

That's nice! Really nice. Like I don't have enough to keep me busy as it is? Yet, even as the warning flashed into his head, his fingers relinquished the card.

Something about Ms. Zoe Callahan had grabbed his attention the moment she'd slid from the truck and wouldn't let go. She wasn't beautiful, at least not in the classic sense. Nor did she appear to be the kind of siren who would be all over his brand new return to bachelorhood. Maybe it was the way her lips turned up at the corners as if she found life amusing and dared everyone else to join her. Or perhaps it was the challenge in her peaked brows, when Jake had questioned her intentions for the classic old home.

What was he thinking? Didn't he already have a houseful of women who tested his peace and sanity? On a daily basis! Had he really just volunteered to add another?

Zoe studied the card then stuck it in her pocket. "Thanks. I just might have to take you up on it. I'm new at the whole home-owner thing."

"Hey! Ms. Callahan! You need to get inside and tell the guys where you want things put." The driver of the van approached with a clipboard in one hand. "And I need your check for the balance due, ma'am."

Before Zoe could turn away, Jake opened his mouth. "You have any plans for supper? You haven't even unpacked yet, and you probably haven't shopped for any groceries, and you're bound to be hungry." He was babbling, and he must sound like an idiot. But her kitchen wouldn't be ready to cook in until sometime tomorrow at the earliest. There was always room for one more at his table.

Zoe's mouth stretched into an engaging smile that warmed him right down to his toes and rewarded him for his impulsive offer. "That would be wonderful." Then she looked at her watch. "What time?"

"Sixish sound okay?" Jake would have to warn Ava that there would be a guest for supper.

"Six is great. Any meal I don't have to prepare myself sounds heavenly." Zoe flashed him another captivating grin and turned back to the van driver.

What have I done? Jake shook his head in disbelief. *The last thing I need is another female in my already crazy life no matter how cute she is. I can't believe I just gave her an open invitation to add her projects to the demands on my time and energy. That place is going to need a mountain of fixing up.* He had the sudden, uneasy conviction that Zoe Callahan's arrival in his life was going to turn out to be even more unsettling than the arrival of the divorce decree.

CHAPTER 2

Zoe wrote the check out and handed it to the driver, then took the clipboard and signed the delivery receipt. When the man walked back to the cab of his truck, Zoe glanced over to the spot where Jake had stood just moments before, but it was empty. Suddenly, the bubbly feeling his warm welcome had induced fizzled away.

She heard childish voices coming from a tree house perched in an ancient live oak growing just beyond the fence that separated the two yards. She noted three bikes, two small and one larger parked neatly in a wooden rack by the garage door. Of course, he's married. What was she thinking? All the good ones were, and even when they weren't, none of the ones worth having ever seemed interested in anything permanent with her. Good old Zoe! A man's best friend when he needed something. But never the woman he couldn't live without.

Not even Porter. Not that she'd wanted anything permanent with Porter either, but once she'd found herself pregnant, she'd resigned herself. In the cultural circles she'd grown up in, an unexpected pregnancy generally precipitated a hurried wedding. Zoe wondered if things might have been different if her mother were still alive. But she wasn't and they weren't.

Zoe banished the unmourned Porter from her mind and thought about what Jake had said about her new house. A sudden jolt of anxiety lanced through her. Had she bitten off more than she could chew? It was old. Really old. And it was big. A lot bigger than she really needed. But it had captivated her imagination — from the elaborately scrolled trim beneath the eaves of the porch out front to the view of the inland waterway from the second story balcony off the master bedroom. And it had history and a ton of charm.

"Where to, ma'am?"

As he hefted his end of the old but serviceable futon her sister had passed along, the younger of the two movers jerked his head in the direction of the house and pulled Zoe's attention back to the task at hand. For the next hour and a half, she didn't have time to dwell on the unknown problems

20

homeownership might have in store for her, or the sexy guy who lived next door. She and the movers hauled all her possessions from the van and stacked them in her new home. She directed the two men lugging the furniture where to put each piece and toted a lot of the boxes herself.

When the van finally pulled away from the house, she opened the passenger door of the truck and invited the dogs to get out. They took their time sniffing their new surroundings before finding a place to relieve themselves. While the dogs rooted about in the shrubs, Zoe gazed up at the place she now called home. With her new neighbor's remarks echoing in her head, the peeling paint on all that trim seemed suddenly more ominous than it had when she'd eagerly signed the purchase agreement.

Just needs a coat of paint, she'd assured herself, having fallen in love with the stately old home full of southern coastal charm. The rockers on the wraparound porch made it feel like a beach house even on this side of the Intracoastal Waterway. She could so easily picture herself sitting there on a lazy afternoon with a tall, sweaty glass of sweet tea, breathing in the salt-tinged air while her baby girl played nearby. The pillars framing the front door gave the house a touch of elegant colonial hospitality, and the beautiful wood-paneled, old-fashioned study had tipped the balance. Zoe had fallen in love with everything, from the tattered flag in a bracket by the front entrance to the afternoon sunlight spilling in the dusty second floor windows from which, on a clear day, you could see all the way to the Atlantic Ocean. Whatever Jolee ancestor had built this place, he'd picked the perfect spot.

Zoe squared her shoulders and called to the dogs as she mounted the shallow front stairs with a cat carrier in each hand. It was a great house and she loved it, even if it was going to need some work. Or even a *lot* of work.

She went back to the truck for Polly, who was muttering unhappily under the sheet draped over her cage. One last trip for the aquarium that held a plastic bag filled with murky water and two frustrated goldfish. She parked the glass cube on the counter in the kitchen and took a moment to gaze out at the overgrown back yard. Beyond the tangle of roses that had been lovingly nurtured who-knew-how-many-generations-back, a glimmer of sunlight bounced off the very blue stretch of the inland waterway. She loved everything about the house!

Reluctantly she turned away from the view

to search for the box with water bowls and pet food. Then she noticed a fruit basket sitting in the middle of the kitchen island, almost hidden by the stack of boxes one of the movers had left there. Zoe smiled as she grabbed the card stapled to the cellophane wrapper.

Welcome Home, the card said in Zoe's best friend's sprawling script.

"Oh, Bree," Zoe whispered, sinking onto a stool. "You're the best."

Zoe peeled the cellophane away from the display, removed a fat strawberry, and popped it into her mouth. Then she propped the card between two bananas and took a third one to eat.

As she peeled the banana, Zoe reflected on the events that had brought her to this place in her life. She took a bite, chewing thoughtfully. The goldfish glared at her with reproach as they hung motionlessly in their temporary confinement, waiting for her to fill their tank with fresh water and set them free. "You'll last a few more minutes, guys," she told them, and then took another bite of her banana.

When all the rest of her friends were being teenagers, Zoe had been mothering six younger siblings. She hadn't had time for hanging out at the mall, or dating, or basketball games, or any of the things most girls her age were doing, but with all except the youngest of her siblings finally out on their own, an unfamiliar sense of freedom had begun to fill Zoe's daydreams. Then, before she could decide where those dreams might take her, she'd gotten careless and ended up pregnant. Porter, the man her father had introduced her to and had clearly hoped would one day become his son-in-law, had turned his back on her when she refused to get an abortion. Even her father had thrown his hands up in disgust because Zoe wouldn't listen to his arguments in favor of placing her baby for adoption as he thought any properly-brought-up young woman should.

Only Bree believed Zoe was doing the right thing — keeping her baby and creating a new life for the two of them. Bree, who'd been Zoe's best friend since they were toddlers; who had stuck by Zoe when the rest of their peers had been out chasing boys and deciding on colleges.

And it was Bree who'd first shown Zoe this house. Bree worked at Kett's Hotel where she'd met the grandson who'd inherited the property from a man he'd barely known. Bree's friendly interest had elicited the information that the grandson was eager to sell the house quickly and return to his life on the west coast.

Zoe had been looking at condos and had been on the verge of making an offer for a unit in the same complex Bree lived in. The quaint little village of Tide's Way was close enough to Wilmington so Zoe would still be close to family. Her commute might be a tad longer, but with a lot less traffic. It was just the sort of old-fashioned small town Zoe had always liked — the kind of place where everyone knows everyone else, and there's never a shortage of busybodies eager to share the latest gossip or advice.

Bree had set up a meeting with the grandson and his realtor and told Zoe it couldn't hurt to just look. Zoe hadn't even waited for a home inspection. She'd dug into her purse and written the man a check while they were still standing in this very kitchen.

A home of my own. Zoe sighed in happy satisfaction, then looked at her watch and jumped to her feet. She tossed her banana peel into the sink until she could locate the kitchen wastebasket. Then she carried the fish tank to the sink and began to fill it. She had an invite for supper, and she didn't want to meet Jake's wife stinking of sweat and covered in dust. She dropped the plastic bag with Cleo and Titus still sulking into

25

the freshly filled tank and headed out to the truck for her suitcase.

As she stood under the spray of the shower, she was glad she'd stopped by after the closing yesterday to turn on the hot water heater. The pelting water felt good drumming against her tired muscles. *Better get used to sore muscles,* she told herself.

Even here in the shower, evidence of the mountain of work ahead of her presented itself in the cracks between the grout. She let her hand glide over the slightly rounded curve of her stomach. Her baby wasn't due until the end of September. That gave her almost five months to get the most urgent projects completed. Of course, she could do this.

Couldn't she?

CHAPTER 3

Zoe crossed the yard and let herself through the gate to her new neighbor's house. It was far newer than her own and a lot more modern in style, but still fit perfectly into the coastal atmosphere. There were only the three houses on Awbrey Circle. The third house had been built sometime in between the other two by another long-dead Jolee, according to the grandson. All three homes had wraparound porches, gabled roofs, and a view of the waterway. Zoe's house had a set of wide, shallow steps leading up to a front porch made more elegant by a row of stately columns, but Jake's had a garage built into the ground level with the living spaces above and a much smaller porch.

It occurred to Zoe to wonder if hurricanes had ever driven the sea this far inland on a storm surge. Her father had warned her about hurricanes, but she'd already been so in love with the house, it wouldn't have changed her decision had she been told that every big storm meant water surrounding the place. She glanced back at her own home in satisfaction and then started up Jake's front stairs.

She cradled the bottle of chardonnay she'd brought in one arm and knocked on the screen door with the other hand. She'd managed to dig out a relatively wrinkle-free, forest-green skirt with a matching silk blouse, so she didn't feel quite the frump Jake had met a few hours ago. She'd tamed the wild curls into a viciously tight French braid that hugged the curve of her head, but even so, wisps had escaped to curl in mutinous abandon. She tried to tuck them behind her ears and waited for her knock to be answered.

A teenaged girl with long, straight, blond hair and deep brown eyes appeared at the door, eyed Zoe through the screen for a moment, then pushed it open. "You must be Ms. Callahan? I'm Ava. Come on in." She shook her hair back over her shoulder and stood to one side to allow passage.

"I, um . . . I brought this to go with dinner, but I didn't know what we were having. I hope it's okay?" Zoe handed over the bottle of wine feeling suddenly awkward. "And please, just call me Zoe."

28

Ava smiled. "Zoe, then." She grabbed the bottle by the neck and made a gesture toward the living room. "Have a seat. Daddy will be down in a minute." Then she winked at Zoe as if they were sharing a secret and hurried back through a wide hallway toward what Zoe assumed was the kitchen.

Zoe wondered what the wink was about as she wandered into the living room. A fireplace graced the far wall with a row of photos arrayed on the mantle. Zoe moved in that direction to study the pictures more closely. Several were of the girl Zoe had just met at various stages of her young life: in a parochial school uniform with her front teeth missing, decked out all in white with a lacy veil and a suitably solemn expression for her First Holy Communion, and the last, a snapshot taken more recently at the beach in a bathing suit brief enough to give her father heart failure. Three more photos were of two little girls so alike they had to be twins — first as infants, then again as toddlers, and one of them showing off the shiny new bikes Zoe had seen parked out front. The largest frame held a family grouping that included Jake, three brothers, and their father, judging by the obvious resemblance. In front of the men, seated on a bench, were three women surrounded by several children. Zoe studied the family photo, then turned her attention to a lone portrait of a very elegant woman in a tailored burgundy suit, flawless makeup, and perfectly coifed blond hair. Jake's mother maybe? She didn't look young enough to be his wife.

"You beat me."

Zoe whipped around guiltily as if she'd been caught poking through papers on someone's desk. "Beat you to what?" Her voice sounded breathless, and she felt even more ill at ease.

Jake wore faded jeans and a bright blue polo shirt. He looked even taller than before and definitely more handsome, if that were possible. His eyes, she noticed now, were gray, but tinged blue with the reflection of his shirt. They were gorgeous eyes, fringed with ridiculously long lashes. Zoe stared, unable to tear her gaze away.

"Only woman I've ever known who could pull herself together that fast and be on time." Jake crossed the floor, a welcoming smile on his tanned face. "You've met Ava, I presume?"

Even more breathless than before, Zoe just nodded. Before she could recover, he turned toward a wingback Queen Anne chair up-holstered in flowered chintz.

"And my mother-in-law?"

Zoe hadn't even noticed the woman sitting in the flowered chair. She'd been totally silent while Zoe perused the photos on the mantle. What could the woman have been thinking of such a nosey visitor?

Jake bent over the woman and patted one hand where it rested on the arm of her chair. "Mom, this is our new neighbor, Zoe Callahan." He straightened and turned back to Zoe. "Zoe, Celia Jolee."

Celia Jolee looked up at Zoe. A smile turned up the corners of her mouth, but a look of vague incomprehension filled her eyes.

"I'm very pleased to meet you." Zoe extended her hand toward the woman.

Celia hesitated a moment, then slowly placed her hand in Zoe's. "Are you my daughter?"

"No, Mom. This is Zoe. She just moved into the house next door." Jake turned an apologetic look toward Zoe. "My mother-in-law sometimes gets confused."

"I'm nothing of the kind, Jake Cameron," Celia sputtered with bravado, then frowned. "Have I met you before?"

Zoe crouched by the older woman's chair and laid her own hand over the elegantly manicured hand Jake had patted just a few moments before. "No, ma'am, I just moved here from downtown Wilmington. I hope we can be friends because I don't know very many people around here yet."

Celia beamed. "Of course, dear. That would be lovely. Have you come for dinner?" She got quickly to her feet and turned toward Jake with a suddenly anxious expression. "It's not my turn to fix dinner, is it?"

"No, Mom. It's Ava's turn. Don't fret." Jake patted her shoulder and then went to the foot of a flight of stairs on the far side of the hall.

"Lori? Lynn? Are you coming? We have company."

When nothing happened, he called again. Zoe saw one small foot slip hesitantly into sight, then another. Slowly two little girls descended, clinging to the handrail and each other all the while studying Zoe with wide, watchful gray eyes. When they reached the bottom, Jake took one small hand in each of his and led them over to Zoe.

"This is Lynn." He placed a hand on one little girl's shoulder. "And this is Lori." He smoothed the other girl's head of cropped blond curls with his other hand. "And this is our new neighbor, Miss —" Jake looked up at Zoe with a frown of uncertainty. "What would you like them to call you?"

32

"Miss Zoe?" Zoe smiled at the twins.

Before either girl had time to respond, Ava strode into the hall and announced dinner.

"It's a disaster," Ava warned. "I'm usually a better cook, but I was trying something new. Oh, and Daddy? Zoe brought some wine. It's on the counter." Then she returned to the kitchen.

The twins bolted after her, and Celia followed them, leaving Jake and Zoe alone.

"Welcome to my world," he said with a rueful grin. "It's full of women. You should feel right at home."

Zoe looked up into the apologetic gray eyes above the lopsided grin and fell hopelessly in love.

CHAPTER 4

Jake stood on his back porch, gazing sight-lessly out over a lawn that needed mowing toward the glimmer of silvery inland water-way that passed well beyond his property line.

The meal Ava had prepared hadn't been nearly as bad as she'd warned them it would be. In fact, the vinegar and herb marinade had been quite tasty, and the steak only a little bit charred from grilling too long. Ava tended to be a perfectionist and her own worst critic. Jake liked her cooking and always let her know when she'd done well, but she let his praise slide off her like water off a duck.

In Jake's opinion, it was hard enough just being sixteen without having to feel like you had to fill in for a mother who didn't care enough to hang around until you grew up. Jake did his best not to demand too much of Ava. He tried even harder not to let her take on too much responsibility. She needed to be her own person. To have the space and freedom to find out who she was, and what she wanted from life. Beyond being Travis's girlfriend, anyway. Jake snorted in disgust.

Travis worried Jake. Travis was so much like Jake had been as a teenager — hell bent on enjoying life and equally hell bent on getting laid. And since Travis seemed to have set his sights on Ava, Jake had every intention of thwarting that goal. Jake had learned his lesson the hard way, and he wasn't about to let his daughter follow in her mother's footsteps if he could help it.

Which was why Travis, who'd stopped by unannounced just as dinner was finishing, was settled on the sofa in the den with his arm wrapped about Ava's shoulders instead of in the back seat of Travis's car parked on some dark, deserted, dead end road. At least the make out session couldn't progress beyond some torrid kissing and a grope or two. Not with Ava's father patrolling the porch outside the sliding glass doors. He'd give them another ten minutes, then go in and break up whatever steamy little scene they had going.

Jake walked to the far end of the porch and noticed the lit upstairs window in the old Jolee homestead. His mind raced back to the oddly expectant look that had lurked in Zoe's eyes as they'd stood on her porch after he'd walked her home. He'd been caught by surprise at his own unexpected and entirely male response. He'd never responded to any woman except Marsha like that. Not even in the two years since she'd walked out on him.

He'd said a hurried good night and hustled home, trying to forget the sudden surge of desire. But Zoe wasn't the kind of woman a man put out of mind that easily. From the sexy package to the sassy confidence. Or the easy, uncomplicated way she'd dealt with Celia, the twins, and Ava.

As they'd consumed Ava's charred southern grilled steak and stir-fried vegetables, Zoe had chatted effortlessly with Celia about memories from long before even his time. She'd engaged the twins in an amusing discussion about the best color to paint Zoe's mailbox and moved on to discuss the merits of a book she and Ava had both read recently. At Ava's urging, Zoe had even managed to get Jake to recount his less than heroic rescue of a mother cat with three kittens when its owner had called the fire department in tears because they were trapped in the attic of her garage. It somehow felt as if they'd all known Zoe for years.

Jake gripped the railing and let out a heavy sigh. If he were smart, he'd do his very best to keep Zoe Callahan at arm's length. That look she'd given him had stirred up needs he'd forgotten he had and wasn't sure he was ready for right now. He didn't want to ruin another woman's life by giving in to his libido with the same lack of restraint he'd possessed as a teenager. Every gut instinct in him told him Zoe wasn't the kind of woman who took sex lightly in spite of the inviting warmth in her eyes. Besides, he had an example to set for Ava and Travis. He was the adult now, and he needed to remember that.

The final divorce decree he'd received that afternoon was sitting on his dresser where he'd put it when he stripped down for his shower. He decided to leave it there to remind himself that screwing around might be temporarily enjoyable, but in the long run, it could mess up your entire life.

Marsha had been beyond pretty. She'd been hot — the kind of hot that drives teenage boys crazy. Which, of course, was why Jake had pursued her in the first place. But long before they'd lost their virginity together in the bleachers above the scoreboard, he'd mistaken lust for love. Love he'd thought would last a lifetime. Lust that had gotten her pregnant and seen them settled into married life before they were even out of their teens.

When Marsha had finally grown up, she'd discovered the last thing she wanted to be was a wife and mother. She'd avoided sex as much as possible after Ava was born, and the twins had been another mistake. Or so she'd informed Jake the night before she left, leaving him miserable and confused. He'd had no idea she was so unhappy, or that she no longer felt anything for him.

Jake didn't understand it any better now than he had two years ago. Perhaps he'd never really been in love with Marsha, even though he'd spent over a dozen years of his life believing he was. Certainly, his reaction to the divorce decree proved he didn't feel anything for her now beyond contempt. And he didn't understand women any better now than when he'd been sixteen.

He barely knew Zoe. He had no idea what her plans and dreams were, but whatever they were, he couldn't be a part of them. They were going to be neighbors. And maybe they could be friends. But that was the beginning and the end of it, so the quicker he got over this shockingly needy physical attraction, the better off they'd both be. He'd almost kissed her good night, for Pete's sake! And he knew without the least bit of doubt, it would have been a kiss with a lot more to it than just a friendly peck on the cheek.

Zoe Callahan was a dangerously tempting woman.

CHAPTER 5

Zoe spent the morning unpacking boxes and daydreaming about Jake. *Nothing will come of it,* she kept reminding herself. *Even if he thinks I'm halfway attractive right now, in another month I'll start really showing, and any interest he feels now will dry up quicker than rain on hot pavement.* But that admonition didn't stop her from remembering the warmth in his gray eyes, or the way they crinkled at the corners when he was amused. Or the flood of electric excitement that raced through her when his hand rested lightly against the small of her back as he escorted her home across the lawn in the dark.

Zoe wasn't used to being treated with such gentlemanly gallantry. Porter hadn't once walked her to her door unless he had expected to be invited in for a nightcap and some sex. Zoe had told Jake she could find her own way home, but he'd insisted. Having discovered that Jake didn't have a wife after all, Zoe had wistfully hoped the courteous walk home might lead to a good night kiss. Although she hadn't flirted exactly, she'd been approachable and willing, yet nothing had happened. They'd stood at the top of her steps while he finished telling a story about the twins, but then he'd turned away abruptly. With a brief wave, he'd taken the steps two at a time and disappeared into the gloom.

Just like one of her brothers. Now wasn't that a dispiriting thought! Zoe gave herself a shake and hefted another box onto the table. "Enough already! You're acting like a moonstruck teenager."

An hour later, having finished unpacking most of the kitchen stuff, Zoe looked around at her new domain and decided she'd been cooped up indoors long enough. She could look for the pots and pans later. Right now, she needed to find a chore out of doors. She needed some sunlight and fresh air.

Then she remembered the twins solemnly advising her to paint her mailbox, *'cause it might fall over if it doesn't get painted!* Lynn, at least she thought it was Lynn that had the tiny birthmark beside her mouth, had lobbied for yellow. Lori had been quick to suggest orange.

41

"Well, it depends on what colors I have, girls," Zoe muttered to her absent advisors as she burrowed through a carton of brushes and leftover paint her brother had donated to her experiment in home ownership. She found a small can of green outdoor paint. God only knew where that had come from since she didn't recall anything painted dark green at Michael's place. A half a gallon of white. A fraction of a pint of the sky blue his front door sported! And then . . . an unopened quart of exterior yellow enamel. "Yellow it is," she said, straightening, then bent again to rummage for a brush. Up against the side of the box, behind the brushes, she found a sheet of orange gerbera daisy decals. *You both win,* she thought, shoving the sheet of decals into her shirt pocket. *I wonder what possessed Michael to buy a bunch of flower decals or yellow paint, for that matter?* Neither was his style. Must have been his wife Connie and whatever she'd had in mind, she'd abandoned for something else.

Jake leaned against the fender of the mini-van with the hood up, contemplating his twins who sat on the bottom step of the front porch. They were communicating in the brief half-sentences that they often finished for each other and hand signals known only to themselves.

They'd always been close, but Jake had been told that twins often were, and until recently he hadn't worried about their preference for each other's company. But last week he'd gotten a letter from the elementary school asking for his decision on separate classrooms when they began kindergarten in the fall, and it suddenly seemed like it might be something he should have thought about.

Maybe he should have been making an effort to invite friends from their day care center over for play dates. Or setting up opportunities for each of them to spend time at other girls' houses on an individual basis. But it had just never occurred to him until the letter from the school arrived.

Jake made a mental note to consult their doctor. Another social issue he knew nothing about. With a sigh, he lowered himself onto the brand new mechanic's creeper his girls had given him for his birthday and returned to the task of changing the oil in the five-year-old minivan Marsha had abandoned along with her family. He'd long ago sold his beloved pickup truck with its big off-road tires and a roll bar in favor of keeping the only vehicle that could transport his

43

entire family.

For several minutes, with his body half under the van watching the oil drain into an old dishpan, he thought about the women in his life and the nagging feeling that he was living on a tightrope, never quite understanding what any of them needed or wanted from him. Only his mother had always been there for him and never asked for more than he had to give. But maybe all men felt that way about their mothers? Finally, the slender column of dirty oil spluttered and stopped. He screwed the plug back in and backed his creeper out from under the van and into the sunlight.

Wiping his hands on a rag, he pulled himself to his feet and grabbed a new jug of oil. He glanced up and noticed the twins had disappeared from the steps. With a start, he looked toward the tree house, then spied them intently watching their new neighbor paint her mailbox.

Zoe smiled at them as she dipped her brush into the paint can. As Zoe spoke, Lynn cocked her head to one side, Lori to the other. Neither appeared to have anything to say in response. Zoe continued the one-sided conversation, her paintbrush steadily coating the mailbox. Once the box itself was newly and brightly yellow, she knelt and went to work on the post. When she was done, she gestured with the brush toward the twins, then toward her house. Eagerly the twins nodded and turned to run back in Jake's direction.

Jake started to ask the girls what they had been talking about, but they dashed past him without stopping, tripped up the stairs, and disappeared into the house. What on earth had Zoe said to send them off with such single-minded determination? With a shrug, he upended another can of oil into his engine.

Whatever Zoe had said was probably based on years of experience. Ava had found an instant cohort and sympathizer when Zoe had revealed that her mother had died giving birth to her seventh child when Zoe had been the same age as Ava was when Marsha walked out. Zoe, like Ava, had ended up taking on the job of woman-of-the-house.

What an amazing coincidence that Zoe should just happen to move in next door at a time when Ava most needed a role model and a confidant who understood. Celia helped out some, but as the Alzheimer's claimed more and more of her memory, Ava had taken on ever more responsibility.

Jake's own childhood had been so very

different. He'd been the baby, and both his parents were still living. Philip, the oldest sibling, was his senior by nine years. Then came Kate and the twins, Will and Ben. They'd all had a pretty carefree time of it, and Jake couldn't imagine what it must be like to be suddenly thrust into mothering six kids when you were barely more than a child yourself.

Yet Zoe didn't act like a martyr. Her cheerful, outgoing personality belied any idea that she felt put upon and used. He wondered what her teenage years had been like. Had she had time for girly things, hanging out with her friends, experimenting with makeup the way he'd seen Ava doing with her best friend? Shopping at the mall and gossiping about who was dating whom?

Had she had a steady boyfriend? Perhaps he should ask Zoe about the boyfriend thing and compare notes about what to expect from Ava. Find out what he should be worrying about from a woman's point of view. Except that might be taking neighborliness a little too far . . . asking such personal questions of a woman he barely knew.

Jake wiped the dipstick on a rag and slipped it back into the engine, then drew it out again. He wished he knew even half as much about women as he knew about cars.

Just as he finished checking the oil level and shut the hood of the van, Lori and Lynn reappeared on the porch, clad in clothes from the dress-up box Ava had put together for them.

Lynn sported long white gloves pulled nearly to her shoulders with a lacy lavender dress that dragged on the ground. Lori had chosen a hat with a long feather curling away from its brim and a burgundy dress only marginally shorter than her sister's. They clutched their favorite stuffed animals under one arm while carefully lifting the hems of their dresses with their fingertips. Jake caught a glimpse of sparkly shoes as they began their descent to the walkway.

Lynn paused at Jake's side and tugged on the hem of his shorts. "We are invited to a tea party," she whispered in awed tones.

"Is that so?" he answered, expecting to see them head toward their tree house. He felt a pang of surprise when the twins traipsed daintily across the lawn in their finery and climbed the stairs to Zoe's porch.

When Zoe met them at the top of the stairs, Jake did a double take. Zoe had changed out of her paint-stained shorts and oversized T-shirt and into a pale pink sundress that set off her slim tanned legs to perfection. She looked young and innocent and unexpectedly pretty. Jake had a sudden inexplicable vision of himself dancing with her. Of the pink dress mingling with the darker fabric of his favorite halfway-dressy slacks. With her wholesome little body pressed against his as they moved to a slow dance tune. Jake ruthlessly cut the daydream off before it went any further and shook his head. *I don't even like to dance!*

Zoe bent to shake each small, gloved hand with solemn formality. Then she ushered them to a card table set up next to the railing and covered with a lacy tablecloth. As Jake watched, a tea set appeared, and something very pink was poured into tiny cups. Lori lifted hers gingerly to her lips and sipped. Jake smiled at the innocent picture. Lynn followed her sister's lead, and shortly a plate of cookies was being passed about. His usually boisterous little girls were behaving with amazingly grownup decorum. Jake wished he were a fly on the wall so he could listen in on the conversation. He would have to ask Zoe what kind of magic she had performed.

Then Ava rushed down the stairs and dashed across the lawn to her bicycle, and Jake forgot all about the twins and their tea party with Zoe.

CHAPTER 6

"Where do you think you're going dressed like that?" Jake demanded, his voice harsher than he'd intended.

Ava jerked to a stop with her bicycle half out of the rack. She wore a skirt made with less material than the handkerchief in Jake's back pocket. She balanced on precariously high-heeled boots that came up to her knees. The neckline of her blouse was unbuttoned far enough to leave almost nothing to the imagination. And if that wasn't enough to set his dad-radar humming, the heavy application of makeup was. The contrast between Zoe's simple pink dress and Ava's outrageous outfit couldn't have been more stark. His daughter looked like a hooker.

Ava finished backing the bike out of the rack and turned to face Jake with a look of defiance on her face. "I'm going to the park." She shoved a bulging soft-sided cooler bag under the rattrap on the back of the bike. "For a picnic."

Jake did his best to control the angry outrage bubbling up inside him. "Not dressed like that, you aren't."

Ava walked the bike toward the street.

"Ava, we need to talk."

"Daddy!" Ava shoved one hip out in a posture of exasperation. The blouse and skirt parted to reveal a smooth expanse of abdomen with something glittering in her navel. "Can't it wait?"

"No. It can't."

Father and daughter glared at each other for several long moments. Then finally, Ava jerked the kickstand down and set the bike on it. She faced him with her hands on her hips and her chin thrust out. She was pushing his buttons, and it felt like she was doing it on purpose. What had happened to the sweet, innocent girl Ava had been just a few short months ago?

"Were you going to tell me you were going out if I hadn't asked?"

"You were standing right there. I didn't think I needed to tell you I was going out."

"And you didn't think you should ask permission? Or at least tell me where you planned to go and when you expected to return?"

"I'm not a little kid anymore, Daddy." Ava frowned. "And it's Sunday. I don't have homework or anything."

"The fact that you *aren't* a little kid anymore is what worries me."

Ava began tugging on her clothing as if she'd suddenly realized its skimpiness might be the real source of his objection. She pulled the neckline of the blouse together, but her efforts did nothing for the shortness of the skirt.

"You never used to care if I went for a ride on my bike," Ava argued in what she probably thought was a reasonable tone, but actually came across as a little defensive and a lot secretive. Jake's suspicions were confirmed.

"That was before you started seeing Travis."

"What's Travis got to do with it?"

"Everything, and don't play dumb."

Ava pressed her mouth into a straight, hard line. "So, I'm meeting Travis? What of it?"

Jake surveyed her clothing, or lack of it, with deliberate thoroughness. "Do you have any idea what that getup will do to Travis when he sees you?"

"Everyone dresses like this." Ava had the grace to color slightly, but her face took on

51

an even more defiant glare.

"I don't really care what everyone is wearing," Jake bit out angrily. "But my daughter is not going anywhere dressed like a hooker."

"And you know what hookers wear how? You visit them much?"

Jake clung to his temper by a thread. "I have never been with a prostitute. Not that it's any of your business if I had, but this isn't about me. It's about you. And Travis."

"How is this about Travis? It's me you're yelling at."

Jake closed his eyes and gritted his teeth. He tempered his voice before speaking. "I'm sorry I raised my voice, but I'm your father, and it's my job to worry about you."

"I don't get why you should be worried about what I wear." Ava drummed her fingers on her thigh and smirked at him as if he were an imbecile.

"You have no idea what goes on in a young man's head, do you? You probably think what you've got on is more modest than that bathing suit your mother bought you, and Travis has seen you in that, so what's the big deal. Well, I'll tell you what the big deal is. There's nothing even remotely modest about that outfit. Any normal young man sees a blouse with half the

buttons undone and a lot of cleavage showing, and all he can think about is how long
it will take him to get all the buttons
undone. Never mind that outrageous excuse
for a skirt!

"Travis will have a boner that neither of
you will be able to ignore the moment you
show up. That's what happens to teenage
boys when girls tease them with their
bodies." The words were harshly graphic,
and Jake knew it, but he didn't know how
else to get his point across. Ava needed a
mother to explain this stuff. He felt so
totally inadequate to the task.

A flicker of doubt crossed his daughter's
face before she looked down. When she
looked up again, a look of resignation
registered on her features. "So, I can't go?"

Jake rolled his shoulders uncomfortably. If
he had his way, he'd shut her up in her
room until she turned twenty-one. But if he
said no to a picnic in the park, he'd just
give her a reason to sneak out behind his
back. Like Marsha had so often done.

"You can go on your picnic. *If* you change
your clothes and wipe that makeup off your
face."

Astonishment showed in Ava's face.

"And you need to tell me where you're
going and when you plan to be home."

"We're going to Tibby Creek Park, and I'll be home before dark." Ava rushed toward him and threw her arms around his neck. "Thanks, Daddy."

Jake returned her embrace. His little girl was growing up way too fast, and it scared the daylights out of him. At least this tryst would be in broad daylight in a public park. "Better go change. Travis is probably wondering if you're still coming."

Ava gave him a peck on the cheek, then turned and hurried up the stairs. Jake felt like he'd dodged a bullet and wasn't quite sure how he'd managed it.

He was still standing by her bike when Ava returned five minutes later, her face clean and young looking. She wore shorts that covered about the same territory as the skirt, but were far less provocative. Her jersey was cute rather than sexy, and the boots had been replaced with sneakers. Jake breathed a sigh of relief.

He crossed his arms and watched her mount the bike. "Before dark. I don't need to worry about you getting run down by a careless driver either." *Or getting hot and heavy in some shadowed out-of-the-way place where anything can happen.*

"I promise, Daddy." And she was off, her slender legs pumping hard to make up for lost time.

Jake watched until she turned the corner and disappeared. Letting go was so hard. Ava had already had to deal with her mother's abandonment, and he wanted to shield her from any more blows life might deal out. But she was growing up, and he was beginning to realize he couldn't always protect her. Some things she would have to learn on her own, and he'd just have to stand by ready to catch her when she fell. But it was hard. A lot harder than he'd ever imagined it would be. He suspected Marsha would have applauded Ava's choice of clothing. Then he wondered what Zoe might have said.

CHAPTER 7

When the merry jingle began, Zoe was unpacking linens and stacking them in the narrow closet in her bathroom. Startled by the unfamiliar sound, it took her a moment to realize it was her front doorbell. She shoved the stack of facecloths into a bare spot on the shelf and hurried down the stairs with the dogs at her heels.

Zoe shushed Scotch's barking and pulled the door open, half expecting to see one of the girls from next door and half hoping it would be Jake instead. It was neither.

Breanna Reagan surged into the house, wrapping Zoe in an enthusiastic embrace. The dogs began a merry dance around their legs, tails wagging in welcome. Bree bent to pet each eager head before stepping back to glance around the cluttered hall. "Still unpacking? Sorry I couldn't help over the weekend. Some friend I am!"

Zoe wiped a hand across her damp brow.

"Family comes first. Was your grandmother surprised? C'mon into the kitchen. My pots and pans have gone AWOL, but everything else is unpacked, and I have a big jug of sweet tea in the fridge."

"Gramma's a sly one, but she put on a good show. If you didn't know her, you'd have thought she didn't have a clue." Bree followed Zoe down the hall with the dogs charging ahead. "So what have you been eating? Takeout?"

"That and stuff I can stick in the microwave." Zoe grabbed two tall glasses from the dish drainer beside the sink and the jug of sweet tea from the refrigerator and plunked them down on the island. As Bree hiked herself onto a stool, Zoe filled the glasses and claimed a stool opposite her friend. "Did you just get back? Where's Sam? Did you drop him at school?"

Sam was Bree's seven-year-old son, born two months after his soldier-father's death in Iraq. Zoe was his godmother and doting, adopted aunt.

"He's coming home with his cousins. He was going to miss a day of school anyway." Bree grinned. "They were stopping in Kitty Hawk on the way, and Sam begged me to let him go with them so he could see the Wright Brothers' plane. Again! A lot more interesting than riding home with boring old Mom, or sitting at a desk when he could get out of it!"

Sam loved anything that flew and vowed he was going to be a pilot when he grew up. "You're never boring, but I suppose I can't blame him." Zoe chuckled.

"Has Porter been by?" Bree asked abruptly.

"I doubt Porter will ever be by," Zoe replied, shrugging. It was almost a relief to know she wouldn't have to see him again. Having become pregnant because she'd been seduced into carelessness on a romantic weekend by the sea, Zoe had reconciled herself to marriage with a man she didn't love and no longer found even mildly exciting. But Porter not only hadn't suggested marriage, he'd disowned his responsibility for her condition completely. "And I'm not sorry. Not really."

"But the man's going to be a father. He should face up to it and share the consequences. He should care at least a little bit."

"Oh, he cares." Zoe plunked her glass down and refilled it. "He cares about his career. He cares about his car. And his money. He especially cares about who he knows, and getting a partnership in my father's firm. I was just a convenience. Only once I got pregnant, I was no longer so convenient."

Bree shook her head, a disgusted look on her face. "The man's a worm. He's worse than a worm except I don't use that kind of language. What about your father? Why isn't he on Porter's case? I mean, he hired the guy, and didn't he introduce the two of you?"

"Daddy probably *is* on Porter's case, but Daddy's still hoping that Porter and I can be maneuvered into getting married, so he doesn't want to come down on him too hard. Daddy's never gotten over the fact that none of his sons wanted to become lawyers and join the firm. He figures a son-in-law is the next best thing, and Porter's a sharp litigator. Just the kind of up-and-coming guy Daddy admires."

Bree made a rude noise. "So I guess he hasn't forgiven you for buying this house yet either?"

"I don't know. He let me take my bedroom set, and he gave me my great-grandmother's dining room table and hutch, but he's probably figuring I'll change my mind once I get moved in and discover that running my own household on an office manager's salary is more than I bargained for. Of course, while the movers were loading the furniture, I had to listen to another lecture about how many couples are dying to adopt an infant. How much better off my baby would be with two parents, and how much better off I'd be without a baby at this point in my life."

Bree tipped her head side to side. "Maybe he'll change his mind once that baby is born, and he gets to hold it. Grandparents are funny that way."

"I can only hope, but Daddy's a major backer for that pregnancy counseling and adoption center. Right now, he's still pretty adamant about me giving the baby up, and he isn't inclined to listen to my feelings on the subject." Zoe slid off her stool. Her father's lack of support hurt, and she didn't want to talk about it anymore. "You have time for some lunch?"

When Bree said she did, Zoe opened the fridge to see what she had to offer. "Thanks for the fruit basket, by the way. That was so thoughtful. Unfortunately, all that's left is the pineapple."

"Never mind that," Bree said, getting off her stool and pushing the fridge door shut again. "I'm taking you to Joel's for lunch. Time I introduced you to a few of my favorite people."

"Joel's? Isn't that the diner across from your condo complex? Haven't we eaten there before?" Zoe recalled the shiny, totally out-of-character diner she'd had breakfast at the day Bree had shown her this house for the first time. Everything else in this little village fit in, even the McDonald's in a refurbished clapboard house. "That place that looked like it could have been plucked off the streets of New York?"

"That's Joel's. And Joel Shaw *is* from New York, in fact. He used to own a diner on Long Island before he fell in love with coastal North Carolina and decided to move. I think the place was some kind of prefab. One day the lot was home to an abandoned fruit stand, and the next day, a shiny new diner popped up like a mushroom. Come on. Grab your purse and let's go. We'll drive the long way around, and I can point out places you might be interested in along the way."

A few minutes later, Bree slowed her Honda Civic to make a right hand turn across from an ice cream parlor. "Best ice cream around," she said, pointing. "The miniature golf place behind it is one of Sam's favorite places." A mile or so later, she came to another intersection and pulled to a stop.

Zoe saw the old gray house with the modest McDonald's sign that she remembered

61

on the opposite corner. "I got a milkshake and a chicken sandwich there the other day but didn't hang around because I was meeting the moving van at the house."

"There's a pizza place on the other side of the VFW hall," Bree told her gesturing with her chin toward the far side of the intersection. "Not *great* pizza, but not bad either, if you're in the mood or a hurry." She turned right onto Jolee Road. Jolee Road, Zoe knew, was the main street through the little village, named after the original plantation house around which this community had grown up.

Bree slowed as she approached a fork in the road. "Abby's Bookstore is a fun place to hang out." She nodded to the far side of Jolee Road. "Big old fireplace with comfy chairs to curl up in, racks and racks of old books to poke though. And Abby is almost as old as the house. Well, maybe not that old, but she knows everyone. And on this side is Emmy Lou's Antiques. Abby and Emmy Lou are best friends, and two nicer ladies you won't ever meet. If you follow the left-hand road up to Kett's where I work and turn left, there's a Food Lion. But maybe you've already been there."

"I have," Zoe told her. "I sort of remembered there being one not far from where you lived, so I started at your place and poked around 'til I found it."

Bree put the car in motion again. She pointed out the library, a low stone building opposite the common that stretched between the diverging roads. At the next fork, the shiny New York style diner appeared. Bree pulled up out front and turned her engine off. "Stay to the right here, and a couple miles further down is Grant's Garage. You ever need work on your truck, that's the place to go. Stu and CJ Grant are the best mechanics around."

"Good to know," Zoe said as she climbed from the car. "My old rattletrap is always needing work. I was thinking of getting a new car with the baby coming, maybe a small SUV, but that was when I was looking at the condo. I think I might need to spend more than I planned on fixing up the house."

Bree opened the shiny glass and chrome door and waited for Zoe to enter. A young woman with neon-green fingernails and huge hoops in her ears grabbed two menus from a rack and beckoned them to follow without uttering a word. She sat them in a booth and promised their waitress would be with them in a jiffy.

"That girl talks like she might have to pay

per word. Not like anyone else I've met around here, most of whom you can't shut up once they get started."

"She's new," Bree said as the girl hurried back to her stool by the door. "Maybe she's one of Joel's grandkids down from the big city."

"Hey, Margie." Bree smiled warmly as the slender, dark-haired waitress appeared. "Meet my other best friend in the world. This is Zoe Callahan, and she just moved into the old Jolee house on Awbrey Circle."

Margie grinned at Zoe, her pencil-thin brows arched in approval. "You are soooo lucky. I just love that house. I wanted to buy it as soon as I knew it was up for sale, but Chuck said no way was he spending the rest of his life fixing up an old house."

Zoe felt her heart contract in alarm. Margie was the second person to hint that Zoe might have jumped at a deal with more problems than solutions, and a house in need of an owner with deeper pockets than hers. But then she remembered the early morning sunlight streaming into her bedroom through the old multipaned French doors that opened onto her own private porch with a view of the Atlantic Ocean.

"I used to deliver Meals on Wheels to the old man, Awbrey Jolee the third. I loved visiting with him. He used to tell me such tales. I swear he must have made half of them up. But he grew up there, lived in that house all his life and died in the same bed he was born in. Imagine that!" Margie rattled on. "But you didn't come in here to listen to me. What can I get you, or do you need a few minutes to decide?"

Bree shook her head and ordered the soup and sandwich combo of the day. Zoe did the same. Margie slipped the pad back into her pocket.

"I hope you'll come out to visit me some day. I promise to be a great listener, and you can tell me all the stories."

"Deal!" Margie stuck out her hand. "Nice to meet you, Zoe." Then she hurried off to place their order.

By the time their sweet potato soup and pastrami sandwiches had been consumed, Bree and Zoe had caught up on almost everything since the last time they'd been together. Almost. Margie had returned several times to check on them, but had to hurry away again because the diner had gotten busy as the lunch hour got underway.

"So, have you met the guy next door yet?" Bree folded her hands and propped her chin on them.

Zoe bit her lip and prayed Bree wouldn't

notice the sudden flush she could feel flaming in her cheeks.

"You mean Jake?" Zoe answered, trying to sound offhand.

"Of course, I mean Jake. You're blushing." Bree smirked. "I wondered how long it would take."

"I —" Zoe glared at her friend. "You know Jake?"

"Not really, but I know his sister, and I've met him a few times. He's single and good-looking. And . . ." Bree let the sentence hang while wagging her eyebrows at Zoe. ". . . his wife was a tramp who ran out on him a couple years ago. Maybe you can fix his broken heart."

Zoe felt herself flushing even brighter and wished she wasn't so transparent. "He's also got three kids and a mother-in-law with some kind of memory issues."

"And you're blushing because?"

Zoe gave in. She never had been able to hide things from Bree. "He's got the nicest eyes." Eyes that had caught her interest the first time she'd looked into them and captured her heart the second time. At least that's how it had felt. Zoe kept telling herself it couldn't be love. Not really. Love at first sight only happened in novels.

Bree's brows rose into elegant arches.

"Eyes? Hmmmm! Do I detect a romance already?"

Zoe sighed with regret. "Not likely. He's definitely good to look at. And he invited me to dinner my first night in the house. But I don't think he's interested. And if he isn't interested now, he's hardly likely to get that way once he finds out I'm pregnant. I mean, he's got three kids already. If he's looking for love, I should think he'd be looking for someone without all the baggage. Someone who isn't going to be big as a whale in a few months."

"Pregnancy is only temporary." Bree dropped her hands into her lap and leaned closer. "So tell me everything."

CHAPTER 8

"Ava tells me you were all over your new neighbor like fleas on a hound dawg," Philip Cameron said as he dropped into a lawn chair next to Jake who was tinkering with the lawnmower.

Jake jerked his head up to glare at his oldest brother. "Ava said *what?*"

"Well, maybe that's not exactly how she put it." Philip took a swig of the beer he'd brought out with him and smirked at his kid brother. "But she seemed to think you were pretty interested. I figure it's just being neighborly for y'all to invite her over for dinner, but walking her home afterward . . . ? That requires some checking into. What's she like? Is she hot?"

"She's okay, but I'm not interested," Jake flat out lied. He hadn't been able to get Zoe out of his mind, but what he'd been feeling was totally out of line, and he was determined not to act on it. Especially if Ava was watching him that closely.

Philip raised his eyebrows and pursed his lips. "Really?"

"Really." Jake picked up the file and began drawing it purposefully along the blade of the mower.

"You know, you're not a monk, and you are a free man again. What's wrong with a little fooling around?"

Jake put the file down and sat back onto his heels. He stared at his brother, wondering how much to say, or not say. He should have just ignored Philip's teasing in the first place and hoped he'd get tired of waiting for an answer. But his brother's face had turned serious and patient. "She's not that kind of woman."

Philip gazed at Jake for a long moment. "Not what kind of woman?"

"Not —" Jake shrugged. "Not easy. Not — She's a sweet, girl-next-door kind of woman. The kind a man marries first and screws after. Not someone who'd be interested in a meaningless affair. And I'm not ready for anything serious."

"Now you're sounding like me. Except I know you. You're Dad all over again."

"What's that supposed to mean?"

"A one-woman man. Dad married the

love of his life, and he's been faithful ever since."

"Yeah, well I married the woman I thought was the love of my life, and look where that got me!" Jake couldn't keep the bitterness out of his voice.

He was over Marsha. *So* over her. But rejection had hurt just the same and eroded his self-confidence. There was no denying, at least to himself, that the feelings Zoe had stirred up, he hadn't felt for any woman in years. Maybe he just hadn't *let* himself think that way about other women.

Philip hesitated. Probably wondering if he should say I told you so, or leave it hanging out there unsaid. He opted for tact. "So you made a mistake. Maybe this woman is different."

"As different as night and day!" Jake stated without hesitation. "Which is why I'm not going to mess around with her."

Philip opened his mouth to comment, but changed his mind, shrugged, and took another swig of beer.

"Any news on your next deployment?" Jake changed the subject.

"Nada." Philip shrugged again. "Right now they've got me on recruiting duty at all the local colleges and high schools. I've heard rumors though. Afghanistan in the fall, maybe."

"Be tough on Dad. Mom too. Another holiday season with their first-born in harm's way. Ever think of getting out?" Jake set the mower back on its wheels, put the file down, and got to his feet. He retrieved his half-finished beer and slouched into a chair next to his brother.

"I'm a Marine." Philip studied the label on his beer bottle. "I've been a Marine since I was seventeen. I don't know anything else."

Jake punched his brother's arm with affection. "I'm proud of you, Philip. Never think otherwise, but I'm still going to pray it's just a rumor. It'd be nice to have you home for Christmas this year."

"It would be nice for a change. Wouldn't it?" Philip lifted his beer bottle in Jake's direction. They tapped bottles briefly.

"Amen."

"Amen! Amen!" Polly rocked wildly on her perch. "Amen! Amen!"

Scotch barked, and Jet circled Zoe's feet, tail wagging furiously.

"Enough, already!" Zoe told her four-footed alarm system as she headed for the door to see who had rung her bell this time.

Ava stood beside the door, rocking from

one foot to the other.

"Hi, Ava. What's up?"

"I hope I'm not interrupting anything?"

"Nothing that I'm not happy to have interrupted."

Ava looked as if she wanted to say something but wasn't sure how to start.

"I've been scrubbing floors," Zoe offered. "Never my favorite activity. You want to set a spell and have a glass of sweet tea?"

"Sure!" Ava grinned eagerly.

Zoe pointed toward the row of rocking chairs she had inherited along with the purchase of the house. "Be right back."

After Zoe had returned with the icy drinks and they'd settled into the rockers, Ava seemed on the verge of saying something, but for several long minutes remained silent. Zoe waited for Ava to get to whatever she'd come to say.

"It must have been hard losing your mom like that," Ava finally blurted.

"It's always hard to lose your mother, however it happens. It's probably just as hard if you're sixty instead of thirteen. I guess it's natural to think of your mother as immortal and shocking to find out she's not."

Ava sighed and ran her fingers over the rivulets of moisture dripping down the sides

72

of her glass. Then she looked at Zoe. "My mom left us on purpose. She had a choice."

"That must have been difficult to understand. At least I knew my mom didn't want to go." Zoe's heart went out to this young girl who so obviously needed her mother at this point in her life. Zoe knew what it was like to be on the threshold of becoming a young woman, then suddenly thrust into the role of mother and homemaker.

"She just took off. No explanations or anything. Like she didn't care what happened to any of us anymore." Ava pushed the rocker hard, letting her hurt and anger show in the rapid movement. "Daddy's always going on about how she still loves us and it's just him she has a problem with, but how could she? How could she just go off like that if she really cared about any of us? How could she do that to Daddy?"

"The relationship between your parents doesn't affect how they feel about you," Zoe tried to reassure her. "I'm sure your father is right, and your mom does love you. She must have had her reasons for the choices she made."

"She didn't want to be a mom anymore. She wanted to be free." The note of baffled hurt intensified in Ava's voice.

"Perhaps something was making her very

unhappy, and leaving was the only way she knew how to fix it?"

"They never argued or anything. Daddy's not like that. He was devastated. I don't think he had a clue she was even thinking about leaving."

Zoe's heart contracted in distress at the picture that leapt into her head of Jake with a look of baffled abandonment in his eyes. She could only begin to imagine how hurt he must have been.

"Your mother never tried to explain it to you?" As soon as the words left her tongue Zoe knew she was getting awfully close to prying into things that were none of her business, but the question was out there, and she couldn't take it back.

"Mom left while I was at school. The twins were at Aunt Kate's house, and Daddy had been called out to fight a big fire out on the island. We came home, and she was just gone. Her clothes were gone. And her computer and all her personal stuff. But no note. No explanations. She didn't even say goodbye to her own mother."

Zoe sucked in a shocked gasp at the callousness. How could a woman do that to her own kids? And her mother? Never mind the man you'd promised to love and cherish 'til death do you part, and whose children you'd borne. "And you never heard from her?"

"Oh, she called late that night when she figured Daddy would be home. But she never said goodbye to us." The bitter angry edge to Ava's words spoke volumes about the bewildered hurt she'd suffered and still did. "And we never saw her again."

"I'm sorry," was the only thing Zoe could think of to say.

"Why should you be sorry? You didn't do it." Ava flipped her hair back with an angry gesture.

"No, but I can be sorry it happened to you. I know how hard it is to grow up without your mom around."

"Are all your brothers and sisters younger than you?"

"All of them!" Zoe reached to set her empty glass on the table beside her chair. "I'm the oldest, like you, so I got to be the mommy whether I liked it or not. And my father didn't share the cooking either."

Ava shot Zoe a look of surprise. "Never?"

"Well, sometimes he'd take us all out to eat. That was his way of giving me a day off. Eventually my sisters got big enough to help, but Daddy never made my brothers join us. That was women's work. He was . . .

is kind of a chauvinist."

Ava chewed nervously on her lower lip. She looked across the lawn toward her own house, then back at Zoe. "Did your father tell you what to wear all the time, and who you could see, and where you could go?"

"I'm sure he would have if there'd been a chance for me to get out of line. But I went to parochial school, so I wore a uniform. And when I wasn't in school, I was too busy doing housework and watching out for my brothers and sisters to go anywhere."

Ava's eyes widened in disbelief. "Ever? Like didn't you have friends you liked to hang with? Didn't you have a boyfriend?"

"I had one real friend. My best friend. She's the lady who told me about this house, in fact. But I never really had any boyfriends in high school. I guess my father would have had a lot to say about that. He's pretty bossy."

"Even now when you're all grown up?"

"Even now." Zoe thought about the royal fight she'd had with her father when she told him about her break up with Porter and her pregnancy. It was the reason she'd been determined to move out of his house and build a new life for herself that didn't include a constant barrage of negative criticism and unfair expectation.

Zoe pushed herself out of the chair and crossed to the railing. She gazed out over the still unkempt back yard to the marshes the bordered the waterway. It had been a momentous decision to spend her inheritance on this wonderful old house in the face of her father's vehement opposition. She turned back to her young visitor. "My father even picked out the man he thought I should marry, and he hasn't been too happy with me since the relationship broke up. Daddy didn't want me to buy this house or move out of his either. But I'm an adult, and I decided it was long past time to start making my own decisions. And my own life."

"Wow! And I thought my father was impossible." Ava sagged back into her rocker, then stood and moved toward the stairs as if preparing to leave. She stopped and hesitated, poised on the top step a moment before turning to face Zoe again. "Daddy says I should dress more like you. I think he liked your pink dress."

Zoe's heart jumped, and a sudden feeling of warmth filled her breast. She'd put the pink dress on hoping Jake would notice, but then he'd been in a heated argument with Ava, and she'd thought her efforts had gone unnoticed.

"Is that what the argument was about on Saturday?" Even while she asked the question, Zoe's mind was still turning over the fact that Jake had admired her dress enough so that Ava had picked up on it.

"He didn't think what I was wearing was appropriate. But everyone dresses like that. He just doesn't get it."

"Well, the outfit was a little extreme." Zoe didn't want to alienate Ava, but neither did she want to say anything that might undermine Jake.

"Yeah, that's what Daddy said. Actually, what he said was that I looked like a prostitute. And he said it wasn't fair to be a tease. But I wasn't trying to tease anyone. I just wanted to . . . I just thought . . . I wanted Travis to think I was pretty. And maybe a little bit sexy. I didn't mean to be a tease about it."

Zoe felt her eyebrows lifting at the image of Jake telling his daughter she looked like a prostitute. "Well, that's a little harsh, but maybe your father has a point." Zoe lifted her shoulders for emphasis and then relaxed again. It felt like she was walking in a minefield. "But you can be attractive without being a tease. Sometimes mystery is more effective than showing everything off."

"Wouldn't that still be considered teasing?"

"It could, I suppose, but if you dress with style and class, I doubt your father would have anything to complain about."

Ava seemed to consider this option. Then she grinned at Zoe with a look of conspiracy lighting her eyes.

"Maybe we should go shopping together?"

Suddenly, Zoe felt trapped. She didn't have a classy outfit in her closet. And what she knew about style could be written on the back of a business card. Sure, she'd had a hand in helping her sisters through the teenage years, but it wasn't like Jake knew that. He had no reason to trust her judgment.

"Please say yes."

CHAPTER 9

"That was fun." Ava grinned across the table at Zoe.

They sat at a little table outside an ice cream parlor surrounded by shopping bags, sipping on milkshakes. Zoe had been more than a little surprised when Jake approved the shopping expedition without question. Even more astonishing, he'd handed Ava his credit card without even mentioning a spending limit. One pink dress seemed hardly enough to base such faith on, but Zoe had done her best not to violate his trust.

She wondered what Jake would think of the clothes Ava had purchased today. All were reasonably appropriate, but whether they'd meet with his approval was something else. Fathers tended to be ultra conservative where their own daughters were concerned. Just to be on the safe side, Zoe had tucked all the receipts in an envelope so anything he didn't like could be returned.

"Thanks for coming with me. My mom —" Ava bit her lips into a tight, hard line, then took a deep breath and relaxed again and went on in a sad little voice. "Mom never took me shopping with her. She just bought things she liked and expected me to wear them whether I liked them or not."

Zoe tried to think of an appropriate reply. She was beginning to really dislike Marsha Cameron for her uncaring disregard for the feelings of her family. It would appear that her insensitivity had begun long before she'd walked out of their lives.

Ava brightened. "At least Daddy's going to like my new bathing suit. He hated the bikini Mom bought me just before she took off. I didn't really like it all that much, but I wore it to please her. Only it didn't matter, I guess. She left anyway." The cloud returned to Ava's face.

"I'm certain your father will approve of the replacement." Zoe hurried to redirect the discussion. Ava had chosen a very flattering two-piece suit in green and blue. A tankini top, at least that's what Zoe thought the clerk called it, and a hot pant–style bottom with little ties on the sides. A lot less revealing than the bikini Zoe had seen in the picture on Jake's mantle, but just as flattering.

"I know he will," Ava agreed. "It doesn't even show off my navel ring. Maybe I'll take it out anyway. It itches. Travis talked me into doing it, but I don't think Daddy would have said yes if I'd asked him."

"He doesn't know about it?"

"Oh, I think he knows. He just hasn't said anything. I guess he figures it's not worth arguing about."

"Maybe he's trying to give you room to grow up."

Ava's eyebrows peaked. "You're kidding? Right? He's all over me about everything else. He won't let me go to the library after supper with my friends. He doesn't approve of Travis. He's always on me about my homework. I get all As and Bs. I don't know why he doesn't trust me to get my stuff done."

Zoe laughed, remembering how often her brothers had avoided homework when they were growing up. "Boys don't take homework as seriously as girls usually do. Maybe your dad just doesn't understand that girls are different. Especially, that you're different. Have you ever talked to him about it?"

"Ava!" A chubby, vivacious brunette hurried up to the table and plunked herself down in a chair, interrupting the conversation. "You'll never guess who I just saw down by the surf shop!"

Ava ignored the urgent question as she spoke to Zoe. "This is my friend Debbie Renkin." With an apologetic shrug, Ava turned back to her friend. "Zoe Callahan is . . . She's my new next-door neighbor, and we've been shopping."

"Oh! Hi." Debbie glanced at Zoe in a distracted way, then back to Ava. "So, don't you want to know who I just saw?"

"I was trying not to be rude," Ava whispered.

Debbie flushed. "Sorry," she mumbled in Zoe's direction.

Ava relented. "It's obvious you're dying to tell me, so spit it out. Who'd you see?"

Whatever else Jake might be missing about teenage girls, he was bringing Ava up to be a considerate young lady. Zoe's estimation of him went up another notch. He was more than just a great-looking guy with a broken heart. He was a pretty decent dad.

"Travis," Debbie answered in a breathy voice filled with outrage. "And you'll never guess who he's with."

"Nope, I guess I wouldn't." Ava tried for nonchalance, but Zoe saw the look of alarm in her warm brown eyes.

"Andrea!" Debbie said between gritted teeth.

Ava's eyes widened, but she didn't otherwise react as if this were unpleasant news. "He has a right to see whoever he wants to see. It's not like we're an item or anything."

Debbie sat back, obviously confused by her friend's reaction. Then she gathered herself together and got to her feet. "Well, I gotta go. My mom's going to be looking for me. See you." She turned to Zoe. "Nice to meet you." Then she hurried away, zigzagging through the tables and disappearing around the corner.

"I suppose we should get going, too. Daddy and the twins'll be home soon." Ava got to her feet and began collecting her bags.

"Is Travis the young man who stopped by my first night in the neighborhood when you had me over for supper?" Zoe asked as they moved toward the parking lot.

"Yeah." Ava strode toward Zoe's truck with total disregard for other cars in the lot and narrowly missed colliding with a woman backing up. She stowed her bags in the truck bed and waited for Zoe to unlock the door. Zoe finessed the key into the rusted old door lock and turned it. Ava climbed in, buckled her seatbelt, and stared pointedly out the side window.

The old truck coughed to life, and Zoe pulled out, negotiating the busy parking lot to the street. Clearly Debbie's revelations had upset Ava more than she wanted to let on. Zoe glanced across at Ava's averted profile. Ava sniffed, and Zoe waited for her to decide if she wanted to confide or not.

Ava didn't look Zoe's way when she finally spoke. "Daddy was right."

Zoe slowed to avoid a car pulling out of a side street, then shot a quick glance in Ava's direction before turning her attention back to the road. "Your father was right about what?"

"About boys and sex."

"Oh?" Zoe queried cautiously. "I'm guessing he knows more about it than either of us. The boy part anyway." Without a doubt he knew more than Zoe did. She'd been too busy taking care of her siblings to date much in high school, so her experience with teenage boys had been mostly limited to what a sister knows about her brothers.

"He told me boys have a one-track mind when it comes to girls. And it's all about sex and how far a girl will let them go."

"Well, I doubt sex is the *only* thing boys think about when they're with girls, but it's probably right up there at the top of the list," Zoe offered as she thought Jake's bald assessment over. She thought about some of the things her brother Michael had confided when he'd first hit puberty. Things that had shocked Zoe at the time, but after watching three more brothers grow up she'd gotten more comfortable with.

"Testosterone is suddenly ruling their lives, and it's not just about their voices changing and having to shave for the first time. Boys are suddenly discovering feelings and urges they never had before. It's natural to want to experiment and find out more. And exciting." *Same deal for grown men as well,* Zoe thought ruefully. In retrospect, the only thing Porter had wanted from her was sex. He'd put on a good act to lure her into his bed, and she'd fallen for it.

The light turned red, and Zoe came to a stop, which gave her a chance to really look at her young companion. "Is this about your relationship with Travis?" Ava blushed and looked down at her lap. "Or about Travis and Andrea?"

"Both, I guess." Ava twisted the fabric of her T-shirt. "Andrea's got a reputation as the school slut. She hooks up with anyone and everyone. At least that's what I've heard. So, if boys are all so set on getting some, and I won't put out, then maybe that's why Travis was with her?" Tears welled up and slid down Ava's cheeks.

Zoe's heart swelled in sympathy. She wasn't so old she'd forgotten how it felt when she'd had a crush on the boy next door. He'd been the first boy to kiss her. And she'd stood there in the shadows behind her father's garage, thinking she was in love. She had believed he felt the same about her, only to find out later that her heartthrob was doing a lot more than just kissing another girl he'd met at a party to which Zoe hadn't been invited.

A car tooted, bringing Zoe back to the present and the fact that the light had turned green again. She took her foot off the brake and waved a vague apology to the impatient driver behind her. Route 17 was not a good place to be having a discussion like this.

"Travis isn't the only fish in the sea. You're a very pretty girl and —"

"But I love him."

The anguish in Ava's voice cut into Zoe with jagged intensity. Zoe wondered if she'd ever felt that strongly about a boy or a man. Certainly not about the fickle kid next door. And definitely not about Porter who she had slept with in spite of not loving him. For a moment, the memory of Jake standing so close she could feel the warmth of his skin flashed into her mind along with the overwhelming desire she'd had for him to kiss her. Had that been just sexual attraction, or had it been her heart's reaction to the look she'd seen in his eyes earlier in the evening?

Thankfully, they were almost home. Zoe breathed a sigh of relief as they turned off the four-lane road onto Jolee. Nothing further was said until she turned into her own driveway. It was hard keeping her mind on driving safely, answering Ava's questions in a responsible manner, and keeping her own feelings out of the mix. At least now she could concentrate. She cut the engine and turned in her seat.

"Look, Ava, it probably feels like love, but there should be more to a relationship than just physical attraction. You should have other things in common that you enjoy doing together. Music and your favorite artists. Mutual friends and activities you're both into. If the only thing Travis wants from you is sex, then it's not about love. At least, not on his part."

"It isn't just about sex. I know it's not. Travis isn't like that. He even said it was okay if I wasn't ready for . . . well, you know. He said he loves me, and he just likes being with me whatever we do. Andrea probably came on to him. Maybe he couldn't help himself with all those hormones and stuff. Or maybe he was just trying not to hurt Andrea's feelings."

Zoe doubted that last rose-colored explanation. Based on the breathless way Debbie had delivered her little bombshell, it was more likely the former, but then, Zoe didn't really know Travis, so she probably shouldn't judge. If Travis had moved on, Ava would find out soon enough on her own. But it was a little alarming to hear that Ava and Travis had actually discussed having sex. No wonder Jake was worried! *Please God, let it be that Travis had moved on and wouldn't be pressuring Ava into anything.* Jake would be out for blood if he knew.

"Have you reassured your father that you're not ready to jump into bed with Travis, or anyone else, for that matter?"

Ava gasped, her eyes growing as wide and dark as the centers of the sunflowers in Zoe's back yard. "Are you kidding? I could never tell Daddy a thing like that."

"Maybe you should. If he knew how responsibly you take such a decision, he might lighten up a little. He's just worried about you. Fathers tend to worry about their little girls. And trust me, you will always be his little girl, no matter how old you are."

Ava chuckled sadly. "Yeah. Daddy's little girl and all that."

"Don't knock it." Zoe wished she'd been Daddy's little girl. Or at least she wished she could remember being so. Maybe once upon a time she had been. Before her sisters arrived. Before her mother died, and Zoe had had to grow up fast and become the surrogate mom while her sisters were treated like princesses. There had been times Zoe had felt more like Cinderella than she liked to admit.

Jake's van turned in past the old brick gatepost, pulled around the circle and into his driveway. The twins piled out and ran toward Zoe's truck.

"Thanks," Ava said, unbuckling her seat-belt. "For everything. It's . . . it's nice to have someone I can talk to. I mean someone older than me. Not that you're old, but you know —"

Zoe smiled at the young woman sitting next to her. "I know. And you're welcome. Come over any time." Zoe climbed down from the truck and then spoke across the hood. "Maybe we can go shopping again. When your father's credit card has recovered, that is." *When nothing I own fits me anymore.*

90

Ava smiled. "I'd like that."

"Think about talking to your father. Seriously. He might be a lot more understanding than you'd guess."

"Miss Zoe! Look what we got!" Lynn almost ran into Zoe in her eagerness.

"Look, Miss Zoe!" Lori waved a sheet of colorful stickers in Zoe's direction.

The chance to say anything more to Ava was lost in the exuberance of her sisters' excitement, but Ava smiled before turning away. "I'll think about it."

CHAPTER 10

Zoe was up to her elbows in dishwater when she heard the knock at the door. *Please, God, don't let it be Jake,* she thought as she wiped her hands on a towel. She made an effort to pull the escaped strands of hair that curled wildly about her face back into her elastic. She felt hot, tired, and frumpy, and not in the mood for company.

Her conversation with Ava had gotten her down, remembering all the lost years of her growing up. And the boy next door she'd been so madly in love with who, it turned out, only wanted to grope her when her brothers weren't watching. And the fact that her father had never had to worry about her dating because no one had ever asked her out. That definitely wasn't going to be Ava's problem. She was pretty as a picture, as Zoe's grandmother would have said. Jake was going to have to fight them off.

Zoe pulled the door open before thinking

to look through the peephole. Jake stood on her porch looking tanned, muscular, and amazingly sexy in cargo shorts and a dress shirt with the collar open and the cuffs turned up. As her body reacted to all that undisguised masculine charisma, Zoe sucked in a ragged breath.

"J—" She swallowed and tried again. "Jake? What's up?"

"I came over to thank you. Can I come in?" He bent to pat the eager heads jostling for space around his legs.

"Sure." Zoe stepped back to leave him room, but the front hall had suddenly shrunk. "I was, um . . . I was just washing the dishes." She twisted the dishtowel in her hands and wished she could act her age instead of like a tongue-tied teenager.

"Don't you have a dishwasher?"

He was definitely standing too close. Zoe edged toward the kitchen and bumped into Jet, stumbled, caught herself, and just managed to cut off the curse that rose to her lips. "I do, but when I turn it on, no water comes into it. I haven't had time to call a repairman." She pushed past the dogs and moved into the kitchen.

"I can look at it for you," Jake offered, following her through the door. "Might be something simple."

"Oh, I couldn't ask you to do that."

"Why not? You took my daughter shopping and got her rigged out in some really decent gear without breaking the bank. I owe you."

Jake squatted in front of the dishwasher and turned a dial. Scotch immediately put two paws on Jake's knee while Jet took advantage of Jake's proximity to lick his face. Jake laughed, fended off the dogs, and pushed the dishwasher door firmly closed. He put his ear to the front panel. "Hmm!" He leaned sideways, going down onto one knee, opened the door beneath the sink, and peered into the gloom underneath it.

"Jet, come here!" Zoe called the dog away when she would have stuck her head under the sink with Jake's.

"Found your problem. I think." Jake reached in, and Zoe marveled at the play of muscles beneath the crisp white shirt. He did something beyond her line of vision, then backed out. "I wish all my problems were that easy."

Water began flowing into the dishwasher. "How'd you do that?"

"There's a valve under the sink, and it was turned off for some reason. Might be because the dishwasher leaks, so keep an eye on it. If you see water creeping out onto the floor, turn it off again. C'mere." He crooked his finger and directed her to come closer.

Close enough for her to see what he wanted to show her was too close for her libido. Now she could smell his aftershave and the clean masculine scent of him. She swallowed and tried to concentrate on what Jake was explaining.

"Just turn this to the right if you see any water where it shouldn't be." He pointed to the valve in question, and his arm brushed against her breast.

Zoe's body immediately ran amok. *I'm having hot flashes. I'm too young for hot flashes. God, he smells good! I'm as bad as Travis, for Pete's sake!*

Jake turned away from the mysteries under the sink and smiled at her. His mouth was less than a foot away, and it looked very kissable. Zoe licked her lips. Jake stood abruptly and leaned back against the sink with both hands gripping the edge of the counter.

Slowly, Zoe got control of herself and straightened as well, being careful to move away as she did. *I'm shameless. I barely know the man, and all I can think about is kissing him.* She pushed herself up onto a stool beside the breakfast bar. *He came to talk about Ava. He clearly isn't as attracted to me*

*as I am to him, and this is getting embarrass-
ing.*

Which thought immediately brought her last discussion with Ava to mind, and the troubling tidbit of information Ava had inadvertently let slip. The fact that Travis had tried to convince Ava to have sex and been turned down. Should she tell Jake, or keep the confidence and hope Ava would tell him herself? Little chance of that, Zoe supposed. Not that she would have told her father such a thing either. Good grief! The very idea made her shudder.

"I had a nice time shopping with Ava. She's a great kid, you know. You must be really proud of her." Zoe was babbling, but couldn't stop herself. Jake just stood there, braced against her sink, not saying anything.

Jake couldn't think what to say. Zoe was telling him something about Ava, but all he could think about was Zoe's mouth and how much he wanted to kiss it. *I gotta get out of here before I do something I can't take back.*

Jake jerked toward the door, then realized he hadn't acknowledged anything Zoe had said. "I, ah . . . yeah, I am proud of her." Now that the kitchen island stood between them, he felt safer. He relaxed and remembered what he'd come for. "Actually, Ava's

96

the reason I came over."

Zoe leaned one hip against the island and looked at him with a puzzled expression in her hazel eyes — eyes that were surrounded by the thickest lashes he'd ever seen. Rich dark lashes, much darker than her red-gold hair. They made her eyes look big and vulnerable. And perfect in her heart-shaped face with the sprinkling of freckles across her nose.

"What about Ava? I mean, other than that she's a great kid?" Zoe prompted.

Jake pulled away from the doorjamb and perched on a stool on the opposite side of the island.

"I don't know how much Ava told you about her mom." Jake folded his arms and rested them on the worn chopping block surface.

"A little. Ava said she left without saying goodbye a couple years ago. That must have been hard for everyone, not just Ava."

Jake shrugged. He wasn't here to talk about himself. "Sometimes I think I'm doing pretty good with her. Ava, I mean. Then we have a scene, and I feel like I'm missing something. She accuses me of not caring how she feels, but it's not that I don't care. Maybe I care too much." He shrugged. "I guess I just don't always understand. I try, but . . . but I'm just her father, so maybe I'll never understand. I don't know."

"Well, she's just a kid, so she probably doesn't get where you're coming from either. Kind of makes you even. But unless you tell her how you *feel,* she can't guess."

The emphasis Zoe put on the word *feel* made Jake uneasy. "But I do tell her how I feel. I tell her I love her all the time, and I tell her I'm proud of her, too."

"Okay, so maybe that was the wrong way to put it." Zoe pulled her lower lip in and bit it, obviously mulling over what to tell him. "Ava and I have been through a similar experience. An experience that makes us different. We talked about how being the oldest is hard sometimes even when your mom is still around. But when she's not, it's even harder. You really just want to be a kid instead of having to fill in for a missing parent. We talked about how that changed our lives and made us different from our peers. But that's only part of what's bothering her. She just feels like she's growing up, and you don't get it."

"I don't get it?" Astonishment at this accusation hit him like a slap in the face. "Did you see what she was wearing the other day? Sweet Jesus! If I hadn't noticed before, there was no way I could have missed the fact

98

that she's growing up in that rig. I wanted to wrap her in a blanket and hustle her back into the house before anyone saw her."

"That's the point I'm trying to make. Ava wants the world to notice she's becoming a woman, and you want to pretend she's not."

"But you can't mean I should let her dress like that?" Jake gasped for breath at the outrageous suggestion.

Zoe reached across the island and placed a hand atop of his. A zing of current ripped through him. His instinct was to yank his hand away, but the soft warmth of hers felt too good. He resisted the equal temptation to turn his hand over and close his fingers around hers. *Friends don't hold hands, chump!*

"No, I didn't mean that." Zoe's voice was as gentle as her hand. "You were right to send her back to change. But you need to make it abundantly clear that you not only notice that she's growing up, but that you're proud of the woman she's becoming. Treat her more like an equal when you can. She's taken on a lot of adult responsibility around your house, and in a lot of ways, she is more adult than child. Let her be a partner some of the time instead of Daddy's little girl. And especially notice the things she does all by herself that don't need direction from you. Like being a good student and being conscientious about her homework. Thank her for taking the initiative when she does something you didn't ask her to do. Would that be so difficult?"

Jake shook his head. It felt like a lecture, but he'd asked for her advice. "I guess not." Reluctantly, he pulled his hand away from Zoe's and stood up. "I am proud of her, you know. She's a really great kid."

"Young woman," Zoe corrected.

"A young woman," Jake repeated dutifully. Ava was his baby. Like Marsha had been someone's baby once. And look what had happened to her. Zoe might be right about treating Ava differently now she was nearly grown up, but damn it! Ava would always be his baby in his heart. He didn't want her getting knocked up by some randy teenager with more hormones than good sense. And he should know better than most fathers just how easily that could happen.

"I think you might be surprised by her views on sex, too."

Mother of God! Could this woman read his mind? The telltale heat of embarrassment surging into Jake's cheeks made him feel vulnerable, but he swallowed his pride and asked, "What *are* her views on sex? Obviously she's shared more with you than with me."

Zoe studied Jake without speaking for a long, unnerving minute. "Don't take it personally, Jake. I doubt there are very many teenage girls who feel comfortable talking about sex with their fathers. Probably not a lot of them who are entirely comfortable talking about it with their mothers either, for that matter. And she probably wouldn't have said anything to me except that we ran into a friend of hers at the mall, and her friend was eager to tell her some scandalous bit of gossip about Travis.

"But she does listen to you, Jake. I know because she asked me to confirm something you told her about boys and sex. Which is how I come to know that she said *no* to Travis when he pushed for more than a few tonsil-tickling kisses."

Jake's fingers curled into fists at the thought of Travis hitting on his baby. His Ava. Jake closed his eyes and counted to ten. Slowly.

"Ava has a good head on her shoulders. You've done a good job with her. Now you need to have a little faith in *her*. Trust her to make some decisions on her own. And let her know you're there for her anytime she needs backup."

When Jake opened his eyes again, Zoe had come around the island and stood in front of him. She had her hands on her hips as she gazed up at him with earnest intensity in her incredible hazel eyes. "She's a remarkable young woman, Jake."

"Yeah. I — she is." Jake swallowed hard against the confusing urge pull Zoe into his arms and hold on tight. "I guess I still owe you one."

Zoe tipped her head, her brow creased. "How's that?"

"Ava needs her mother, and I can't do anything about that. But you've helped me see the error of my ways from a woman's point of view. I appreciate your honesty."

"And I appreciate having a dishwasher that works. So we're even."

"Not even close." Jake moved toward the front door, and Zoe followed him. As he stepped onto the porch, he remembered the envelope he'd been instructed to give her. "Almost forgot. The twins asked me to give you this."

CHAPTER 11

"Jacob Andrew Cameron. Come down out of that tree house this instant!"

Jake cringed at the sound of his godmother's voice and glanced at Zoe. He'd been praying for the last half hour for a good excuse to get away from the tight confines of his daughters' tree house where he'd been attending a tea party in Zoe's honor. The scent of Zoe's shampoo and the softness of her skin every time her arm brushed his kept triggering thoughts he had no business thinking. *Be careful what you pray for,* his father's words echoed in his head. *You just might get it!* What he'd gotten was Aunt Catherine.

"Jacob!" his godmother demanded again.

Jake unfolded himself and moved toward the ladder. Unfortunately, that meant crawling over Zoe.

"Sorry," he muttered, working his way across her.

Zoe folded her knees tight to her chest and leaned back against the wall of the tree house to give him more room. "Is something wrong?" she whispered.

Jake sighed. "Something's always wrong according to Aunt Catherine."

"Jacob!"

"Hold your horses, Aunt Catherine. I'm getting there as quickly as I can." When she spoke to him in that tone of voice, he felt about ten years old. It was embarrassing to say the least and irritating at the best of times. This wasn't the best of times. He shoved his feet through the opening and lowered himself to the ground without needing to use the ladder.

Catherine Cameron waited impatiently at the foot of the tree. Her elegantly coifed head was artificially blond, and her nails were professionally trimmed, painted, and buffed. In spite of the heat and humidity, she wore a tailored navy blue suit and high heels with a burgundy scarf and matching handbag. According to Jake's godmother, appearances were everything.

"Are you ever going to grow up and act your age?"

"Not if I can help it," Jake replied flippantly. Once upon a time he'd made an effort to answer as he knew she expected him to, but it had never resulted in her approval, so he'd long ago given up trying.

"Don't be rude." Catherine turned with a haughty sniff and began walking toward the house. "I need your opinion."

Jake snorted. His godmother always *needed* his opinion, but never took his advice. He wondered why she bothered. As they approached the porch, Jake's mother-in-law was making her way down the stairs.

"Hello, Celia," Catherine greeted the other woman.

Celia frowned. "Do I know you?"

"Of course, you do," Catherine answered with barely curbed impatience.

"Aunt Catherine!" Jake hissed in warning. He held his hand out to Celia. "Where are you going, Mom?"

"Out to the garden. I thought I'd sit in the gazebo and wait for Richard."

The gazebo had been destroyed in Hurricane Bertha, and Richard had been gone even longer. Jake's heart ached for his mother-in-law. For two years, drugs had kept the Alzheimer's at bay, but recently things had seemed to take an alarming turn for the worse. How much longer before she didn't even remember who he was?

"I don't think Richard's coming today," he said gently. He drew her hand firmly into the crook of his arm and steered her in the direction of the old oak tree. "Why don't you sit in the chair under the tree where it's shady. There's a nice breeze, and you'll be comfortable there."

Celia looked up into Jake's face with a beaming smile. "You are such a dear boy. I do think that would be nice. Thank you."

Jake didn't even bother to glance at his aunt. He didn't want to see the patronizing impatience on her face. He settled Celia in an old Adirondack chair, asked if she would like a glass of sweet tea, and when she declined, left her there while he dealt with whatever his aunt had come to discuss. *What Zoe must be thinking about all this,* flashed through Jake's mind, but he didn't have time to dwell on it at the moment.

Zoe overheard the conversation going on below her with a mixture of distaste toward the unseen woman, pity for Celia, and sympathy for Jake. She'd caught a brief glimpse of the woman as Jake dropped to the ground and recognized her as the woman in the photo on Jake's mantle.

What was wrong with Jake's aunt that she didn't understand that Celia couldn't help her failing memory? For that matter, how could she treat her grown nephew with so little respect? Not that Zoe's father was any better. *I guess Jake and I have something in common after all,* she thought as she accepted another cup of tepid chamomile tea from Lori and a cookie from the plate that Lynn held out.

Zoe was still thinking about Jake and his aunt when she climbed the steps to her own porch twenty minutes later and found Celia sitting in one of her rockers.

"Celia." Zoe dropped into the other rocker. "I'm so glad you've come for a visit." *Does Jake know she's here?* "May I get you something to drink?"

"I believe I would like a glass of sweet tea if it isn't too much trouble." Celia rocked gently, her gaze drifting from Zoe to the yard beyond.

"Yes, ma'am. Coming right up." Zoe hurried inside and grabbed the phone. She dialed Jake's number while reaching for a glass and then waited impatiently for him to answer.

"Hello?"

"Hey, Jake. Did you know Celia's sitting on my porch?"

Zoe heard Jake sigh. "I thought she was still under the tree. Can she stay with you for a few minutes longer? I need to get my aunt taken care of, then I'll be over." The sound of Jake's voice, even over the phone, sent a lovely warm feeling tingling through her. But she heard frustration and maybe a hint of sadness in his tone. She could relate to that. That was how she felt every time she had to listen to one of her father's harangues.

"Sure. No need to hurry. I wasn't going anywhere anyway."

Quickly she hung up and filled the glass from the pitcher in the fridge, then headed back to the porch. "Here you are," Zoe said, pressing the tall glass into the older woman's hands.

Celia brought her gaze back to Zoe. "Have you seen Martin yet?"

"Martin?" Zoe felt her eyes widen in surprise at the suddenly clear and intense tone of Celia's question. Zoe had never heard of anyone named Martin and had no idea to whom Celia might be referring.

Celia leaned forward to whisper confidentially. "Martin grew up here."

Well, that explained not having met the man. He was another memory from Celia's past.

"Martin's great-great-grandfather built this house, you know."

Zoe hadn't known. But who was Martin? Other than another Jolee family member?

"Martin was a soldier," Celia went on, as

if reading Zoe's mind. "He went off to fight in Korea. He never had a proper funeral because his body never came home. But his spirit did, and he sometimes appears around people he likes. This is the only home he ever knew, so I guess it's natural he'd want to be here."

"How do you know all this?" Zoe felt more curiosity than alarm at the idea that the ghost of a young soldier might be skulking about her house.

"I married Martin's brother." Celia smiled wistfully. "Richard was too young to fight in that war. He went to Vietnam instead. We were married as soon as he got out of the Army. Richard built a house for us right next door, and Marsha grew up in that house." Celia frowned. "But she's gone now, too."

Zoe still had a hard time wrapping her heart and mind around the idea of a woman who could turn her back on her entire family. Falling out of love with one's husband was distressingly common, but to leave an ailing mother and three daughters behind? How could any woman be so uncaring and selfish?

A wistful look of rejection clouded Celia's features, and Zoe hurried to banish the unwanted memory. "Tell me about Martin.

What's he like?" Might as well get the facts straight before she encountered any ghosts that might be lurking.

Celia had lived on Awbrey Circle her entire adult life. In a house her husband built on Jolee land. And Jake is apparently living in his mother-in-law's house rather than the other way around. I bet Celia could tell a lot of interesting old stories. If she could remember them.

Celia's smile returned. "Martin was so handsome, and he was such a sweet man. He was older than me. He was always nice to me, but he never noticed how we had so many things in common." Celia sighed, then brightened again. "He loved animals. I love animals, too, you know. He had a dog named Pounce and a cat called Whiskers, and he fed the wild animals, too. Deer would walk right up and take food from his hand."

If ghosts really exist, I guess I can expect a visit one of these days. I've filled his house with half a dozen animals. Maybe I should set up bird feeders and start tossing nuts out for the squirrels.

"He would never hurt you." Celia patted Zoe's hand. "So you needn't worry. But, sometimes he forgets to close the doors."

Jake appeared and took the stairs two at a

110

time, interrupting Celia's wandering memories. "Hey, Mom. Ready to come home yet?" He bent to kiss Celia's powdered cheek. Then he looked at Zoe. "Thanks. Now I really owe you."

A number of possible ways Jake could reward her flashed through Zoe's mind, but all were X-rated. She chided herself for her silliness. "I've enjoyed our visit. Celia told me all about Martin."

Jake rolled his eyes. He apparently didn't believe in Celia's ghost.

"She told me that she's lived in this neighborhood most of her life."

"All her life," Jake corrected. He gestured with the sweep of an arm, taking in the three homes that graced the little neighborhood. "Celia grew up in the Cliffords' house and married the youngest son of the man who inherited yours. When they married, her husband, Richard, built the house I live in. Celia's maiden name was Clifford, and Bill Clifford is her father's much younger brother's son. So Bill is her cousin, and I think that makes Bill's son Danny her second cousin, or is that first cousin once removed? I can never get that straight. Anyway, we're all related somehow."

"All except for me." Zoe suddenly felt left out. Which was absurd. She had a family of her own. Just because they lived in Wilmington proper, and she'd moved to this little bedroom town where the old Jolee Plantation land once stood, didn't mean she didn't still belong.

"Well, they adopted me, maybe they'll adopt you. You can be an honorary Clifford, or a Jolee if you prefer. Personally, I'd stick with Clifford. I know you've met Danny. I've seen him playing with your dogs, but have you met Bill and Carrie yet?"

"They had me over to supper the other night." Zoe got to her feet. "I'll have to ask about the adoption option next time."

"Jake?" Celia stood and frowned at Zoe. "Why am I here?"

"You came to visit, Mom. Would you like to go home now?"

"Yes, I think that would be best. I don't think I should be here when Martin comes."

Jake glanced at Zoe and shrugged.

"Please come again, Mrs. Jolee. I've so enjoyed your visit and hearing all about Martin." Zoe bent to kiss the older woman's cheek.

Celia looked pleased with the familiarity and reached up to tuck a stray curl behind Zoe's ear. "Please, just call me Celia. You'll take good care of Martin?"

"You can count on me, ma'am."

As she watched Jake guide his mother-in-law across the lawn, Zoe realized she should have asked if it was all the doors Martin tended to leave open or just one in particular. Then she gave herself a mental shake. *There is no ghost, you idiot. I've been here the better part of a month. Surely I'd have noticed a ghost leaving doors open before now?*

By the end of the week, Zoe was no longer so sure about the house not being haunted. The first morning after Celia's visit, when Zoe had come down to breakfast, she'd found the front door ajar. She'd closed it carefully, trying to picture herself shutting and locking it the night before. But the more she thought about it, the less certain she was about what she remembered or didn't remember.

Two days later the French doors in the study were open, and the long lacy curtains wafted gently in the morning breeze. That incident had been pretty easy to justify since the afternoon before Zoe had stopped on her way home from work to get the new bird feeders. After she'd hung them along her back fence, she distinctly recalled standing at the porch railing admiring her magnificent view of the waterway and the dunes beyond. But when she had retreated to the study to watch out the partially open doors as the birds began to discover their new feeding stations, a squirrel had shown up. His antics as he tried to hang upside down to shake seed out of the feeder had made her laugh out loud, which prompted Polly to join in with raucous laughter. Zoe'd had to restrain Jet from taking off in a mad dash to catch the squirrel before it made it back to safety. She must have gotten sidetracked by the dogs and forgotten to return and latch the doors.

Besides, she kept telling herself, *if there were really a ghost, wouldn't the dogs have barked at it?* Scotch at least. He barked at everything. Even the cats had continued strutting about with their noses in the air as if they owned the place with no one and nothing to challenge that belief. Surely, the cats would have noticed an unexplained presence in the house and meowed their disapproval. Wouldn't they?

On Thursday, after a quiet day at work, Zoe decided to organize the closet under the stairs. At the far corner, hidden in the shadows, she found a box and dragged it out to investigate. Old newspapers with headlines from significant dates in history filled most of the box. Neil Armstrong's first

114

steps on the moon. The assassinations of JFK and Martin Luther King. Zoe scanned through the yellowed reminders of America's past, then at the very bottom of the box she found a framed photo of a young man in uniform. Zoe carried the frame to the kitchen and cleaned the glass. He was a handsome young man, dressed in old-fashioned army greens. Was this Martin Jolee? Or perhaps his younger brother Richard?

For reasons she didn't totally think through, Zoe took the photo into the living room and set it on the mantle next to a wedding portrait of her parents and a group snapshot of her siblings, her sister-in-law, and her nephew taken the previous Christmas.

Zoe's gaze lingered over the group photo, marveling for the zillionth time how beautiful both her sisters were and how different she was. Erin and Kelly had smooth ink-black hair and clear ivory complexions, while Zoe's flaming red mop frizzed out of control and a thousand freckles marched across her face. She was definitely the changeling in the family. No wonder no man had ever looked at her with desire in his eyes.

With a sad snort of self-mockery, she

returned her gaze to the young soldier.

"Are you Martin?" she asked the silent, solemn man. "Did you leave my doors open? Because if you did, I'd prefer you leave them shut. You can come and go any time you like, but if you don't mind, could you please make sure to close the door after you?"

Zoe laughed out loud at her absurdity, and Jet tipped her head at the sound of Zoe's voice.

"I know." Zoe scratched Jet's ears. "How dumb is that? Talking to a ghost. The picture of a ghost even!"

The following morning, the kitchen door was ajar.

CHAPTER 12

Zoe had just finished painting the cabinets a clean, crisp white when a soft knock came from outside her kitchen door. Scotch started barking. Hoover began to wag his tail, and Jet ran to find a toy. That meant friend, so Zoe hurried to open the door. Scotch dashed out and immediately began dancing around Jake's legs. With a tool belt slung around his lean hips and a tank top that showcased his muscular torso, he looked wonderful. Zoe pushed the inevitable mop of escaping curls back into her elastic and wondered if he'd ever get a chance to see her at her best, rather than at her frumpiest. Then she noticed his eyes.

She stepped aside and invited him in. "Don't tell me Celia's ghost was haunting you, too?" Smudges of exhaustion colored the skin beneath his eyes.

"Martin wouldn't bother me, even if I did believe in his ghost. This the door that's giving you problems?"

"This is the one. Doesn't want to stay shut, but you didn't have to come over today to fix it. It could have waited."

"Waited for what?" Jake's eyebrows rose into questioning little arcs. "For someone to break in and rob you? Or worse?"

"I didn't think this was that kind of neighborhood."

"It isn't, but a woman alone . . . I thought you'd want to know the doors could be secured. Besides, no point in putting it off."

"But you look like you didn't sleep much last night."

"Got called out to a fire. I'm used to it."

"Oh, my gosh. Was anyone hurt?"

"No, thank God. Someone left the burner on under the fryer at the Crab Shack down by the bridge. That place was a tinderbox. If you'd been awake, you'd have been able to see the glow in the sky. But we managed to contain it to just the one building. Place is a total loss, but no one was there at two in the morning, so no one got hurt."

"And I never got to try the crab cakes. I heard they were the best."

"They'll rebuild. I'll take you out to celebrate when they reopen. Now, what's up with the door?"

Had Jake just asked her out for a date?

Albeit, some unknown date in the future, but still . . . Her heart fluttered excitedly.

"The door?" Jake prompted, looking at her oddly.

Right! The door was the real reason he'd come. Not to ask her out. "I — I thought maybe I just forgot to shut it the first time. But after Celia told me about Martin and how he leaves doors open all the time, I began to get a little spooked." Zoe shrugged. "It just keeps happening. I push the door shut, and if I stand there long enough, it opens again all by itself."

Zoe reached past Jake and shut the door firmly, then waited. A minute stretched into two, and then suddenly, with a faint click, the door popped open and began to swing inward.

"See? No ghost! But it beats me why it won't stay shut."

Jake hunkered down into a squat and began tinkering with the lock mechanism. Twice he pushed the door shut and waited until it popped open again. Jet sat next to him, all attention riveted on the door, and each time it opened, she swiveled her gaze to Jake as if making a point. Jake patted her head, then stood. "Don't worry, girl. We'll get it sorted out."

"Just the house settling." Jake turned his

attention to Zoe. "I only wish my problems were as easy to solve as yours."

"That's what you said last time, but they don't seem all that easy to me. When I bought this place, I never imagined all the things that could go wrong. Maybe I should have listened to my father after all."

"What? And miss all the fun of home ownership? Think of it as an adventure." Jake smiled, and some of the tiredness seemed to leave his eyes. "Besides, this house has history."

"I just never appreciated what my father's checkbook could do for getting stuff fixed." And that was the humbling truth. Her father had warned her about the costs, but she'd ignored him, thinking she'd just take care of things herself. How hard could it be? At least that was the attitude she'd focused on as she'd cruised through the hardware store picking out tools she thought she might need. It had never occurred to her that she might not have a clue how to use the tools when problems arose.

Jake ducked outside and came back with a long wooden toolbox — the old-fashioned kind, open on top with a rod for a handle. Zoe noted two handsaws neatly lined up along one side, an enormous hammer and a smaller wooden mallet, a level, a plumber's wrench, a cordless drill, several cans with screws of different sizes, and a miscellany of things she didn't even know the names of, never mind their function. Her own shiny new tool kit seemed laughable now.

Jake rummaged around in the box and hauled out a tool that looked like an overgrown screwdriver. A very sharp one.

"What's that?" Zoe gestured to the tool in Jake's hand.

"You've never seen a chisel?"

Zoe made a face. "I've got a lot to learn, haven't I?"

Jake pulled a screwdriver out of his tool belt and knelt by the doorjamb. "Well, if you live here long enough, you'll get lots of opportunity. This house is over a hundred and fifty years old. You're going to find things giving up the ghost on a regular basis." He snickered. "Bad choice of words. I meant it's to be expected that stuff will need fixing or replacing with frustrating regularity."

He turned back to the jamb and began unscrewing the latch plate. Jet settled in to watch.

"So, how do you fix a sagging house?" Zoe bent down next to Jet to get a better view of the proceedings.

Jake tipped his head up to look at her, and

her breath caught in her throat. His gray eyes were so incredibly dark in this light. And more than just tired, they looked haunted. Even if he didn't believe in ghosts, something was bothering him. She wanted to put her arms around him and make whatever it was go away. She straightened abruptly. They hardly knew each other. What would he think of such a familiarity?

"I, ah . . . I need to wash my brushes before I can't get the paint out." She hurried to gather up her brushes and moved to the sink.

Jake didn't appear to notice her hasty retreat. He set the plate and screws on the corner of the counter and then picked up the tool he called a chisel.

"The problem," he explained as he worked, "is that houses tend to settle no matter how long they've been standing, and things get out of whack eventually. Right now, the latch plate on the doorjamb is off by a hair. So, when you shut the door, instead of the spring pushing the bolt all the way into the slot, it gets caught just part way in. Besides that, the door itself has warped a little and doesn't want to stay shut. Eventually the tiny hold the bolt had when you first pushed it closed slips, and the door swings open again."

Jake positioned the chisel and tapped it with the mallet. Tiny slivers of wood fell free. He tried shutting the door, then opened it and repeated the process. This time he sighed in satisfaction and began reassembling the latch.

As she ran hot water to wash her brushes, Zoe watched out of the corner of her eye. Absorbed in watching Jake work, it was several moments before she realized there was no hot water forthcoming. She turned the faucet full blast. Still no hot water.

"Rats!"

Jake whipped around to look at her, a frown creasing his brow. "You okay?"

"I'm fine. But apparently my hot water heater isn't." She began sloshing the brushes in cold water.

Jake piled his tools back into his box and tried the door again. This time it stayed put. "Well, I've settled this problem. Want me to take a look at the hot water heater? If it's gas, maybe the pilot's gone out."

Zoe gazed at him, her shoulders slumping. "I hate to keep asking for favors, but I'm not sure I even know where to look for a pilot."

"Not a problem," Jake answered nonchalantly as he headed for the utility closet.

"Not a problem for you maybe," Zoe muttered.

Maybe buying this lovely old house wasn't the smartest thing she'd ever done. But no way was she ready to admit her father might have been right. She wasn't going to throw in the towel that easily. She finished cleaning the brushes and laid them on a piece of old newspaper to dry out. Then she slumped onto a stool in front of the island to watch Jake.

He seemed to be taking a lot longer to relight a pilot than Zoe thought it should. Not a good sign. After removing and replacing two panels and tinkering with some dials, Jake finally shut the closet door and settled onto a stool opposite Zoe.

"It's electric, and you need new heating elements. I'd run up to the Home Depot in Wilmington and get you some right now, but I have to take the twins to a doctor's appointment. I can pick them up on the way home and get them replaced either tonight or tomorrow after church."

"Are the twins okay?" Zoe was instantly diverted from her own problems.

"Sure, it's just a regular checkup. Doc Meredith knows some parents have a hard time getting their kids in on a weekday, so she has hours every third Saturday."

"Oh. She's their pediatrician?" Zoe made a mental note to look up Doctor Meredith. She wondered if that was the doctor's first name or last. Zoe was going to need a good doctor for her baby.

"Actually, she's a GP. But she's great with kids. The best around. The twins love her. So does Ava." Jake slid off the stool and bent to pick up his toolbox. "Well, I'd better get going." He was out the door before Zoe could offer another round of thank yous.

Then he stuck his head back in. "If you want to take a shower, feel free to come on over. Ava will be there. She'll grab you a towel or anything else you might need." Then he was gone.

Zoe finished buttoning up one of her favorite oversized shirts. She opened the door, hoping to let the steam out of the small bathroom and clear the mirror so she could see her reflection and brush her hair. Ava, sitting on the edge of her bed sorting through a shoebox, looked up as Zoe appeared.

The bathroom had no door into the hall. Instead, it had two doors into the bedrooms on either side. One opened into Jake's bedroom, and the other door led to Ava's bedroom. It seemed like an odd arrangement, but Zoe decided that Ava's small room might originally have been intended as a nursery, which would explain the unusual setup. The twins and Celia shared the other bathroom, which did open off the hall, but Celia had been using it when Zoe arrived.

"Can I use your mirror?" Zoe asked Ava. "I've steamed up the one in the bathroom, I'm afraid."

"No problem. It's been doing that lately. Daddy's waiting for some part to come in so he can fix the fan in the vent." Ava pushed the lid back on her shoebox and shoved it under her bed.

Zoe managed to get the tangles worked out and started to put her hair into a scrunchie. Then the elastic inside it snapped, and the scrunchie shot across to the far side of Ava's dresser. Zoe grabbed for it and noticed a frame lying face-down on the dresser. Without thinking, she picked it up and set it facing forward. Ava, much younger than she was now, sat on the lap of a stunningly beautiful woman with Jake posed behind them.

Zoe swallowed painfully. Jake's wife had been drop-dead gorgeous. Zoe spoke without thinking. "She's beautiful!"

Ava snatched the photo from Zoe's hand, yanked open a drawer and shoved the frame under a pile of underwear, and then slammed the drawer shut. "Beauty is as beauty does. Isn't that how the saying goes?" Ava's face was a mixture of anger and longing.

"I'm sorry, I didn't mean to —"

"Not your fault. You didn't know."

Zoe watched the play of emotions on Ava's face as she worked through whatever bad memories Zoe's words had evoked.

"You should cut your hair."

Startled by the abrupt change of topic, Zoe jerked back to look into the mirror. "Cut my hair?" Slowly she turned her head one way and then the other, studying her reflection with more care than she usually took. "I've never cut it. Not really."

Ava stepped behind her and lifted the heavy, damp mass of Zoe's hair and bunched it loosely behind her head. "It'd look really nice. You have such beautiful curls. If your hair was short, it would be perfect with your face."

"You really think so?" Zoe had never thought about what she might look like with short hair. Her sisters wore their silky black hair long. They didn't have Zoe's curls or frizz to deal with, but Zoe had always considered long hair essential. Porter had told her he liked it long. Then again, the only time he'd said that was when she'd spent half a week's paycheck getting it straightened and three hours at the salon before their date.

What would it be like to have short hair? She couldn't even begin to picture how she would look with short hair, but the idea, once planted, began to sprout like Jack's beanstalk.

"I could cut it for you, if you like."

Zoe felt a momentary pang of apprehension. What if she didn't like it? What if it came out horrible? "I —" *Why not?* She'd already considered the problems her hair would present once the baby was born. "Let's do it!"

"You're kidding, right?" Ava sounded totally taken aback by Zoe's abrupt acquiescence. "You'd let me cut it off. Just like that?"

"If I hate it, it'll grow out again. But on the other hand, you might be right, and I'll love it." Now that the decision had been made, Zoe was anxious to put it into action before she lost her nerve. *Just wait 'til Bree finds out!* Zoe had never done anything drastic without consulting Bree, but this time . . . Zoe smiled at herself in the mirror.

"Cool!" Ava continued to sound awed that Zoe was actually going to let her do something so radical, but she hurried into the bathroom, and Zoe heard her rummaging around in a drawer. When she returned, she pulled her desk chair out and directed Zoe to sit in it. She draped a sheet around Zoe's shoulders. "Want to watch?"

So Zoe watched as twenty-seven years' worth of hair fell in clumps to the floor. Her head felt lighter with each snip, and the transformation was astonishing. Suddenly Zoe could see the heart shape of her face softened by the loose curls rather than flattened the way it appeared when she pulled everything back into a ponytail or a braid or half hidden by an unruly tangle of frizz.

"Ta-da!" Ava whisked the sheet off and stood back. "What do you think?"

Slowly Zoe got up and approached the mirror. Cautiously she ran her fingers through the curls, fluffing them a little. The result was so unexpected. Ava had been so right. The curls were perfect for her face. Then she turned back to Ava to express her amazement and thanks and found Ava staring at her with a tight expression clouding her face.

"You don't like it?"

"I —" Ava swallowed. "I like it. I like it a lot."

"Then why are you looking at me like I've sprouted horns?" Zoe had a pit of dread settling into her stomach and didn't even know why. It couldn't be the hair. The curls were everything Ava had promised. Zoe ran her hands through her newly-shorn hair again, loving the way it felt. But Ava looked so distressed.

"Are you —" Ava glanced down, then back up. "Are you pregnant?"

CHAPTER 13

Zoe's breath caught in her chest with painful suddenness. Zoe had begun to really show about three or four weeks ago, but the judicious choice of clothing had hidden it. Just now, when she had reached up to touch her curls, her shirt must have hiked up and revealed the unmistakable swell of her growing belly.

"I am." No use denying it. Ava would have found out eventually. Jake would know next.

"But there's no Mr. Callahan."

Zoe couldn't decide if there was condemnation in Ava's question, or just curiosity. She decided to be honest and treat Ava as an equal. That was the advice she'd given Jake not so long ago — accept the fact that Ava was growing up and treat her accordingly. Ava would make her own judgment about Zoe, but at least she'd know Zoe hadn't treated her like a child.

"Porter didn't want to be married. He

didn't want to be a father either."

Ava sank down on the side of her bed and gazed up at Zoe with open curiosity. "Did you mean to get pregnant? Or was Porter one of those guys you were talking about who only want one thing and don't spend much time worrying about the consequences?"

"No and yes. No, I didn't mean to get pregnant. And apparently yes to Porter and his motivations."

"Well, if you didn't mean to get pregnant, how did you let it happen? I mean, you're old enough to know how to get stuff."

Zoe turned the desk chair toward the bed and sat down. Innocent though she was, considering the discussion they'd already had about boys and sex, Ava deserved the truth. "I am, and you're right. I should have been protecting myself. I thought I was in a different kind of relationship than it turns out I was. I got careless, and . . . well, here I am. About to become an unwed mother. I guess I'm not the best example of how to conduct one's personal life and relationships."

"But what about this guy, Porter? Don't you love him?"

Zoe took a deep breath. Confession was supposed to be good for the soul, but looking into the guileless eyes of this young woman, Zoe wondered if she should be confessing to her at all. Now that she'd started, though, there seemed no reasonable way to end the inquisition.

"I wanted to love him. My father wanted me to love him. But it just didn't happen."

"Then how come you were — you know . . . ?"

"Intimate?"

Ava nodded, a fiery flush surging up her neck and into her cheeks.

"It's kind of complicated. I shouldn't have let it happen, but I did. Porter was the first man who really seemed interested in me, and it was exciting. I was flattered, and I really wanted to fall in love, but . . ."

"But, what?" Ava's brows puckered. She folded her hands in her lap, waiting for Zoe's explanation.

"Like I said, it's complicated. First off, you have to understand that my father always planned for my brothers to become lawyers and join the firm. Only none of my brothers wanted to be lawyers, and my father was pretty disappointed. Then Porter came to work for him, and when my dad brought him home for dinner, Porter met me. Before long, he asked me out on a date. I never figured my dad for a matchmaker, but I think he got the idea that if Porter and I got married, Daddy would finally get to add *son* to the company name.

"I know it's not an excuse, but I let my father's attitude convince me that Porter and I were meant to be. When Porter invited me to spend the weekend with him at a classy resort in Hilton Head, it seemed —" Zoe hesitated, remembering how it had felt to be treated like someone's princess. "It felt special and very romantic. And it was. Or would have been if we'd really been in love, but we weren't."

"Is that when it happened?" Ava glanced at Zoe's belly, then back to her face.

Zoe looked away from the assessing, questioning eyes. It hadn't happened then. Not until weeks after that disappointing weekend. But how could she tell this young girl about those other nights she had let Porter follow her to her bedroom, take his pleasure, then leave her to stare into the dark, feeling used and empty? How could she admit to being such a total fool for thinking Porter loved her and that one day she would learn how to love him back?

"I was careless and stupid." Zoe avoided answering the question.

"Why stupid? You're old enough to get married and have a family."

"I know. And I would have married Porter if he'd asked. But he didn't. When I told him about the baby, he got upset and insisted I get an abortion. Then, when I refused, he said he wanted nothing more to do with me, or the baby, and if I tried to insist it was his, he'd sue me for entrapment or something along those lines."

Ava gasped, her eyes widening in outrage. "What a bastard!"

Zoe nodded. "Yeah, he's that. But he's a boring one so I'm better off without him messing up my life any more than he already has. I guess I should have told you about the baby the day we went shopping, but . . ."

"Are you happy about it? The baby, I mean?"

"I am now. Actually, I'm kind of excited about it now that I'm used to the idea."

The frown lifted from Ava's brow. "Then I'm happy for you."

Unconsciously, Zoe curled her hand about the firm little mound of her growing uterus. Her mind flitted back over the last few months and the myriad feelings this pregnancy had filled her with. First dread, then panic, and finally acceptance. And with acceptance, once she'd stood up to both Porter and her father, had come happiness.

"Can you feel it moving yet?" Ava glanced

135

toward Zoe's middle, her eyes alight with interest.

"For a few weeks now. Just a little flutter. Like a butterfly." And that sign of life had blossomed instantly into a love like Zoe had never expected or felt before.

"Is it moving now?" Ava's glance was more pointed and less self-conscious this time.

"No, not at the moment. I guess she's sleeping."

"Wow, so you already know it's going to be a girl. Do you have a name?"

"Molly Ann."

"Molly Ann," Ava repeated softly. "So, what did your father say? Was he really angry with you? For — for getting pregnant, I mean? He must be totally pissed at Porter."

Zoe's pleasant moment of shared wonder jerked to a halt. Jake thought she was a good influence for his daughter, but that was about to come to a screaming stop. How could an unwed mother possibly be considered a proper role model for a teenager on the verge of exploring her own sexuality? Jake would probably ban her from his daughter's life all together. Just when she'd begun to feel like the Cameron family was becoming friends she'd enjoy for a lifetime.

"I didn't tell my father what Porter said. I didn't think it was fair to Porter to get fired over it. I mean, the whole thing is more my fault than his, and —"

"That's a load of crap!" Ava leapt to her feet and paced toward the door, then back. "You didn't get pregnant by yourself. He should get fired at the very least! Especially for the way he treated you!"

"But Porter never once mentioned marriage, and I knew he wasn't keen about kids. I should never have slept with him at all. It's my mess, and I have to live with it." Might as well be totally honest. Make sure Ava got the message that safe sex was the woman's responsibility, regardless of the circumstances. And that abstinence was even wiser. "Bottom line, it's my responsibility."

"Is your father good with that?"

"He thinks I should give the baby up for adoption."

"But you can't do that!"

"No. I can't." Zoe covered her stomach with both hands. "I could never do that."

"Can I be like" — Ava paused, pursed her lips, and then rushed on — "like an honorary aunt? Or something?" She reached out and grasped Zoe's hands and squeezed. "I feel like we're sort of like sisters. You know?

So, that would make me sort of like an aunt. Right?"

Zoe hesitated, thinking of Jake's reaction, but then saw the first hint of disappointment in Ava's eyes. Ava felt rejected by her own mother, and Zoe wasn't going to let her feel rejected again. Not if she could help it. She returned the pressure of Ava's hands firmly.

"Oh, Ava! That would be so much fun. I love having you for a friend, and a woman can never have enough sisters. Molly will be so lucky to have an honorary aunt living right next door. As long as it's okay with your father."

Would Jake be okay with it? Zoe wouldn't blame him if he wasn't enthusiastic about his very impressionable teenage daughter hanging out with an unwed mother-to-be. Zoe wasn't exactly the kind of role model a conscientious father would choose for a girl he was having a hard enough time just acknowledging was becoming a young woman. Zoe would understand if he did his best to discourage it. But it would hurt.

She stood in the dark, gazing out her bedroom window at Jake's house, wishing she'd told Jake about her pregnancy earlier instead of trying so hard to hide it. All the reasons she'd had for not wanting him to find out before seemed stupid now. After all, they were just friends, so why should it matter to him personally if she was pregnant?

But as friends, she should have been the one to tell him, not Ava. Wearing oversized shirts and not saying something when she'd had the chance seemed so dumb in retrospect, because she'd known he'd find out eventually. She couldn't hide it forever. And now she might have jeopardized the friendship that had grown so quickly between them. Trust was so important, yet so terribly fragile.

If only she hadn't fallen in love with him. That's why she'd been reluctant to say anything. She hadn't meant to fall in love, but it was like trying to un-ring a bell. And in spite of all evidence to the contrary, she'd continued to hope he might feel a spark of attraction in return.

Except that men didn't fall in love with women who were carrying another man's baby. Zoe wiped angrily at the tears that had begun to dribble down her face.

"But I should have told him," she whispered into the darkness of her lonely bedroom.

CHAPTER 14

"Daddy? I know Mom was already pregnant, but was that the only reason you got married? I mean, you were going to get married anyway. Right?"

Jake had just come down from tucking the twins into bed and found Ava curled up on the couch with a paperback novel in one hand, a can of soda in the other, and the dog sprawled beside her. Her question stopped him in his tracks.

"We talked about it. We talked about getting married after we graduated college, that is. But then you happened." He moved to the chair across from the couch and sank into it. *Where is Ava going with this question?*

"So, you would never walk out on a woman you'd gotten pregnant, right?"

Jake's heart began to thud in painful apprehension. "I cared about your mother very much. I would never have walked out on her, pregnant or otherwise."

"But if you hadn't loved her, would you still have gotten married?"

"Of course I would have offered to marry her. Why all the questions?"

"And you definitely wouldn't tell her to just go get an abortion. Right?"

"What is all this about?" Jake's heart clenched painfully. Was his baby pregnant? Had everything Zoe told him been wrong? Had Travis worn Ava's resistance down, and then told her to get lost once he'd had his way with her? When was the last time he'd seen Travis, anyway? The facts were adding up, and Jake didn't like the sum. "Ava, are you pregnant?"

Ava gaped at him. Then a look of indignation flashed across her face. "Daddy!"

"Well, are you?" He had to know. He didn't want to know, but he had to. Jake tried to calm himself. It took a moment for him to realize that Ava was shaking her head *no*. Relief flooded through him so quickly he thought he might faint.

"Travis and I were never really *that* together. I don't know why you're jumping to all the wrong conclusions. Considering that Travis thinks I'm such a baby, and all." A cloud of unhappiness came into Ava's eyes, leaving Jake even more confused than before.

"I'm sorry, kitten. I didn't mean — look, if you're trying to get back at me for something, it's working. So please, tell me what this is really about." Jake still felt light-headed, and his heart jerked erratically as it slowed to something closer to normal.

Ava looked at her hands and fiddled with her book. Then she patted the dog and cleared her throat as if she'd gotten something lodged in it. "I didn't mean to scare you, Daddy. I'm — I'm still a virgin, if that's what you're dying to know."

Zoe was right after all! Thank God! "I'm sorry. I shouldn't have jumped to such a thoughtless conclusion." He took a deep, steadying breath. "So who *are* we talking about? Your mother and me, or one of your friends?"

"A friend."

"Has your friend told her parents?"

Jake's hands trembled. *Must be the aftermath of shock. Some other father is going to go through that roller coaster I've just been on, only his ride won't have as happy an ending. Poor bastard. It only took me all these years to understand how Richard Jolee must have felt when I got Marsha pregnant when we were just seventeen years old.*

142

"Yeah, she did," Ava admitted carefully. "But her father told her abortion would be compounding a sin, and she should put the baby up for adoption so she could get her life back on track."

"Is he forcing her to have the baby?"

"It's Zoe I'm talking about, Daddy. She's old enough to tell her father to take a hike."

For the second time that night, Jake's heart jumped into his throat. Zoe pregnant? Beautiful, funny, sexy Zoe? Pregnant? How had he not noticed?

"You'd have found out sooner or later anyway, but I told you because Zoe thinks you won't want me hanging around with her anymore. I really like her, and I know she likes me. She listens to me, and she cares about what I think." Ava leaned toward Jake with eager intensity in her young face. "Please, Daddy. We can still be friends, can't we? Just because she's having a baby doesn't have to change anything. Does it?"

"Of course, not!" Jake assured his daughter, his brain still reeling. In the short time Zoe had lived next door, she had become more than just a friend to his little girl. Actually, as Zoe had so strenuously pointed out, Ava wasn't a little girl anymore, even if he still thought of her that way. And Zoe listened to Ava's teenage dreams and angst. Ava was always welcome in her house. And he knew from his conversation with Zoe that Ava felt comfortable going to Zoe to ask difficult questions about things Ava couldn't come to him with. Pregnancy or not, he suspected Zoe would continue to be a good influence on his daughter, giving her things he couldn't and filling the gaping hole where her mother should have been.

"Friends should stick together," he finally said, dragging his attention back to his daughter's worried expression. Ava probably needed Zoe more than Zoe needed a teenager adding to her problems, but who was he to make that decision? "Especially now."

Ava grinned in relief. "I know she's got Bree and her sisters, but Zoe told me she likes doing stuff with me. 'Cause we've both been through the same kind of stuff, and we understand what it's like. Not having a mother, I mean. And she's going to need all the friends she can get when the baby gets here. Being a single parent and all. But I guess you know all about that part."

Jake opened his mouth to make an observation about how Zoe had gotten into such a pickle and then shut it. Another thought had just occurred to him. Maybe there was more upside to this than down. Maybe watching Zoe grow big and uncomfortable would highlight the less pleasant results of careless, unprotected sex. And after the baby arrived, being around Zoe when sleep was hard to come by and any semblance of her former life disappeared would be an eye-opener. It would give Ava some very strong reasons to stick to her guns the next time Travis or some other randy kid wanted to get into her pants.

"We haven't known Zoe all that long, but she really has become a good friend, and friends don't take off when you need them most. I'd have been disappointed in you if you didn't stick by her."

"And can I borrow your credit card again? I want to take Zoe shopping this time. I want to help her pick out some really cute maternity clothes."

Only half thinking about it, Jake pulled out his wallet and slid out the credit card. He offered it to his daughter. "Just remember I'm not made of money. Okay?"

Ava snatched the card, then surged off the couch and wrapped her arms about Jake's neck. Just as quickly, she backed off and kissed him on the cheek. "Thanks, Daddy." Then she grabbed the book she'd been reading and headed for the stairs.

Jake watched her go, feeling like he'd just gone a few rounds with a punching bag that fought back. He tucked his wallet back into his pocket and thought of Zoe. How was she going to manage pregnancy and all that entailed as well as keep that big old house together all by herself? Jake wondered about Mr. Callahan. What kind of father was he? Jake knew he lived in the historic part of Wilmington, which wasn't that far away, but so far as Jake knew, the man had not even been to Zoe's house. In spite of his disapproval, would he be there for his daughter if Zoe really needed help?

Well, one thing was certain. Jake knew how to be a good friend, too. As his daughter had pointed out, Zoe was going to be a single parent, and Jake knew what that was like. At least, he knew what it was like to be a single dad. That had to count for something. Besides, there were things he could do that Ava couldn't. He made up his mind to do what he could to make sure things ran smoothly at the old Jolee house, fixing anything that needed fixing. Maybe fixing things that didn't. And another thing was for sure — Zoe definitely wasn't going to do any more painting. Paint fumes weren't good for a pregnant woman or her baby. If he couldn't convince her to put the rest of her painting projects off until after her baby was born, then he'd just have to find time to do them himself.

Jake reached out to run his hand down the silky head of the retriever. Taffy licked his hand, then put her head back on her paws and stared at Jake with her liquid dark eyes.

"Friends hang together," Jake told the dog. "Right?"

Zoe was folding laundry in her bedroom with afternoon sunlight streaming across the floor when the dogs began their routine: Scotch barking his fool head off, Hoover scampering for the door with his tail wagging, and Jet began hunting for a toy to present to whatever friend was headed her way. Polly squawked just because the dogs were barking. Zoe figured it must be Danny, who loved coming over to play with the dogs, but when she crossed the hall and stuck her head out the front window, it wasn't Danny after all.

Jake strode up her front walk with a stack of boards balanced easily on one shoulder. Zoe stretched out the window in an effort to see below the overhang of her porch roof. Jake's toolbox sat on her bottom step. What on earth was he up to now? She hadn't reported any new malfunctions.

Quickly, she retreated back into the room, then hurried down the stairs and yanked the front door open. Jake was nowhere in sight. She stepped out onto the porch, but he wasn't there either. The toolbox, however, still sat on the bottom step, and the stack of boards leaned against the railing.

Zoe sat down on the top step to wait for Jake to show up and explain. She had some explaining to do herself, she was sure of it. Because by now Ava must have told him about the baby.

Zoe was glad that she'd chosen to wear a dress to church that morning, one that made her feel at least halfway pretty. With her new hairdo and the sunny yellow dress with a flare to the skirt, she'd studied her reflection in the mirror and been pleasantly surprised. The cut of the dress didn't show off the growing belly. At least not too much. But it did highlight her breasts and legs. Two of her more attractive attributes.

When she saw Jake loping across the lawn with a pry bar in his hand, Zoe got up to go meet him.

Jake spied Zoe coming down the stairs and jerked to a stop halfway up the front walk. She looked fantastic. How could she possibly be pregnant and still look so sexy?

When had she cut her hair? He loved the way it curled about her face. It made her eyes seem even bigger than they had appeared before. And that dress!

"Hi, Jake." Zoe turned to gesture toward the lumber he'd stacked against her railing. "I came down to see what you were up to. I don't remember calling you to report any new disasters."

Jake looked from the lumber to Zoe. She looked gorgeous. He wondered if she had any idea how terrific she looked. No wonder he hadn't noticed. Pregnancy looked good on her. Her skin had a fresh, healthy glow to it, and the new haircut just added to the allure.

"Jake?" Her eyebrows repeated the question.

"I . . . um . . . Your railing needs fixing."

"My railing?" Zoe spun on her heel and returned to the steps. "What's wrong with my railing?"

What's not wrong with it? The whole thing was so loose he'd spent half the night worrying about her grabbing it for support and falling, hurting herself and the baby being born too early. Babies born too early didn't have a chance, and he wasn't about to have another little life get snuffed out before it had a chance. Once was enough to last him a lifetime.

Zoe placed a hand on the railing and started to jiggle it. When the post broke without a whimper, she jumped back with a squeak of surprise.

Jake lunged to grab the railing as it toppled toward her. "That's what's wrong with it!"

"Oh, my!" Zoe eyed the railing in disbelief. "I had no idea it was so rotten. How did you guess?"

"Ava mentioned it. She said she was worried about you falling." Not half as worried as he'd been after he'd found out Zoe was pregnant. Not that she couldn't have been just as hurt without being pregnant, but somehow her condition just made it seem more ominous.

Zoe paled. "I guess I'm lucky someone didn't take a spill and sue me."

"Lucky," Jake agreed. Lawsuits had never occurred to him when he'd contemplated the results of someone falling. But he supposed, with her father being a lawyer, that might be the first thing she'd think about.

"What can I do to help?"

"In that rig?" Jake took another thorough inventory of the sexy yellow dress and wagged his eyebrows.

Zoe flushed, as if embarrassed by his scrutiny. "I'll go change."

150

"No need." The point was to look out for her, not get her involved in projects that could get her hurt.

"But I should do something . . ." Zoe made a face. "It's my problem you're fixing. And speaking about my problems, there's something I need to talk to you about." Zoe sat down on the second step and looked up at him. Her big eyes looked wary and worried.

Jake wanted to give her a big hug and tell her he already knew about her problem and that there was nothing to look so worried about. But maybe that wasn't what she was going to tell him.

"I know about the baby," he offered, trying to make it easier for her.

"Could you sit down? Please?" Zoe patted the step next to her. "It's hard enough without having you looming over me like a disapproving judge."

Jake plopped obediently onto the step. "I'm not disapproving. I'm hardly in any position to sit in judgment."

Zoe pinched a pleat of yellow material and began twisting it. "I should have told you before. I'm sorry I didn't."

"I'm sure you had your reasons. Look, Zoe —" Jake reached over to stop her from destroying her dress. He pulled one small, yet capable hand back into his own lap and wrapped his other hand around it. "I know it's probably none of my business, but where's the father? How come he's not here looking out for you?"

Zoe felt the warmth of Jake's concern flood through her with the same calming effect as his big hand cradling hers. She'd tossed and turned all night for nothing. She hadn't lost his friendship or his trust. He made her feel as if she could tell him anything.

"It's kind of a long story, but the short version is that Porter doesn't want to be a father." Zoe recalled the day she'd told Porter and remembered the look of utter distaste on his face. She'd been dismayed back then. Afraid and uncertain. But she'd had time to realize she didn't need Porter. In fact, didn't want him in her life at all. Or her child's.

"So he's not taking *any* responsibility?" Jake sounded disgusted.

Zoe turned her head and met Jake's troubled gaze. "He doesn't love me, and I— I'm —" Zoe looked back at her lap, unable to face the concern in those quiet gray eyes. "I'm better off without him."

"It's not going to be easy being a single parent. I should know," Jake offered gently.

His thumb traced steady circles on the back of her hand as he spoke. "It's really none of my business, and you don't owe me any explanations. Not about Porter or about your decisions. But I just wanted you to know you've got friends next door. Ava was worried I'd think she shouldn't hang out over here anymore, but — but she's wrong. Unless she gets to be a pest. If she's over here too much, just say the word and . . ."

Jake swallowed and his Adam's apple bobbed. ". . . and I'm your friend, too. Anything you need. Just ask. I'm good at stuff like putting cribs together. I'm a good listener, too. And I know how to change a diaper and do some floor walking when you're about ready to go out of your head, and you need a break. You just gotta ask because I'm not such a good mind reader. Okay?"

Tears stung Zoe's eyes. She blinked them back and stared even harder at her lap. Jake might not want anything more than simple friendship, but for no reason at all, he seemed to care more about her welfare than Porter ever had. And he was offering to help out, no strings attached.

Jake bent to peer up into her face. "You okay?"

Zoe lost the battle with her tears. "I'm not

usually such a watering pot." She sniffed and dashed the tears away with her free hand.

"Pregnancy does things like that to a woman," Jake answered with easygoing acceptance. He let go of her hand and dug in his pocket, then produced a clean white handkerchief. He handed it to her and waited while she dried her eyes. "Now there are a few other things we need to discuss. Like paint fumes and mowing the lawn and —"

Zoe's phone rang. She jumped to her feet, and Jake stood as well. She hesitated. The phone rang again. "I'll be back," she mumbled and hurried up the stairs.

"Yeah, you and Schwarzenegger." Jake watched her go.

Finally, he glanced down at the fallen railing and started to figure out where to begin.

CHAPTER 15

The repair of the railing on Zoe's front stairs led to replacing the railing around three sides of her wraparound porch. Shortly after that project was completed, Zoe was gathering bags of groceries from the bed of her truck when one of the garage doors pulled loose from its hinges. It crashed into the back of her pickup, causing Zoe to drop the bags as she jumped backward with a squeal of startled fright. Jake, who'd been wheeling his rubbish bin back up his drive, came running, a look of horror on his face. After they'd both calmed down, he surveyed the problem and took on another big project, toiling away in the evenings after work.

The rotten doorjambs had been replaced first, then the doors rehung. With that repair completed, Jake had stalked through the house, poking into every nook and corner, assessing, muttering to himself and taking notes on a clipboard. Over the next few weeks, he replaced several shelves in the pantry because he claimed they were loose and could easily tumble down with everything on them. Loose boards on her back porch had been nailed down. A railing was installed on her cellar stairs. A new lock replaced the faulty one Jake had discovered could lock all by itself and could have resulted in Zoe being trapped in her own bathroom.

And every repair had been accompanied by a lecture on safety. Jake had begun to sound like Zoe's father, except that Jake was clearly more concerned with Zoe's physical safety than his own convenience. His insistence that the chemicals in fresh paint weren't good for her baby meant the kitchen walls remained a faded shade of green. But when she'd protested that the spare room was too dark and dingy for a baby, Jake had taken over that project after banishing her from the house one whole Saturday. He even confiscated her old lawn mower and added her lawn to his whenever he got on his ride-around mower.

Jake treated her like a concerned and bossy older brother. Zoe appreciated his caution and admitted she'd have had a hard time getting any of the projects done without his help, but she didn't want an older brother. She wanted him to notice her as a woman. She wanted one of those charged moments when they seemed to become suddenly, physically aware of each other to turn into something more. She wanted to feel his lips on hers. She wanted him to take her into his arms and make her feel desirable in spite of her growing belly. In spite of her too-big mouth, the detested freckles, and the fact that she'd never be beautiful.

Plain and simple, she wanted him to want her as much as she wanted him.

Zoe hadn't expected to fall in love. Not the heart-stopping, melting kind of falling in love she'd read about in novels. She'd tried, really tried to be in love with Porter, but they'd never really clicked, and she'd given up hoping she would ever know the wonder of being in love. Then she'd met Jake, and everything had changed.

Falling in love hadn't been filled with romance, kisses that burned her soul, or the euphoria all her favorite heroines experienced. The depressing truth was that Jake obviously didn't feel the same way about her. Fixing up her house could hardly be classified as romantic. For her, falling in love had brought a longing that grew harder to hold inside every day.

She was going to have to get over it. Mooning after a man who wasn't interested wasn't attractive. Or healthy.

Lunch over, Zoe hauled herself out of the rocker and straightened her shoulders.

Her dogs ambled up the stairs and came to see if there was anything left on her tray. Zoe shared the bits of crust she'd deliberately saved for them and gave each a scratch behind the ears.

"Time to stop daydreaming about the impossible and get back to work, guys." Zoe gathered her lunch dishes and headed into the house. She deposited them in the sink and climbed the stairs to the guest bedroom where she had set up her sewing machine.

Her black tomcat, whom she'd named Vicar because of the little square patch of white on his throat, had parked himself smack in the middle of the carefully folded sewing project. She shooed him away, and he retreated to the bed where he sat glaring at her with arrogant disdain.

"Oh, don't look so put out," she told the cat as she brushed black cat hair off the pink and white fabric.

Zoe hummed as she hemmed the new curtains for the baby's room. She'd already finished a quilt for the crib she hadn't yet purchased and matching cushions for the old rocker she'd found at a yard sale. She paused and admired the pattern of flowers and teddies that ran along the border of the pink-striped material. Maybe she should try making a teddy bear, too. She'd never tried sewing a stuffed animal, but it might be fun.

"Zoe!" Jake's shout came out of nowhere and was just as abruptly joined by Scotch's frantic barking. Vicar leapt off the bed and darted beneath it. Jake sounded angry. "Zoe?"

Zoe rose hastily from her chair and headed for the hall with Hoover shoving his way past her, beating her to the stairs. "I'm up here, Jake." In her rush to find out what Jake wanted, Zoe turned the corner too fast, and the little braided rug at the top of the stairs skidded sideways. The last thing she saw as she lost her footing and began to fall was the horrified look on Jake's face.

If Jake hadn't already let himself into the house and been standing at the foot of her stairs, Zoe would have tumbled headlong all the way to the bottom. He scrambled up the last few steps and caught her in mid-flight.

Heart pounding, he sank onto the step with her in his lap. "Da—" he bit off the cuss he'd been about to utter. "You scared the crap out of me."

"I — I don't know what happened." Zoe sounded shaken.

"It's my fault." His blood pressure must be off the charts. He should have gone looking for her instead of shouting as if the house were on fire. If she got hurt and went into labor way too soon, this time, it *would* be his fault.

His breathing still came in ragged gasps, and his heartbeat thrummed erratically when Zoe slid off his lap and made her way to the bottom of the staircase. She was blushing furiously. "S-sorry. I'm not usually such a klutz."

"Are you okay?" Jake took a visual inventory. Looking for what, he wasn't sure.

"I'm fine." Zoe glanced down at herself, then back at him. "I'm fine," she said more firmly.

Jake prayed she was right.

Zoe's brows knit into a frown. "Why were you shouting?"

"I —" Why had he been shouting? *Crap! Celia!* "Celia's gone missing. I need you to watch the twins. Are you sure you're okay?"

"I'm fine." Zoe put heavy emphasis on the *fine*. "What do you mean Celia's gone missing?"

"She's wandered off, and I can't find her."

"Oh, no! Jake!" Zoe's eyes widened in

concern. "Why didn't you say so right away?"

"When you fell, it pretty much went out of my mind."

Zoe headed for the door. "How long has she been missing?" She was clearly less affected by her tumble than Jake. He already knew he was going to have nightmares about it.

He caught up to her in two strides while he explained that he'd just gone out shopping for new sneakers for the twins and that Ava had gone to a friend's house. Celia had never wandered away before, except over to Zoe's house, and it hadn't occurred to him to worry about leaving her this afternoon.

"But how long?" Zoe asked again as they hurried up Jake's front stairs.

"I don't know." Jake tried to recall exactly what time it had been when he'd left Celia sitting in her rocker with a crossword puzzle book in her lap. "An hour maybe."

In the living room, Jake squatted beside his daughters where they were busily putting on their new sneakers. "I've got to go out for a bit. Miss Zoe's here. You be good, okay?"

"Yes, Daddy," they chorused in unison.

He planted a quick kiss on the top of each head and stood up again.

On the verge of asking her yet again if she was sure she was all right, he stopped himself. "Thanks, Zoe." He turned to leave.

"Jake?" Zoe's voice stopped him as he was just about to hurry out the door. "Do you have your cell with you?"

"Yeah." He checked the holster on his belt to make sure.

"Good. I'll call you if she wanders home on her own." Zoe placed a hand on his forearm and squeezed. "Good luck."

Without thinking about it, Jake bent his head and touched his lips to Zoe's. Thankful for her instant understanding of the urgency that gripped him. Thankful that he wasn't alone in his worry and panic. "Thanks."

Zoe set grilled cheese sandwiches in front of Danny and the twins and filled three glasses with milk. She'd made a sandwich for herself, as well, but didn't really feel like eating it. It had been almost three hours since Jake had dashed out the door. He'd called several times to see if Celia had come home on her own and report his own lack of success. In spite of his obviously growing alarm over his mother-in-law, he continued to ask how Zoe was feeling. Each time she reassured him she was okay and tried to find words to encourage him with regards to Celia. It had been a long three hours.

The Cliffords had pulled into their driveway an hour ago, and Bill and Carrie had joined in the hunt, leaving Danny to entertain the twins. Zoe wanted to be out there herself, but she was in charge on the home front. She'd just have to wait and pray. But waiting was hard.

She imagined Celia, confused and lost and becoming more bewildered as time went on. Zoe knew that Celia got confused easily, often forgetting names and sometimes faces. But she hadn't known that Celia's problems were perhaps bigger than just old-age forgetfulness.

Zoe chided herself for not knowing. For not having discussed it with Jake before now. Now that she thought about it, their conversations always seemed to be about what Zoe needed except when they were comparing notes on teenagers and discussing Jake's concerns about Ava and her crush on Travis. Zoe felt guilty that she hadn't been more aware.

She'd been too absorbed in how alive Jake made her feel when he was around that she hadn't paid the slightest notice to his problems with his mother-in-law whom he clearly loved. Friendship was a two-way street, and now it seemed like all the traffic had been coming all her way.

"Hey, Zoe!" Ava rushed into the kitchen. "What are you doing here? Hi, Danny. What's up? Where's Daddy?" She plopped down in a vacant chair. "Can I have a sandwich, too?"

"Celia's wandered off. Your father, Danny's parents, and your Aunt Kate are out looking for her." Zoe pushed her untouched sandwich across the table.

"Oh, no! Where is he? Do you know where he's looked already? I'll go help." Ava ran an agitated hand through her blond locks, the sandwich ignored.

"He's got his cell. Why don't you call him before you go charging off?" That's all Jake needed — to finally find Celia and then come home and discover his daughter was out somewhere alone in the descending darkness.

Ava fumbled her cell out of her shorts pocket and hit a speed dial number. At that same moment, the phone on the kitchen wall rang. Zoe snatched the receiver out of its cradle. "Cameron residence."

"It's me. We found her." Jake sounded exhausted, but enormously relieved.

Zoe sank back into her chair, overwhelmed with relief. "Thank God. Ava just got home,

164

and she was about to rush off to join you. If you hear a beep, it's her trying to call you." Zoe touched Ava's arm. "It's your father." She pointed to the house phone. "They've found your grandmother."

Ava turned her phone off and sat down. This time she did pick up the sandwich and take a bite.

With Celia safe, Zoe discovered she was hungry as well. But now she might as well fix a real meal because the search party was likely to be just as famished. She hauled out a pot and began filling it with water. Spaghetti would be easy and quick.

By the time Jake, Celia, Kate, and the Cliffords had returned to the house, Zoe and Ava had the table set and dinner ready to serve. They invited Kate to stay, but she said she needed to get home and fix dinner for her crowd. She gave Jake and the girls a hug and disappeared out the door while Zoe began setting out the food.

As everyone bowed their heads, Jake offered up thanksgiving for having protected Celia on her solo ramble and for directing Bill and Carrie to the spot where Celia had chosen to stop for a rest. Once the food was passed about, the general chatter of a convivial supper began.

Zoe reached for the bread sticks, and her

fingers touched Jake's. He didn't jerk away this time as he had so often before. In a little suspended bubble of time, they studied each other across the table as if no one else were there.

She saw worry in his eyes. The problem of Celia wandering off was probably going to get worse, and his concern was understandable. But there was something else in his gaze as well. Something Zoe couldn't define. She remembered the feel of Jake's lips on hers and wondered if he was remembering it, too.

CHAPTER 16

"You look like hell!" Philip observed as he slid a tub of cookies onto Jake's kitchen counter. "These are from Mom. What's with the bags under your eyes?"

Ava looked up from the backpack she was loading books into and turned to glance at Jake as if she hadn't noticed his tired eyes before her uncle mentioned them.

"Nothing a good night's sleep won't cure."

"And you can't get out of sleeping at the fire station tonight?"

"It's my night on. Doesn't mean I'll get called out, though." Jake pulled his windbreaker on and grabbed his own backpack. "Ava, go tell your grandmother we're leaving and remind her that Uncle Philip will be staying for the night."

Ava loped off to the television room.

"Not that Celia will remember. She'll still probably be surprised when she trips over you on her way to bed." Jake was glad his brother was free to stay the night, and he hadn't had to tell Ava she couldn't sleep over at her friend's house. Celia's little excursion the other day had shaken up his routine and left him scrambling to figure out how to make everything work. Maybe he'd have to give up the volunteer fire department.

"Am I pulling an all-night watch?" Philip poured himself a cup of coffee and slid onto a stool. "Has she been wandering in her sleep, too? Is that why you're looking so haggard?"

"So far, no nighttime expeditions. You should be fine." Jake debated telling Philip about the dreams that kept him tossing and wakeful, but was saved from making any awkward confessions when Ava bounded back into the kitchen.

Ava grabbed her backpack, gave her uncle a peck on the cheek, and headed for the door. Jake stopped long enough to grab a handful of his mother's signature honey and spice cookies, then followed Ava.

"The nightmares are back?" Philip's question stopped Jake halfway out the door.

"Yeah," Jake answered, not turning to look at his brother.

"That baby wasn't your fault."

"I know. I'm over that. It's — look, I gotta

get going."

"I don't report in until noon tomorrow. Talk it out over breakfast."

Jake turned to look at his brother. Maybe it would help to put the frayed wisps of his dreams into words. Get some perspective and think rationally instead of waking every night with his heart hammering so hard his chest hurt and the echoes of a woman sobbing tearing at his brain.

Philip could be the biggest tease in the world, but he had a serious, caring side, too. And he probably knew more than most men about the ravages of senseless nightmares. Anyone who had seen as much of war as Philip had to have nightmares far worse than the ones messing with Jake's mind.

"There's nothing wrong with me." Jake fought the urge to admit the truth.

"Never said there was," Philip answered mildly. "But nightmares can be a bitch."

"Breakfast, then. And Philip? Thanks."

"What's wrong with me, Bree?"

"You're falling in love with the guy, and you just wish he felt the same way. There's nothing wrong with you." Bree picked up the ball that had landed at her feet and tossed it to a gap-toothed boy who'd come running after it. The boy scooped it up and

169

gave them a brief smile before heading back to first base and tossing the ball to the pitcher.

Bree and Zoe were sitting in the bleachers watching Bree's son Sam's little league team at their weekly practice. The guilt that had been eating at Zoe since Celia's wandering episode had grown, and Zoe had finally broken down and shared her self-reproach with her friend.

"But he doesn't. And I know it. He just wants to be friends." Zoe stated what she knew to be the truth of the matter in a carefully neutral tone. Making herself take the truth to heart was more difficult. "I've never had a man for a friend before, and I'm not sure how to go about it."

"Same as any friend." Bree stretched out an arm and pulled Zoe against her side in a quick hug. "You treat Jake the same as you treat me. And you don't go on a guilt trip every time you find out about some problem he's got that he didn't feel like sharing." Bree squeezed Zoe's shoulder again, then let go to reach for her water bottle. "So, how long has he known how serious Celia's memory problems are? Is it Alzheimer's do you think?"

"I don't know. Jake didn't say much. But I know he's worried. At first I thought it was just because she'd wandered off, and he didn't know where she was, but later, after she was back home again, I could see it in his eyes. How worried he still was, I mean."

"Did you ask if he's consulted a doctor? Maybe there are drugs that can help."

"I didn't suggest anything. That's just it. What kind of friend is so wrapped up in their own wants and feelings that they don't bother to see what the other person is dealing with?"

"You're determined not to cut yourself any slack over this, aren't you? Lighten up. You're the best of friends. I'd never have made it through the last few years without you, and you know it."

"That's different. You're a woman. And I've known you all my life."

"How's it different?" Bree made an exasperated gesture with her hands. "Look, tonight, after you know the twins are in bed and his evening is more or less his own, wander over and knock on his door. Take a bottle of wine with you if you need a crutch, and ask him to come out and share it with you. Then you can introduce the possibility of consulting a doctor for Celia."

"I'm pregnant. Or did you forget? I'm off wine for the time being."

"You're making excuses. And you don't really need the wine anyway. Just go over there."

Zoe tried to picture herself waltzing up to Jake's front door and inviting him to come out to chat. She always felt comfortable around Jake, and he was easy to talk to, but that was when he approached her, not when she shoved her way into his problems.

"If it were me, would you feel so unsure of yourself?" Bree persisted.

Zoe knew she wouldn't. She shook her head.

"Okay, it's decided then. As soon as Sam's practice is over, I'll drop you off at home, and you'll walk next door. Better yet, I'll drop you at Jake's door. You'll have less time to get all self-conscious."

"Hey, Zoe. What's up?" Jake didn't seem surprised or the least bit awkward about her unannounced arrival. He pushed the screen door wider and stepped out onto the porch. "Something on the fritz again?"

"No. For once! Can we talk?" Zoe backed away from his overwhelming height and magnetism.

"Sure. Twins just went to bed, and Ava's busy with homework. What do you need to talk about? Are the twins being too chummy? Or maybe it's Ava who's making a pest of herself?"

Jake strode toward the porch swing and dropped himself into one corner. Zoe followed and curled up on the other end, tucking her feet under her. He stretched his long legs out and leaned back, his thigh pressing lightly against her knee. Zoe pulled herself into an even smaller ball and tried to ignore the way his closeness made her feel.

"Your girls are great company, and I love having them around. Even with all the livestock, it's still a big house for just me. I just wondered . . ." Zoe tailed off, still not sure if her opinions would be welcomed. "I came over to see how things were going with Celia. Since the other night, I mean."

Immediately, Jake's face clouded with concern, and his body tightened out of its casual slouch. "I wish I knew. She's never done anything like that before, and it scared me."

"I don't blame you. I was scared, and she's not even my mother-in-law. I was just thinking — have you — have you consulted her doctor? I mean, what if she has —" Zoe broke off, suddenly not wanting to suggest anything as serious as Alzheimer's. "What if there's something out there she could take that would help with her memory?"

Jake covered his face with his hand and rubbed his eyes, then slowly drew his hand down to his mouth. Briefly, he returned Zoe's gaze before looking away. "I know what you were going to say." He dropped his hand back into his lap. "You were going to say Alzheimer's. It's like the big C. And yes, that's what she has. But she's already on something for it."

"Oh." Zoe didn't know what to say next. Her whole focus had been on the fact that Celia could have been suffering from any of a dozen other things less ominous than Alzheimer's. She had done a Google search and had convinced herself she might be worrying about a worst-case scenario for nothing.

"I've known for a few years now, but when she first got the diagnosis, the doctor put her on this medicine, and she seemed back to her old self in just a couple weeks. But then . . ." Jake still wasn't looking at Zoe, but rather at a scrap of paper he'd found in the folds of the swing cushions. He fiddled with the paper, flicking the corner of it with his thumbnail.

"It not just the wandering," he finally added. "Celia used to do most of the cooking, but in the last year or so, Ava and I have been taking turns so I didn't notice —" He broke off and looked at Zoe with distress in his eyes.

"Didn't notice what, Jake?" Zoe prompted gently.

"I found her in the kitchen a couple days ago holding the fridge door open with all the cold air falling out. I asked her what she was doing, and she told me she was trying to decide what to fix for dinner. I closed the door and told her it was my turn to cook. She insisted that she always cooks dinner, so I told her it was a special night. I took her back to the den and turned *Judge Judy* on. She settled right in, and I thought that was that. But after I went to check on the twins and got back to the kitchen, there was Celia with the fridge door open again. And we went through the entire conversation like we'd never had it before." He pulled his feet in and hunched forward, elbows resting on his knees. "What am I going to do, Zoe?"

Without thinking, Zoe reached across the space that separated them and put her hand on Jake's shoulder. His head jerked up, and his gaze met hers. As the impact of that intense gray stare shot through her, Zoe's heart began to race. But the pain in his eyes overrode all the other things she felt. She wanted to pull him into her arms and comfort him like she would have had he been one of the twins. Then he turned his head and jerked his shoulder away. He rolled the bit of paper into a ball and threw it with force into the dark beyond the railing. "It's not fair."

"No, it's not, but hoping it's just temporary won't help her, Jake."

Abruptly, he shoved himself to his feet and crossed to the railing. He stood facing away from her, his hands braced on the railing, staring out into the dark, every line in his body taut. *Was he angry because she was butting into his problems uninvited?*

Then he turned back to her, gesturing helplessly with his hands. "I don't know what I'm going to do. Philip covered for me last night, and my mom's been by during the day to check on Celia, but I can't keep asking them to rearrange their lives all the time."

Relieved that he wasn't shutting her out, Zoe got off the swing and closed the small distance between them. She laid a hand on his forearm. "Make an appointment with her doctor. Maybe there's something else they can try. I'll babysit for you if you need me to. There's no point in worrying about all the possible scenarios you might face. Get the doctor's advice, then decide what next. And don't be afraid to ask *me* to help out. That's what friends are for." Then she

176

tiptoed, kissed him quickly on the mouth before he could pull away, and hurried down the stairs toward home.

CHAPTER 17

Jake pushed the screen door open with one elbow. He carried a mug of coffee in each hand. "Lynn didn't even make it through the first book. Lori crashed in the middle of the second one." He held one of the mugs toward Zoe.

Zoe reached for the offered mug. "I suppose this is that decaffeinated stuff."

Jake nodded.

"Might as well have just brought me a glass of water," Zoe muttered.

Jake, about to join her where she sat on the top step, hesitated. "You want me to get you water instead?"

"Sorry, no. I'm just being a grump because all my favorite beverages have been declared off limits. No wine. No coffee. No beer. Just this tasteless excuse for coffee."

"If you're sure," he said, smiling briefly as he folded his long legs and sat down next to her. "Besides, I'd hardly call you a grump.

178

Thanks again for picking the twins up at day care." Jake took a sip of his coffee and swallowed. "You didn't have to fix supper, too."

"Ava did most of it. I just helped. As for the pickup, I enjoyed it. Lori and Lynn showed me some of their artwork and the tunnel thing." Zoe laughed, a musical, friendly sound that he'd come to love. "It's like a giant gerbil cage for kids."

"It's their favorite part of the place."

"I was pretty impressed with the entire center. I put Molly's name on the infant list for next year, and I've got a fistful of paperwork to fill out once she's born."

"I don't think you'll be disappointed. My mom found the place for me. When Marsha took off I was right in the middle of a big project on the other side of the Cape Fear River, and I couldn't take a lot of time off. So my sister babysat while Mom did the legwork checking out my options. The twins fell in love with Miss Win and the play yard on their first day there." He set his mug down and stretched one leg out to reach into his pants pocket. "Speaking of the twins, Lynn asked me to give you this."

Zoe took the small wad of paper Jake held out and unfolded it. She chuckled as she studied the childish rendition of the kiddie

179

maze, then sobered again. "So, how did the doctor's appointment go?"

Jake sighed. His interview with Celia's doctor was the reason he'd asked Zoe to pick the twins up on her way home from work. There had been no chance for Zoe to question him with everyone present around the dinner table, and he'd been glad for the reprieve. He hadn't wanted to think about the decisions he was going to have to make regarding his mother-in-law. He should have known Zoe would follow up.

"Lately it seems like I've been doing nothing but sitting in front of one doctor or another discussing my family's mental health issues." And if he didn't start sleeping better, he'd be visiting the station shrink himself before long. Talking with Philip had been reassuring on some levels, but it hadn't banished his irrational fear that something bad was going to happen to Zoe and cause her baby to be born too early.

Zoe looked up, her eyes wide with concern, almost as if she'd been reading his mind. "Doctors? Plural? Who — ?"

"I was in to see Doctor Meredith about the twins a few weeks back."

Zoe's brow furrowed, and Jake hurried to explain.

"They start school in September, and I

got a letter from the Early Education Co-ordinator's office asking me if I wanted to have them assigned to separate classrooms. I know they're close, but I thought that was normal, and I just didn't know what the best answer was."

Zoe shrugged one shoulder. "Hard choice! What did Doctor Meredith say?" She put her half-finished mug of coffee aside and wrapped her hands around her knees.

"She thinks they're pretty well adjusted, and they'd probably take either decision in stride."

"So, will you separate them?"

"No." He shook his head. "Not this year anyway. I figure the switch from the less structured environment of day care to a full day of school is going to be stressful enough. No need to add to it. Besides, I'm not sure I'd survive it."

Zoe grinned. "What do you mean, survive it?"

"I'm a pushover for a woman in tears. I just can't feature myself walking out and leaving them in separate classrooms crying their eyes out. I'd probably end up bawling myself, and God knows what the teachers would think then."

"They'd think you were a father who cared about his kids' feelings. That's a good thing." The look in Zoe's eyes was a curious mix of tenderness and longing.

Jake wondered if she was thinking about her own little girl growing up without a father. Maybe Porter would have a change of heart once his baby was born. Jake recalled the moment he'd first held Ava and the enormous, unexpected bubble of love that had welled up inside him. He couldn't imagine any father turning away from the trusting, wide-open gaze of his newborn infant, even if he hadn't wanted a child to start with.

Jake hadn't wanted to be a father. Not at eighteen, anyway. He'd had plans. College. See the world. Hang out with the guys and enjoy a few footloose bachelor years. Even start his own company. But all that had changed when Marsha told him she was pregnant. They'd married right after gradu-ation, he'd moved from his parents' house to hers, and he'd gone to work for his father instead.

At the time, he'd thought he was in love and hadn't given much thought to all the might-have-beens. As the reality of being a married man with a baby on the way had settled in, he'd tried not to be jealous of his unattached friends. He'd done his best not to resent the long, hard hours starting out on the bottom rung of the ladder in spite of being the boss's son. Then the nurse had put that tiny wriggling bundle into his arms just moments after Ava's birth, and none of it mattered anymore. He'd loved that little mite more than he'd ever believed he was capable of loving anyone. Maybe the same thing would happen to Porter and take away the sadness in Zoe's eyes.

"I bet the twins will love school, no matter how they get settled in." The wistful look had faded from Zoe's face, replaced by a furrowed frown of concern. "But, how did you make out with Celia?"

"The doctor changed her meds. He says a switch in medication often brings a noticeable improvement. So I'm hoping . . ." Hoping for a change dramatic enough to avoid thinking about the rest of the doctor's advice.

"And if it doesn't?" Zoe's voice was soft and laced with an understanding compassion.

"He said I should start looking at assisted living options." There! The words were out, and suddenly they were painfully real, eclipsing even the nightmare-inducing worry about Zoe.

"And you don't want to think about it." Zoe glanced back at the house, then returned her gaze to his. "How long has it been since she was first diagnosed?"

"About five years since the official diagnosis, but we think it might be a lot longer. Marsha used to totally lose patience with her because Celia would get so mixed up. That was back when Celia understood enough to retaliate, and they'd end up yelling at each other."

"That had to be hard," Zoe murmured.

"It was harder at the time because Celia knew what was happening to her. All her life she'd been so easygoing, and she never used to lose her temper. But at the start of this it was like, all of a sudden, she'd be snapping at the girls, or Marsha, or me. Usually over nothing at all. But I think it wasn't so much about being angry at anyone so much as it was about being scared. She knew she was losing herself, and it scared her. Now she's kind of gotten past that. The only person she snaps at now is my Aunt Catherine, but my aunt usually deserves it."

"So maybe she's beyond being upset about the idea of a home?"

"I don't want to put Celia in a home. She —" He had to clear his throat. "Celia's been like a second mother to me. She's always been there for us. She took care of us. She took care of me, even when what I really deserved from her was contempt. Now it's my turn to take care of her." He wasn't going to abandon her. Not like Marsha. He was better than that.

"I wouldn't expect you to feel any different. That's the kind of man you are. But taking care of a parent with Alzheimer's is tough no matter how much you love them. And sometimes it's better for them to consider a home. Better for their safety. And —"

"Celia held our family together," he said, cutting Zoe off. "I didn't know it back then, but she was picking up all the slack. I was off working to support us, doing the manly thing. And Celia was being the mom to my kids so Marsha could play tennis and golf and have lunch with her unmarried friends. It wasn't until Celia got sick that I suddenly realized just how much she'd been filling in and letting Marsha go on as if she were still a teenager without a care in the world. As soon as it became clear that Celia couldn't manage it anymore, that's when Marsha took off."

Jake plowed his fingers through his hair. Anger rushed through him with searing intensity. He should shut up and not say anything else, but resentment and anguish drove him on. Words spilled out like a damn had burst. "Marsha never wanted to be a mother. She never wanted to be my wife either. She stopped pretending as soon as things fell apart, and it looked like she might have to grow up and be an adult for a change. How can a woman do that, Zoe? I mean, I get it that she didn't love me anymore, but how could she abandon her own kids? Her own mother?"

"Doesn't she ever come to see the kids or Celia?"

Jake shook his head. "Never. Not since the day she walked out. She called just the once to tell me it was over, but that was the last time I talked to her. I don't even know where she is except somewhere in Arizona."

"You're kidding! What about the divorce? Didn't you have to discuss that?"

"As far as Marsha is concerned, there was nothing to discuss. She wanted out and asked for nothing from me. I didn't get a choice."

"I see." Except it didn't sound as if Zoe did see. Jake couldn't blame her. He still had a hard time understanding Marsha's callous disregard for her mother and her children. And that wasn't the whole story.

He took a deep breath and began to explain in a calmer tone.

"When Celia realized she was sick, and

things were only going to get worse, she put everything in my control. I guess she knew her daughter a lot better than I ever did. Celia put the house and all the rest of her assets in trust for the girls with me as sole trustee. She gave me power of attorney and made me her executor. Marsha was furious."

"I guess that would tend to create a rift. But considering what you've told me, I can only admire the strength and wisdom Celia showed in choosing you over her daughter to manage her affairs."

"Marsha sulked for days and refused to even talk to her mother. Then she just up and left."

Zoe was quiet for so long, Jake wondered if he'd said too much. She probably had no desire to hear him vent about Marsha. Besides, he hadn't meant to dump all that anger and frustration out on Zoe. She didn't deserve it. It had just been easier to fume about Marsha than face his problem with Celia.

"It's not really about Marsha, and I'm sorry for the outburst. I'm over her, and I should be over all the anger, I guess. I thought I loved her once. Maybe I did, I don't know. But I guess what I'm really angry about is all the hurt she left behind for the girls and for Celia."

Zoe nodded her head understandingly. "Ava vents about it sometimes, too, but I think, on the whole, she's a pretty well-adjusted kid, doing a pretty good job of coping. The only time the twins talk about her, it's as if she was a visitor they once had and liked. Kids are more resilient than we give them credit for."

"Celia's not a kid. What about her?"

Jake realized Celia had never shared much of what she'd felt about her daughter's departure. She'd just gone on doing the best she could in spite of her memory problems. And he'd planned to make it up to her one day.

"It's just that I wanted to take Celia to Paris. Not to some lousy nursing home."

"Paris?" Zoe lifted her eyebrows. "Why Paris?"

"She always wanted to go to Paris. She and her best friend talked about it a lot. They talked about going when the last of their kids were out of school. Just the two of them. They had a scrapbook of pictures they'd been collecting for years: the Eiffel Tower, the Cathedral of Notre Dame, the Louvre, the Arc de Triomphe, Versailles, and a dozen other places. They talked about a river cruise on the Seine and going to the opera. It was a dream they'd had since they were girls, I think."

Zoe picked up her mug and put it to her lips, but then set it down again without drinking.

"Is that cold? You want a fresh mug?"

Zoe shook her head. "I assume they never got there?"

"Her friend did. But Celia stayed home to take care of Ava and Marsha. It's my fault. If I hadn't gotten Marsha pregnant, she'd have gone off to college, and Celia would have gone to Paris with her friend."

Jake was a little appalled at his admission. He'd never admitted out loud to anyone how guilty he felt about how different things might have been for Celia had he not let lust get in the way of good sense.

"I can see how you might feel it's your fault. But really? Why didn't Celia just put the trip off a few weeks or months and go later? Surely Marsha could have managed without her once Ava wasn't a newborn. Every other new mother in the world manages. Even teenage mothers."

"Marsha didn't want to manage without her! She whined and cried, and Celia gave up her trip. She gave up her life!" Jake shut his mouth abruptly, aware that once again, he'd let anger over things in the past erupt into the present where they had no business. "I just wish I'd taken Celia to Paris sooner. While she still remembered her dream."

Zoe felt the anguish in Jake's voice clear down to her own soul. She'd done things she regretted. Like sleeping with Porter. Except if she hadn't, there wouldn't be any Molly, and she already loved the little being growing inside her with fierce intensity. She couldn't imagine not having Molly in her life.

"Sometimes things happen for a reason. If things had been different, Celia might have gone to Paris, but you wouldn't have Ava. Would you want to change that?"

Jake dropped his forehead into the palms of his hands, blocking out the scene around him as if he were trying to picture such a life. He shook his head without lifting his face. "No." His admission was muffled. "But I still wish I didn't have to think about nursing homes."

"Celia doesn't need a nursing home. At least not right off. Have you ever been inside an assisted living home, Jake?"

"No," he admitted, then raised his head and looked at Zoe. "But I've been in a nursing home, and I hated every minute of it. My grandmother used to get parked in a chair with a table that held her captive for hours on end. Every day. For three years. I was pretty little at the time, but even so, I saw and understood the helpless despair in her eyes. No," he repeated. "I don't like the idea of putting Celia in any kind of a home. It's not the same as being with a family who loves you."

"I've never had to make such a choice for anyone I loved, and I'm not sure I wouldn't feel the same as you, but . . ." At the bleak look in Jake's eyes, Zoe wanted to reach out and hug him, but refrained.

"Look, Jake. On Sundays I deliver flowers from the altar at church to shut-ins. A couple of the people I visit are like Celia, and they live in protected environments within an assisted living facility. It's nothing like the nursing home you remember from your grandmother's day. Why don't you come with me this Sunday and check it out?"

"But she belongs with us," Jake insisted.

"She belongs where she'll be the safest," Zoe countered gently. Jake clearly had no idea what an assisted living facility was like. He was thinking with his heart, not his head. "It wouldn't be like you'd never see her. Or like she isn't still part of the family. It's like she has her own apartment, and you can visit anytime you like. And you can take her out anytime you want, too. Take her out to dinner and her favorite restaurant. Bring her to the house for parties and holidays or just because you want her around. Like on weekends, maybe, when you're not working and the kids are home from school. But when you can't be here to watch out for her, she'll have a place where she's taken care of and protected."

"That's what her doctor said, but . . ." Jake scrunched his shoulders up, then dropped them.

Zoe reached across the dark span that separated them and placed her hand on his forearm. "The best place I've visited is less than five minutes away. They have a great staff that engages the residents in all kinds of activities. They have movie nights. Bingo games. Cards and crafts and picture puzzles. There's a lovely outdoor area that's entirely enclosed. They can sit out there and enjoy the sun on nice days.

"Come with me this weekend," she urged. "Maybe the meds will bring about a big improvement, and it will turn out you don't need to do anything right now. Maybe you could even take her to Paris in a month or two. But eventually you will have to consider a home. Wouldn't it be nice to know what your options are?"

Jake gazed at Zoe in silence. Light from the front hall illuminated the strong planes of his face and glittered in his eyes. "You seem to care an awful lot. How come?"

It was on the tip of Zoe's tongue to say, *because I love you.* Instead, she said, "Because we're friends. And because I like Celia."

As they gazed at each other in silence, Zoe felt the pull that Jake always had for her. This man who was so capable. So gentle. So caring. And so torn up by the things life had done to him and those he loved. He was the man she'd been waiting for all her life. She was as incapable of pulling herself away from his magnetism as the moon was of breaking out of the earth's orbit.

When he leaned slowly toward her, Zoe knew he was going to kiss her. She wanted to close her eyes and be surprised by the touch of his mouth on hers. But she kept her eyes open. She watched him close the distance. Watched the play of emotions across his face. Probing the depth of his eyes, she hoped to see her love returned.

When his lips did touch hers, they were soft and ever so gentle. Just a brush of his flesh against hers. Excitement raced through her as if he'd lit off fireworks. She saw a flare of heat in his eyes in the brief moment before he closed them. Then he kissed her again.

CHAPTER 18

Jake knew he shouldn't be doing this. He shouldn't be kissing her. Shouldn't be holding her like this. His emotions were so close to the surface these days, and it had been too long since he'd been with a woman. Zoe was there. She was desirable and willing. And he could so easily end up taking them both to a place he shouldn't go.

He'd be taking advantage of her. And that was the last thing he wanted. But her mouth tasted so sweet. The way she melted against him just made him want to hang onto her forever.

Forever!

There was no forever! Jake dropped his arm and stood up abruptly. "Sorry. I shouldn't have done that."

He glanced down at Zoe. He saw the hurt in her eyes. Hurt he'd brought upon her. This had to stop. She was too vulnerable. She was his friend.

"Please, Jake. Don't be sorry. I'm not."

He reached down to take her hand and pulled her to her feet. "Then I won't be sorry either. But your friendship means a lot to me. I don't want to mess it up."

"I don't think you can mess it up. We haven't known each other that long, but our friendship means a lot to me, too." She cupped his cheek with one hand. Her fingers were cool against his skin.

"You're a very special guy, Jake. I treasure whatever it is we have going between us, so please don't be sorry. I —" She pressed her lips together for a moment, then the corners of her mouth turned up in a sweet little smile. "Good night, Jake. And don't forget to think about Sunday."

She tiptoed and quickly kissed him on the lips. Then she hurried down the steps and faded into the night just as she had done a few nights ago. He watched her reappear in the circle of light under the lamppost at the end of her front walk. She mounted her front stairs with a skipping step and headed for her door. At the last moment, she turned and blew him a kiss. Then the screen door slapped shut behind her, and her porch light went off.

Jake sank back onto the steps, thinking about what had just happened. Like an unseen wave that took one by surprise on the beach, desire had slammed into him, soaking and shocking in its power. But Zoe was his friend, not his lover.

He'd never had a woman as a friend before, and he wasn't sure just how to act. But he was damned sure that the notion of friends with benefits didn't work in the long run. Sooner or later one or both parties got hurt.

Zoe had burst into his life, bringing a houseful of animals and more problems than he could have thought possible. But somehow none of that mattered, because she was so full of life and optimism. She seemed wise beyond her years and generous to a fault. She glowed with something that came from within. Something he was incapable of putting words to, but felt inescapably drawn to. He felt as if he'd known her for years instead of mere months. He felt like he could tell her anything and she'd understand. That kind of friendship was rare, and he didn't want to lose it. He'd told Philip he wasn't going to mess around with her, and he meant it.

He'd just have to behave with her like he did with his friends on the fire crew, or the guys at work. Like he did with any of his other friends. But the memory of her mouth melting beneath his lingered and made him squirm. Maybe just being friends with a woman wasn't really possible after all.

Zoe leaned against her door in the darkened hall with her fingers pressed against her lips. Lips Jake had just kissed. A kiss that had not been about passion, yet she'd sensed that passion lurked beneath the surface. Why had he pulled away from her and leapt to his feet so abruptly? What kind of signal was she sending that made him back off every time they got close?

She'd wanted him to kiss her. How could she have made her desire any clearer? Could she have been mistaken about the passion after all? Jake said he treasured their friendship and didn't want to jeopardize it. So maybe that really was all he wanted from her.

Zoe thought about the other men she'd known. Not that she had all that much experience to review. She laughed at herself, but there wasn't any humor in it.

Starting with her father who needed someone to take over running the household, they'd all wanted something. The boy next door had wanted the thrill of feeling a girl's breasts. Male acquaintances in high school had been pretty much interested in getting help with their homework. Bree had set Zoe up on a blind date once, but after Zoe balked at making out in the back seat of his car, he hadn't asked for a second date. Porter had just wanted a convenient bed partner and maybe a leg up in her father's firm. But none had ever wanted to be her friend. Not until Jake.

Zoe had never had a male friend. A man she could be herself with. Who made her laugh and shared her political and religious views. Someone comfortable enough in his own skin to share his problems with her and wasn't afraid to admit to his mistakes. Not only had she never had a friend like Jake, she'd never even known a man like Jake. Jake was special.

Zoe sank to the floor, sliding her back slowly down the panels of the door.

She wrapped her arms tightly about herself and relived the intoxicating feeling of watching Jake's mouth descend on hers and the wonderful sensation of homecoming as he'd pulled her close. She'd wanted the kiss to last forever.

But Jake apparently didn't share such a desire. Otherwise, why would he jump to his feet, putting instant distance between them as if kissing her was forbidden?

Would friendship be enough? Could she

live next door to a man to whom she felt so physically drawn without always wanting more?

CHAPTER 19

With a display of flowers clutched in each arm, Jake followed Zoe through the automatic doors. He didn't want to be here. Ever since his discussion with her, he'd avoided thinking about it, but common sense told him to take Zoe's advice and check out his options.

He had driven past the Safe Haven Assisted Living Facility every day since it had been built more than five years ago and never really thought beyond the construction of it. He might have bid on the project except that at the time bids went out, he had been swamped with work, so the details weren't familiar to him. Even as he'd watched it grow from another lost parcel of the old Jolee plantation to the sprawling, low profile, red-brick building it was now, he hadn't considered what it would look like inside.

It definitely surprised him. Instead of the

201

antiseptic feel of a hospital, it looked more like the lobby of a four-star hotel. If Zoe was right, and he ended up liking the place, he suspected it would turn out to be way out of reach financially. Outside, the raw new brick half-hid behind a lush wall of thick green shrubs and half grown maple trees. Inside, at the center of the spacious foyer, a small fountain bubbled merrily, adding an air of serenity and elegance.

Several groupings of comfortable-looking chairs were set around coffee tables strewn with colorful magazines. At the far end, beside a currently unlit fireplace, an elderly man in a wheelchair smiled at his equally elderly companion who perched on the edge of a chair with her hand clasped in his. Jake guessed they were husband and wife. Closer to the fountain at the center a woman who looked old enough to be a centenarian chatted with a much younger woman while a toddler dragged his fingers through the water, making motorboat sounds with the tip of his tongue protruding between his lips.

Beyond the fountain, wide sliding doors opened out into an enclosed, open-air courtyard. A paved pathway led away from the building and branched out to meander through a well-manicured lawn punctuated in places with stone benches. Slender brown trunks gave evidence of more young maples, their canopies out of sight from where Jake stood. Hydrangea bushes laden with heavy blossoms added bright splashes of color.

Jake hesitated by the doorway to the courtyard to watch a small, dark woman in a maroon uniform who sat on one of the stone benches chatting with a white-haired gentleman. A dog wearing the bright orange vest of a therapy animal had his paws resting on the old man's thigh while the man fondled the dog's ears. It was such a pleasant, comforting scene that Jake was hastily revising his long-held antipathy toward homes for the elderly.

"This way." Zoe caught his attention and pointed toward a pair of closed elevator doors.

Jake took one last look at the old man and the dog before hefting the floral arrangements he still carried to a more comfortable position and turning to follow Zoe. "This place must cost a fortune."

"No more than a nursing home. Less than most, in fact." Zoe punched the *Up* button.

"I thought you said the Alzheimer's unit had a self-contained outdoor area. Do the residents have to navigate an elevator to get to it? I should think they might get confused and forget how to get back."

The door slid open. Jake and Zoe stepped inside. Zoe pressed two. There were only two floors, but Jake guessed elevators were required with so many folk in wheel chairs.

"Sometimes they do come down to the main courtyard, either with someone on the staff or a family member, but they have a private deck connected directly to the entry-controlled unit. It's on the roof of the main dining area with a fantastic view of the inland waterway. On a clear day you can see as far away as the ocean. One of the ladies I visit is nearly always outside, watching for boats passing through the waterway and speculating on where they are from and where they might be going. The unit has its own kitchen and dining area too, but some-times —"

The elevator door slid open, interrupting Zoe's description, and they moved out into a hall that looked as much like a classy hotel as the foyer had. To their right a set of doors with small windows in them closed off the hall beyond. Zoe punched a string of num-bers into a box on the wall, and the door lock clicked. Zoe pushed the door open and held it for Jake to pass through.

"Sometimes wh— ?" Jake started to ask what Zoe had been about to say when the elevator had delivered them to their floor, but then noticed the large travel posters decorating the walls. He stopped in stunned surprise, recognizing the Eiffel Tower lit up brightly against an inky night sky. Next to it, another poster depicted a sidewalk café with menu items written in French in the window. He took two more steps and studied a third poster of a tourist boat cruising on the Seine at dusk.

Slowly, Jake pivoted, glancing at each of the remaining posters in turn. The Louvre with its famous glass pyramid. The Pont-Neuf bridge decorated with sculptured heads. The Champs-Élysées in the rain dotted with brightly colored umbrellas. There were more that Jake couldn't identify, but they were unmistakably scenes that could be seen only in Paris.

"What is it?" Zoe returned to his side and followed his gaze.

"It's . . ." Jake had to clear his throat. "It's Paris."

Zoe did the same three-sixty Jake had just executed, then looked up at him with a growing grin of delight. "So it is! You know, I never paid much attention to them before. I mean, I've been coming here almost since I moved in, and I've seen the posters, but I just never stopped long enough to think about them. Amazing! What my friend Bree would call a *God's incidence*."

Jake looked down at Zoe's eager face through the fronds of ferns protruding from one of the arrangements. "A *God's incidence*?"

"She doesn't believe in coincidence. She says there is always a reason for things, even if we can't always see it, and that's when God is arranging things. So — *God's incidence*." Zoe did another little pirouette, her hand gesturing to the posters as she spun. "You wanted to take Celia to Paris, but maybe you will bring Paris to Celia instead."

It's not the same, Jake's heart stubbornly insisted. But still — the coincidence left him feeling a little dazed. What if God was directing him to this place? Jake closed his eyes against the overwhelming feeling of inevitability that he didn't want to face.

"Maybe," he muttered, turning his back on the posters. He strode off down the hall in an effort to escape the feeling. "Then again, maybe not."

Zoe hurried to keep up, but didn't argue with him.

In his haste, Jake didn't pay much attention at first to the rooms as he passed, but eventually he slowed and looked around. Even here in the lockdown ward, the place seemed more and more like a hotel and less and less like the nursing home Jake remembered.

"Here we are." Suddenly Zoe veered left into a room filled with sunshine and people. At tables scattered randomly around the room, residents were eating some kind of pudding or sipping coffee.

"Miss Zoe!" An elderly woman set down her coffee cup and stretched her hands toward Zoe. A warm smile creased her wrinkled face.

"Hello, Mrs. Warren." Zoe took both of the woman's hands and bent to kiss her cheek. "Look, I've brought a friend to visit today."

The older woman craned her neck to look past Zoe to where Jake stood with his arms still full of flowers. She wiggled her eyebrows at Zoe. "Is he someone special?"

Zoe's cheeks turned pink as she glanced toward Jake. "Put the flowers on the counter and come on over." She slid into a vacant chair next to the woman. "He's very special. He's my very good friend, Jake."

Jake felt the scrutiny of curious gazes as he deposited the flowers on the counter and then joined Zoe and her companion at the small table by a sliding door onto the private outdoor area Zoe had told him about.

With the introductions taken care of, Mrs. Warren began talking about her grandchildren. Photos were produced for Jake's inspection. Soon the soft babble of other conversations resumed, and Jake felt less conspicuous. He was able to relax and admire Zoe's ease with this lady she'd met only a couple months ago.

A dark-haired, well-built, young man dressed in the same maroon uniform as the woman in the courtyard wheeled in a cart and began clearing the tables of the remains of lunch. He took the time to chat with the people still sitting at the tables, and they clearly enjoyed his banter. He appeared to be telling them jokes because at one point a little bald man with a Santa Claus beard erupted into belly-jiggling chuckles. Everyone smiled at the young man making his rounds, and several of them waved at him as he departed.

This was definitely *not* Jake's grandmother's nursing home.

Zoe got to her feet and kissed Mrs. Warren on the cheek again. "Shall I put your flowers on your dresser?"

"If you wouldn't mind, that would be so very nice, dear," Mrs. Warren replied in her soft southern voice. Then she turned to Jake, who'd realized they were preparing to move on and had gotten to his feet. "It was a pleasure to meet you, young man. I do hope you will come again."

"Yes, ma'am," Jake answered automatically. Then, without thinking about it, he copied Zoe and bent to kiss the old woman's cheek.

The smile she bestowed on him told him how much she appreciated his response. It made him feel warm inside, as if he'd done a good deed. In a way, he supposed he had. Not that he'd gone out of his way to do anything special, but the twenty minutes they'd spent chatting with her had clearly brightened Mrs. Warren's afternoon.

Zoe grabbed one of the vases filled with flowers, and Jake picked up the other. He followed her out of the dining room and down the hall to a room that he assumed belonged to Mrs. Warren. It was furnished in dark oak with a pale orange afghan thrown over the back of a battered old rocker and a pastel floral bedspread on the bed of roughly the same vintage as the rocker. A barrage of photos lined the dresser: a large, very old wedding photo, several graduations, a few weddings, and a myriad of children dressed in everything from school uniforms to Halloween costumes. Mrs. Warren clearly had a large family. Jake wondered how often any of them came to see her.

When Zoe had arranged the flowers she'd been carrying on a small round table near the window, she headed for the door again. "Now we go to visit Durbin. You won't understand much of what he says, and he won't remember seeing you five minutes after we've gone, but he likes the company, anyway. We'll leave those flowers in the television room for everyone to enjoy."

As they strode down the hall, Zoe leaned close and asked, "So, what do you think so far?"

"It's not much like I imagined." If he hadn't been carrying the flowers in that arm, he'd have taken her hand in his to keep her close. She was like a ray of sunshine. She made everyone she touched feel good. Including him.

"Didn't I tell you?" she asked with an impish grin.

"You did. At least you tried. I guess I wasn't in a mood to listen."

"I understand where you're coming from, so I'll forgive you. This time. Here's the TV room."

The television room was far busier and noisier than the dining room had been. Two women playing cards in the corner were arguing over whether one of them had cheated. Another maroon-clad man held a skein of bright red yarn stretched out between his large hands while a diminutive little woman wound the yarn into a ball. And a child of about four was pushing a small toy racecar along the back of a couch with appropriate sound effects while his mother chatted with a dapperly dressed older man.

Three more men parked in front of the television were cheering on a batter who faced a left-handed pitcher and had three men on base with two outs. Jake couldn't help being distracted long enough to see if the guy would get a hit or strike out. When the ball sailed into the stands in fair territory, all three of the men watching erupted into cheers. By the time Jake tore his attention away from the television, Zoe had already arranged the flowers on a side table and was headed back out the door. Jake gave the men a thumbs-up gesture and then followed her.

"It's not always that crazy in there," Zoe told him. "But it's Sunday afternoon. And there is Durbin. He was a jockey back in the day, and that's about all he talks about. Horses and racing." In a small alcove to one side of the hall, a trio of easy chairs was grouped against the wall. A man no bigger than Ava, yet wrinkled like a prune with dark skin and a full head of white hair, perched on the middle chair.

Durbin's conversation, as incomprehensible as Zoe had predicted, was entirely about horses. Also as predicted. But Durbin hadn't required any response. He was just happy to have someone to talk at, and Zoe made all the right sounds in all the right places. When they got up to leave, Durbin winked at Zoe in a way that suggested he'd once been a ladies' man as well as a horseman. Then he happily returned to his worn copy of *American Turf Monthly*.

As they waited for the elevator, Zoe smiled encouragingly. "So, you want to stop by the office and see if anyone is in? Maybe they have some printed information you could take home with you to read."

"I suppose," Jake said as he put a hand to Zoe's back to usher her into the elevator. He hoped the office would be locked up, and he wouldn't have to talk to anyone. Not today. He still wasn't ready, even though Safe Haven had turned out vastly different than his expectations. The posters of Paris unnerved him as much on their way out as they had when he'd first seen them. "Do you come here every Sunday?"

"No, just on my week to deliver the altar flowers, but sometimes I stop in on my way home from work. One time a client brought a bunch of helium balloons into the office for my boss's birthday. He didn't want to keep them, so I brought them here. The old folks loved them. Durbin thought it must be a birthday party, and he was disappointed there was no cake. But most of the residents thought it was fun. So, I stop in from time to time, and I usually try to bring something unexpected."

"Unexpected like what?"

"One time I brought a bunch of foam balls, and they had a grand time tossing them at each other. Then the staff got into the game and found a couple laundry baskets to shoot at. Everyone loves to play. Doesn't matter how old or forgetful you get."

"You are a remarkable woman, Zoe Callahan."

Zoe grinned. "Yes, I am."

There was that spark of sassy confidence that so attracted Jake. He'd rarely met a woman who seemed so unaware of how attractive she was, and yet could still be so self-possessed and happy with herself.

He was still marveling over the mystery of Zoe when she veered away from the lobby as they stepped off the elevator. She stopped in front of a closed door and looked back at Jake, her mouth turned down in an exaggerated pout.

"We'll have to come back."

"We?" Celia was his problem. In spite of Zoe's interest and support, this was his struggle.

"Well, one of us anyway." Zoe shrugged, ignoring Jake's pointed *we*. "The office is usually closed when I come by after work, too. But maybe on my lunch break I could run over and ask for you."

As they headed back toward the lobby, Jake considered her offer. Considered what it might be like to have someone who shared his fears and heartache. Wasn't that what friends were for?

"Isn't that a little out of your way?"

Zoe shrugged, still smiling. "I like to get out of the office on a nice day. Any excuse is as good as another."

The automatic doors swished open, and they stepped out into the sunshine. "Well, then, considering the construction project I'm on right now is on the other side of Wilmington, I'll take you up on it. Thanks."

As they stepped off the curb to cross to his van, Zoe looked up at him with an oddly curious expression on her face. She was

214

probably surprised by his sudden capitulation. He certainly was. But something else seemed to be lurking in that clear hazel gaze. His heart suddenly skipped a few beats.

Then she tripped, and his heart slammed into overdrive.

"Zoe!" Jake reached for her, but connected with nothing.

Zoe sprawled onto the pavement with a grunt. Her purse skittered ahead of her. Jake dropped to his knees beside her. "Are you okay?" It was his fault. She had been looking at him, not where she was going. "Where are you hurt?"

Zoe rolled over and sat up. "Another ruined pair of pantyhose." She touched her knee where it had begun to ooze bright drops of blood. "Ouch."

Jake fumbled for his handkerchief, then began blotting the wound. His heart still raged wildly in his chest, and his brain had begun processing the possible ramifications of Zoe splatting onto her belly like that.

"Help me up, Jake." Zoe reached for his hand. "This is embarrassing."

Jake ignored the outstretched hand and scooped her up into his arms. He strode toward his car, wondering if he should suggest she call her doctor.

"Jake? Put me down. Now it's getting really embarrassing."

He set her on her feet next to the van and hurried back to grab her purse. "Here." He pressed it into her hands. He pulled his keys out of his pocket and reached past her to unlock the car. His hand shook. When his second effort to put the key into the lock failed, Zoe's hand closed around his and took the keys away. She unlocked the door and handed them back.

"Are you sure you're good to drive?" She looked at him quizzically.

"I'm fine to drive. You're the one who just took a spill. What if something happened to the baby?"

"I'm mortified, if you must know. But Molly is fine."

"But that fall —"

"I'm not a piece of porcelain, Jake. I'm just . . ." Zoe's voice trailed off, and the look of embarrassment left her face. Her hazel eyes went dark, and she swallowed audibly.

In the next instant he was kissing her as if he might never stop. He cradled her face with both hands and angled her head, opening his mouth and running his tongue along her lips.

When she responded, his blood raged

216

through his body, humming and singing with building excitement. He nibbled and teased. Zoe leaned into him and teased back. He forgot where he was. He forgot about the spill she'd taken. He forgot he wasn't supposed to be kissing her.

When she crooned softly in her throat, the world came crashing back. Jake swallowed hard and drew back. Slowly he let his hands drop to his sides and stepped back. Zoe stared at him with wide, startled eyes for several long moments. Then she wordlessly folded herself into the van.

Jake shut the door and headed around to his side of the van, but had to stop halfway there to catch his breath. He'd known Zoe Callahan was a dangerously attractive woman the first day they'd met. He just hadn't known how dangerous.

Zoe let her head fall back against the headrest, eyes shut tight. Slowly her heart eased off its frantic runaway pace, and her lungs began to function normally again. She felt totally disoriented and very close to tears.

Just a half dozen heartbeats ago, she'd been caught up in the most incredible kiss she'd ever experienced. Although their bodies had not even touched, there had been nothing but passion in Jake's kiss this time. His hands had been warm and gentle on her face, making her feel treasured and appealing in a way she'd never felt before. And all the while his mouth had been doing things that made her ache everywhere with hungry desperation.

Then he'd backed away so quickly that if she hadn't had one hand braced against his chest and the other clutching the top of the van's door, she'd have fallen on her face.

She expected to hear the door open and then feel the car dip as Jake hauled his big frame into the driver's seat. But the silence lengthened and nothing happened. Zoe opened her eyes.

Jake stood with one hand on the hood of the van gazing down at his feet. *He's probably wondering what on earth possessed him to kiss the klutz. Maybe he's rehearsing another apology. Or maybe he's feeling all the same things I am and wondering why he stopped himself.*

What is it that keeps coming between us?

Molly kicked hard. Zoe jerked her gaze down to her belly and watched as some part of Molly's anatomy arced across the protruding surface of Zoe's blue, jersey-covered stomach. Then the baby was still again.

Is that what's stopping you, Jake? Another man's baby? Zoe pressed her palms against her eyes and gulped back a sudden sob.

Life wasn't fair. She'd finally met the man she'd been destined to fall in love with, and she was pregnant with another man's baby. A man she hadn't been able to love, and who'd lost interest in her the moment he found out she was pregnant. Jake could hardly be blamed for not wanting to take on the responsibility for another man's child.

He can't be blamed for not wanting me either.

CHAPTER 20

Zoe stirred, not wanting to let go of the dream.

Moonlight lit the beach with a soft aura of romance. Waves chuckled against the shore and sent sheets of water running up the sandy slope, but their blanket was their private little oasis in this shadowy land of enchantment.

Jake was touching her, exploring the contours of her body, his hand stopping briefly to caress the rounded bulge of baby and belly. It didn't seem to matter that she was pregnant and her body distended with the growing baby inside. The love in Jake's eyes was hot with passion, and he was telling her . . .

What had he been telling her?

Zoe opened her eyes. Immediately the dream retreated into wispy recollection. No beach. No moonlight. No Jake. She looked about the room and wondered what had disturbed her. It was still dark out and not time to get up yet. Maybe it was that other perk of pregnancy — several nightly trips to the toilet.

Zoe climbed out of bed, carefully flexed her skinned knee, and padded into the bathroom. Afterward, she washed her hands, filled a glass with water, and took a drink. Then she headed back to bed. Jet lay stretched across the hallway at the top of the stairs, which seemed odd because the dogs usually slept downstairs. Then Zoe noticed light seeping out from under the door of the nursery. She didn't remember leaving the light on in there. She definitely hadn't closed the door.

With her heart thumping erratically, she tiptoed to the door and silently pushed it open. Jet got to her feet and leaned against Zoe's leg. Celia sat in Zoe's rocking chair, eyes closed, humming so softly the sound was almost inaudible. Zoe's heart lurched. The change of meds apparently wasn't helping. Jake was going to be crushed.

"Celia?" Zoe moved slowly into the room. She didn't want to startle the older woman. "What are you doing? It's the middle of the night."

Celia looked up at Zoe, her eyes misted as if she were seeing something in her memory.

"Martin's baby was crying. Martin wasn't here to take care of her, so I came to help." She glanced down at her arms.

That's when Zoe noticed that Celia held Zoe's threadbare old teddy in her arms as if it were an infant. She rocked gently, crooning to the teddy bear. Zoe vacillated between staying and talking with Celia in hopes that the present would return to her consciousness, or hurrying back to her own bedroom to call Jake. Zoe opted for calling Jake.

Within minutes, Jake was at her door, dressed in pajama bottoms and a T-shirt with his hair standing on end. "I'm sorry," he said as he hurried through the door Zoe held open for him. "How long has she been here?"

"I don't have any idea. I was asleep when she came in. Did Martin have any kids?"

Jake halted abruptly and glanced down at Zoe with a frown furrowing his brow. "Yeah. Marsha's cousin, Donna. Why?"

Zoe turned toward the stairs. "Celia's in the nursery rocking my old teddy bear. She thinks it's Martin's baby. And she said Martin wasn't here to care for her."

Jake started up the stairs to the room he'd recently painted for Zoe's baby. Neither of them had known the room had been used as a nursery before, but apparently Celia had. "Donna is considerably older than Marsha. She was born after her father left for Korea. Martin never even knew he had a daughter."

Jake felt a gnawing despair growing in his gut. Celia would have been just a teenager at the time, but she must have been involved in caring for the infant. Now her memories, receding ever further into the past, were of a time even before she'd married Martin's younger brother, Richard. The new medicine wasn't proving to be as effective as the first one had been. Things were spiraling out of control.

Celia looked up when Jake slipped into the room. She still held the bear. Her face registered momentary confusion and then cleared. "Martin! I knew you'd come home as soon as you knew Donna needed you."

Jake knelt in front of his mother-in-law, his heart aching with sadness. "I'm not Martin," he said as gently as he could. "I'm Jake."

Celia reached to touch his cheek. Her lips curved up in a smile of infinite sweetness. "Of course you are." Almost immediately her face clouded again, and she looked around her in confusion. "Why am I here?"

"You came to check on Zoe. You were worried about her, but she's fine, and it's time to go home now." Jake took the bear from Celia's arms and handed it to Zoe. Then he put a hand under Celia's elbow and urged her to her feet.

"Is there anything I can do?" Zoe hovered, looking worried and helpless. As helpless as he felt.

Jake shook his head. "Thanks for calling me instead of the cops when you found someone in your house in the middle of the night." He guided Celia toward the stairs.

"The dogs never barked, so I never really thought to be afraid. I just wondered why the light was on. And of course, as soon as I saw it was Celia, who else would I call?"

"You are a remarkable woman, Zoe Callahan." Jake followed Celia down the stairs. "I hope she didn't ruin the rest of the night for you."

Zoe held the door while Jake ushered Celia out into the night. "Don't worry about it. I won't have any problem getting back to sleep. I never do."

"Well, good night. And thanks. I —" He hesitated, wanted to say something more, but what was there to say? He'd said thanks. And good night. But she gazed up at him with an eager, expectant look in her lovely hazel eyes. He almost kissed her, but stopped himself before impulse became action. "See you tomorrow, maybe." Then he hurried after Celia.

Jake stared up into the shadowy darkness of his bedroom, hands folded behind his head, listening to the soft sounds of Celia sleeping next door in Ava's bedroom. Safe for now. He had roused Ava and sent her to sleep in Celia's bed for the remainder of the night, then convinced Celia to sleep in Ava's bed. He felt easier being close enough to hear if Celia wandered again. But what about tomorrow night? And the night after that? He couldn't stay awake every night listening. And what about the times he got called out to a fire?

He closed his eyes. They were heavy with weariness, but sleep was far away. Visions of Parisian posters flitted through his memory, taunting him with heartbreaking choices and promises not kept.

Jake rolled over and punched his pillow to fluff it up. He pressed his face and tired eyes into the cool percale fabric, but the images didn't go away. He rolled onto his side and bent his knees.

Abruptly he lifted his head. He couldn't hear Celia. He slid his feet to the floor and crossed the room in three strides, passed through the bathroom, and slanted his head against the partially open door to the next room.

Total silence.

Then he thought he heard the rustle of bedclothes. He stuck his head all the way into Ava's room and heaved a sigh of relief to see the small irregular shape of Celia facing away from him. Silently he retreated to his own room again. He stood at the window, staring across the lawn to the fence that separated his yard from Zoe's, remembering her gentle insistence that keeping Celia safe might be a difficult decision, but it would be the loving choice if the new meds didn't work.

And it was clear they weren't working. Celia's doctor had increased the dose, but even that attempt to halt the course of the disease had had little effect. Jake had been hoping for another remarkable reprieve like the first medication they'd tried almost three years ago. What could have triggered this seemingly sudden decline after nearly three relatively stable years?

The words to a familiar Psalm filtered into Jake's head. *The Lord is my shepherd . . .* he muttered the words out loud. "So lead me. Tell me what I should do. I've got all these questions and no answers."

Then it occurred to Jake that perhaps

226

tonight's misadventure had been his answer. Perhaps the answers had been around him all along.

Two days ago, he'd come in from mowing the lawn and been assaulted by the reek of burning plastic. Dashing for the kitchen with his heart in his throat and his cell phone out ready to dial 911, he'd discovered the source of the stench with a mixture of impatience and dismay. Celia had tried to reheat a leftover serving of lasagna. But rather than putting the plastic container in the microwave as she had always done before, she'd turned on the regular oven. The plastic had melted of course. It had dripped down through the oven rack and plopped onto the bottom of the oven in big soft drops where little blue flames danced with merry abandon. Celia herself had forgotten all about the snack she'd been reheating and had wandered off to the den and *Judge Judy.*

Jake returned to his bed and flopped down wearily. He thought about the posters again — all the places Celia had dreamed of visiting lining the pale green walls of the Safe Haven Alzheimer Unit. He thought about the attentive maroon-clad staff chatting and visiting with the residents, joking with them and making them smile. He thought about the fact that Zoe had known about Safe Haven, had visited it often, and knew the people who ran it. And more importantly, he considered the phone call he'd had from the director just before quitting time yesterday to let him know that a room would become available in two weeks if he was still interested.

Jake closed his eyes and tried to will away the problem and let sleep come.

It seemed like just moments later he jerked to wakefulness again, his shirt soaked with sweat and his heart hammering. With wide, aching eyes, he stared into the dark, but instead of his familiar bedroom walls, he saw only Zoe's frightened face. Her terrified voice echoed in his brain.

"I think the baby is coming, and it's too soon."

CHAPTER 21

Jake called to thank Zoe again while she was finishing her breakfast. She scooped up the last bit of grits, popped the spoon into her mouth, and put her bowl on the counter. Cradling the phone under one ear, she began to assemble her lunch. She was running late after sleeping through her alarm.

Jake sounded exhausted as he told her about the call from Safe Haven and his decision given last night's escapade.

"Are you going to be okay with this?"

Zoe finished slathering peanut butter on a slice of bread and slapped a second slice on top. She listened to his brief account of how he'd wrestled with his options after bringing Celia home again in the wee hours, sensing that his decision had been a lot harder to make than he made it sound. She shoved a banana into the bag along with the sandwich, wishing she had the time to go over and talk with him in person. To look into his eyes and make sure he was okay with it. Perhaps her boss wouldn't be too upset with her if she came in more than just a little late?

"I told the woman I'd stop by with a deposit today."

"I know it's not easy, but I think you're doing the right thing."

She heard Jake sigh. Then, "I know. I just — I know it's best. Hey, look, last night I noticed you didn't have a crib yet."

Changing the subject. Obviously he didn't want to talk about Celia anymore. "Just haven't gotten around to it. I suppose I should though. I mean, Molly could make an early appearance and catch me out. Right?"

Jake made an odd noise as if she'd given him bad news and wondered why her joking comment should trigger such a reaction. Then she remembered his worried concern when she took that spill in the parking lot.

"Jake? I'm kidding."

"Yeah, well . . . What I was going to say was that I have two perfectly good cribs sitting in my garage I doubt I'm ever going to need again. They're the kind that convert to youth beds. If you're interested, that is . . ."

"If they're convertibles, how come the twins aren't using them?"

"They wanted princess beds. With canopies and ruffles." Jake snorted, softly.

Zoe pictured him assembling beds with tall frames while the twins pranced around with excitement. "If you're sure, I'd love to borrow one."

One less expense to wrangle out of her already tight budget. Her father had been right about the financial drain the upkeep of a house would turn out to be. She couldn't afford to be choosy if a decent crib was available for free.

"Right then. I'll bring it over tonight. And, Zoe? Be careful. Okay?"

As soon as Zoe got home from work, she hurried up to the little room she had designated as Molly's. She moved all the boxes of baby clothes her sister-in-law had passed along to make room for the crib. She'd barely finished when she heard Jake's footsteps on the porch stairs.

"The mattresses were pretty shot, and they got tossed out, so you'll have to get a new one," Jake said as he leaned the headboard, footboard, and rails against the wall. Then he disappeared back down the stairs and returned with the spring and the toolbox that Zoe had become so familiar with.

"I could probably do that myself," Zoe of-

231

fered as Jake began to sort through the hardware he'd dumped out of a tattered manila envelope.

"Yeah! You probably could." He raised his eyebrows at her, then turned to root through his toolbox and came up with an adjustable wrench. "But I'm here, and I've got all the tools, so I might as well save you the trouble."

Zoe sank into the rocker. Watching Jake work was something she found vastly enjoyable no matter what the project was, but watching him set up a crib for her baby tugged at a desire buried deep within. She wished Molly was Jake's baby, and that he would be around for a lot more than just putting a crib together. She'd seen the way he was with his own girls, and she jealously wanted that for Molly.

Zoe wanted to see her infant cradled in those big capable hands while Jake sang lullabies in his deep, sexy baritone. She wanted Molly to have a daddy to give her baths and read to her at night. To teach her how to tie her shoes and to ride a bike. A father whose eyes would get glassy with tears as he watched her receive her college diploma. A father to give her away at her wedding. She wished with all her heart that Jake was Molly's father instead of Porter.

But it wasn't just about what Zoe wanted for Molly. Zoe wanted what she'd had in her dream last night. She wanted Jake to be as much in love with her as she was in love with him.

Thinking about the dream, and what they'd been doing in it, Zoe felt a sudden wave of longing rush through her. She watched his dexterous fingers find and fit bolts into holes he couldn't see, then quickly tighten the nuts as the crib came together. All of a sudden, all she could think of were the things he could do to her body with those sensitive fingers. A blinding memory of the kiss they'd shared in the Safe Haven parking lot rocketed through her along with all the heady desire it had provoked. Zoe couldn't sit still and watch any longer.

Lurching out of the rocker with a flush heating her cheeks, Zoe mumbled something unintelligible and bolted from the room.

A short while later, Jake found her standing by the porch railing, where she'd been gazing blindly out over the waterway. He set his toolbox on the top step and approached, looking worried. "Something wrong?"

Zoe shook her head. "Don't mind me. I'm a little emotional lately."

Jake settled his butt against the solid new

railing he'd installed just a couple months back and peered at her with concern still clearly visible in his gray eyes. "I hope it wasn't anything I said."

Zoe winced. *It was something I was thinking!* "No! It was just . . . I can't believe I'm really going to be a mother."

Jake grinned and glanced at Zoe's very pregnant belly. "Believe it! I don't think there's much doubt. How are the birthing classes going? Your friend Bree is going to them with you, isn't she?"

Bree was Zoe's labor coach. And she was a good one. At least it seemed that way in the classes, and Zoe had no reason to think Bree wouldn't be just as effective in the labor room. But at her last class, Zoe hadn't been able to stop herself from looking around at all the solicitous husbands, soon-to-be fathers. She'd envied the women as they accepted the fluffing of pillows and the counting of their practice panting punctuated with loving little kisses and casual endearments.

She had closed her eyes and tried to imagine that it was Jake holding her hands. And Jake's comforting strength steadying her shoulders. When she'd opened them again, and it was still Bree smiling at her in encouragement, Zoe had wanted to cry.

She looked away quickly lest Jake see the longing in her eyes. "Bree's always been a friend I can count on. I'm lucky to have her. Lucky to have Ava, too." With her emotions back under control, Zoe turned back. "Ava made shopping for maternity clothes an adventure instead of a chore. I really enjoy her company."

"Ava's changed a lot since you showed up." Jake ran a hand through his hair, making it stand up like it had when he'd arrived straight from his bed clad only in his pajamas.

Immediately, Zoe felt the same tug of amusement and desire she'd felt in the middle of the night. She wanted to reach out and smooth the tufts of hair down again.

"For the better, I mean," Jake continued, oblivious of the thoughts running through Zoe's disobedient brain. "You've been a good influence on her. She's been a lot easier to talk to." Then he snorted and flashed Zoe a rueful grin, his teeth white against his tanned skin in the growing dusk. "Of course, it might just be that you've been a good influence on me. You've taught me how to appreciate Ava and the young woman she has become. We were luckier than we knew the day you moved in next door."

"It's been a two-way street — Oh my!" Zoe peered at her stomach in surprise. She grabbed the railing and cupped her belly with the other hand.

"What is it?" Jake sounded alarmed.

Molly kicked again, then squirmed. "It's Molly. She kicked me."

Jake bent at the waist and spoke to Zoe's belly. "Hey, Miss Molly. Be nice to your mother." Then he glanced up at Zoe. "Kind of amazing, isn't it? There's this little person in there. And you made her, all by yourself. Well, almost all by yourself."

Zoe stared down into Jake's warm gray eyes and felt like she was falling. How had she ever thought gray was cold and hard? His eyes. His smile. Everything about him was warm and comforting. She felt as if nothing bad could ever happen to her so long as Jake was there to catch her.

Molly turned, and Zoe's belly bulged alarmingly. Jake reached out, then hesitated. "May I?"

Zoe nodded, bemused to be sharing this oddly intimate moment with Jake.

Jake gently rested his hand over the bulge. Molly obligingly moved again and then was still. This time, when Jake looked up at Zoe there was something else in his eyes that hadn't been there a moment before. Slowly

236

he straightened, his hand still curved warmly over her belly. Then he bent his head and covered her mouth with his.

Zoe swayed toward Jake's broad chest, and he caught her against him with his free arm, pulling her close. Very quickly the tender moment of wonder was eclipsed by a wave of fiery desire. Jake's kiss deepened, and he shifted to hold Zoe with both arms. She ached for the swimming, swirling feelings of sexual awareness to intensify and blossom. She so wanted Jake to be in love with her.

Jake wasn't sure how he'd gotten from marveling over the movement of Zoe's baby to the realization that he was sexually aroused. It didn't matter that Zoe was enormously pregnant, he hadn't been so turned on in years. Or maybe ever. This shouldn't be happening. What was wrong with him? Zoe was his friend.

He dragged his mouth away from hers and sucked in a ragged breath.

Zoe's eyes were dark with desire. Her breathing as uneven as his own.

He wanted this woman. He wanted all of her. He wanted — God! What did he want? As he'd kissed her, and she'd melted into him, an image of them naked in bed, with her spooned into the curve of his body while he covered her swollen belly with his hands had filled him with such a sharp stab of longing that it hurt.

But he couldn't lose her friendship. It was too precious. He couldn't give in to this. Whatever this was. He wasn't going to mess around with her. He couldn't.

Jake dropped his arms and stepped back. "We can't do this."

"Why not?" she whispered in a husky voice. She swayed toward him again.

"I can't." Jake planted both hands on her shoulders and held her away. "I can't take advantage of you. Not like this."

"I'm an adult, Jake. You're not taking advantage. What's wrong with wanting each other?"

Jake released her and ran an agitated hand through his hair. "It wouldn't stop at wanting. We let this go any further, and we both know where we'd end up. And it'd be great." It would be better than great. But it would be the worst thing he could do to her. "But it would be wrong. You're not that kind of woman."

"What kind of woman am I then?" Zoe's eyes flared with something different. The desire he'd seen in them just a moment before had been quenched and replaced with uncertainty.

"The Cinderella kind," he spit out in frustration, and immediately regretted it. He hadn't meant to sound so rude or hurtful.

"What's that supposed to mean?" Her question stabbed at his heart.

"You believe in fairy tales." He softened his voice, trying to take the sting out of his words. "You want happy-ever-after. But this isn't love. This is — I don't know what it is, but it's not a fairy tale. We're just friends."

"Friends can be lovers, too." Zoe sounded more confused than hurt. "I know I'm as big as a whale and not very desirable right now, but I —"

"You are more desirable than any woman I've ever known. If you weren't, we wouldn't even be having this conversation. But there's Molly to consider."

"What about Molly?" Zoe's voice had taken on a hint of desperation.

"She's not my kid. I'm just . . . not . . . I can't . . . I — I'm sorry."

He turned and fled.

CHAPTER 22

Zoe stood frozen in shock as Jake snagged his toolbox and took her front steps in three giant leaps, as if he had a fire to get to. He bolted across the lawn, through the gate and up his driveway, the toolbox banging against his thigh. He didn't look back.

When he'd disappeared into his garage, and the door had come down with a *thunk* of finality, Zoe finally turned away and went into the house. She climbed the stairs with leaden feet and returned to the nursery and the newly installed crib, her heart crushed. She picked up her worn old teddy bear and slumped into the rocker. Clutching the much-loved remnant of her childhood tightly against her chest, she hugged it hard, desperate to stifle the empty feeling of loss.

She no longer doubted that Jake found her physically attractive. Although exactly why he was attracted to her was a mystery. But he didn't love her. He just wanted to be friends, and he didn't want to mess it up with sex.

His hot and cold behavior suddenly made sense. It made sense that he wouldn't let their friendship blossom into something more. It made sense that every time something hot and heady flared up between them, he ran for cover. She was just a handy neighbor who could help him sort out his family problems in return for tasks he was good at. Apparently he wasn't good at relationships. Maybe there was a good reason Marsha had walked out on him — good enough to leave her own children behind.

It shouldn't have surprised Zoe. Every man she'd ever thought was important in her life had used her. Had wanted her for what she could do for him, rather than loving her for the person she was inside. Jake was just the most recent.

First it was her father, who treated her sisters like little princesses while Zoe had become her mother's replacement. She hadn't been the scorned stepsister exactly, but even so, her value to her father seemed more rooted in the cooking, cleaning, and overseeing of her siblings, than in pride and love for his firstborn. Zoe tried to remember the last time her father had hugged her or told her he loved her, but the scene between them when she'd told him she was unwed, unengaged, and pregnant had been pretty typical.

Then there'd been her affair with the newest lawyer in her father's firm, the man her father had wanted her to marry. When she first met him, Porter had seemed excitingly different. He'd told her she was pretty, something she knew she was not, but it was nice to hear anyway. They'd enjoyed the same movies, read many of the same books, and they liked the same restaurants. Porter had been the only man she'd ever slept with, and that had been exciting at first, too. But then she'd gotten pregnant, and everything had changed.

When she'd told Porter, he'd demanded she get an abortion and began outlining *his* plans for *his* future. That's when Zoe had realized they didn't have so much in common after all. She'd also realized there had never really been any love between them. For her, it had been a heady whirlwind of lust and the kind of attention she'd never had before. For him, she'd been the means to an end. A way to curry favor with her father.

But Jake had seemed so different. That first night looking up into his rueful gray gaze, Zoe had felt her heart expand with feelings she'd never experienced with anyone else. Before she knew it, she was helping Jake figure out how to deal with his teenage daughter. She'd become Ava's confidant, although that hadn't been hard. Ava's age put her closer to being Zoe's peer than her daughter. To be honest, their friendship probably would have happened without Jake in the picture.

When Jake needed a babysitter, she'd been happy to help out. The twins were great fun. She loved spending time with them and hadn't thought about how Jake might be taking advantage of the situation.

And then there was Celia. Not that Jake had asked for Zoe's help with Celia. He'd been genuinely distressed by Celia's failing memory and sincerely apologetic every time Zoe had gotten drawn into helping deal with another crisis.

Maybe it's me! Maybe I just don't have a life of my own, so I volunteer myself to be part of everyone else's! And Jake didn't turn me away until I wanted his heart.

Maybe, it was time for her to grow up.

Time to stand on her own two feet and stop believing that there was a soul mate out there who would love her for herself. Someone who needed her to make him whole, not just to make his life comfortable. A man she could trust to be there when *she* needed *him* rather than the other way around. She should've learned that lesson already because everyone who'd ever been important in her life had, sooner or later, failed to be what she wanted them to be.

Tears welled up and began trickling down her face into the matted brown fur of the teddy bear. Zoe didn't try to stop them. Jake had been right about one thing. She *had* wanted the fairy tale. And in spite of all the signals he had sent to the contrary, she had gone on hoping Jake would be her prince. She'd taken neighborliness for interest. Believed friendship could grow into some-thing deeper. And interpreted his kisses to mean more than just physical desire. She *had* believed in the fairy tale. But fairy tales only happened in books.

"Just because you're in a rotten mood, I don't get why I should be getting punished." With a spatula clutched in one hand, Ava planted her fists on her hips and glared at her father.

"You're not getting punished," Jake said evenly. "I just need you to babysit tonight."

"I've been Gramma-sitting all week. Now you want me to stay in on Friday night, too?

You know it's Bethany's big party tonight. And Travis is taking me. I just can't stay home. Not tonight!"

Ava's aggrieved tone had merit. She hadn't once complained about staying around to make sure Celia didn't wander off while he was at work. And it was her summer vacation, after all.

"Why don't you ask Zoe?" Ava turned away to flip the pancakes she was making for breakfast.

Sorrow and embarrassment filled Jake's breast. He couldn't ask Zoe. He also couldn't tell Ava why. "She's probably busy."

"Zoe's never busy. Or haven't you noticed? Outside of us and Bree, she hasn't got a social life. Besides —" Ava broke off to plunk a platter of pancakes on the table. "Breakfast is ready!" she called. Then she set a tub of margarine and a jug of syrup next to the platter as the twins slid into their seats and began tugging pancakes onto their plates. Ava turned back to Jake. "Besides, Zoe owes you. All the work you've done around her house and mowing her lawn and repairing the railing and stuff."

Zoe didn't owe him anything, and he knew it. He liked working with his hands, and he enjoyed riding around on his mower. If anything, his being over there so much of the time had probably given Zoe the wrong idea in the first place, raising expectations he had never intended.

Aunt Catherine insisted a man and a woman couldn't be friends without one or both of them getting hurt. But he'd gotten so used to ignoring her, the reality of her assertion hadn't sunk in. Not until he'd seen the shock in Zoe's eyes when he'd made that stupid remark about Molly not being his kid.

"Zoe doesn't owe me anything. I'm sorry I forgot about Bethany's party. I'll figure something else out." Jake sat down and stacked a half dozen pancakes on his plate. "Maybe I can change the appointment. Are you free tomorrow afternoon?"

Ava studied him for a long minute. The unusually acute expression in her eyes made Jake want to squirm. For an uncomfortable moment she looked just like his Aunt Catherine, sizing him up and finding him lacking.

"Yeah. I'll be around tomorrow. I guess." She took her seat and carefully cut a pancake in half, transferring one of the halves to her plate. She poured a miniscule amount of syrup onto it and took a bite. Then she put her fork down and looked across the table at Jake. "Did you and Zoe have a fight?"

"No." It hadn't been a fight. It had been more like lobbing a hand grenade into an undefended camp.

"Then why can't you ask her to babysit?"

"Because."

"How come whenever I'm the one getting the third degree, *because* is never a good answer?"

Lynn's and Lori's heads swiveled from Jake to Ava and back as if they were at a tennis match.

"We had a misunderstanding." *And I said something really unforgiveable.*

Ava opened her mouth, then shut it again. She took another bite of pancake. Then shrugged. With one final forkful, she got to her feet and dropped her plate in the sink. It was Jake's job to clean up when Ava cooked.

"Just so you know" — Ava hesitated in the doorway — "I don't really mind watching out for Gramma, and I don't have a problem with babysitting the twins tomorrow, but you need to make it up with Zoe. She's my friend, and I don't want you messing it up. I don't know what you've said to her, and maybe it's none of my business, but you'd better apologize."

247

Jake didn't like being lectured to by his daughter, but he deserved it, so he kept his mouth shut. Her footsteps echoed down the hall and up the stairs to her room. The twins studied him appraisingly.

Then Lori piped up. "Are you and Miss Zoe mad at each other?"

"No. We aren't mad at each other." *I just broke her heart.*

"Can we still ask Miss Zoe over for a tea party?"

"Of course, you can invite her over for a tea party." Jake withered under Lori's questioning.

"And we can still see Molly when she gets borned?" Lynn added her query to Jake's growing pile of sins.

"Yes, you'll still get to see Miss Zoe's baby when she is born."

Apparently satisfied that their world was still functioning the way they expected it to, the twins mumbled their excuses and hurried from the room. Jake stared at his uneaten breakfast.

He'd never been so wrong. Or so willfully blind.

Four days without seeing or even talking to Zoe had opened his eyes. He'd been fooling himself for weeks with the fiction that he only wanted friendship. He'd tried to convince himself that what he felt for her was just lust, and lust he knew from experience would disappear once the novelty had worn off. But it wasn't just lust or her growing pregnancy would have squashed his desire. Especially considering that he wasn't responsible.

It had been idiotic to imply that he wouldn't love Molly. The matter of genetics would never stop him from caring deeply for any child in his care. But Molly was Zoe's child. He would love her for that reason alone. His claim to the contrary had been a cheap shot — the desperate shot of a coward afraid to take the chance of getting hurt again. Or maybe it was the blind panic of a man who knew he wasn't good enough to measure up to everything Zoe believed him to be.

It was too late to tell himself not to fall in love with her. He'd been blindsided by that, too. He'd been so busy convincing himself that what he felt for Zoe was just lust and what they had going between them was friendship, that he'd totally missed the fact that she'd moved into his heart as well as his neighborhood. Somewhere between that ridiculous tea party in the twins' tree house and putting his hand on Zoe's belly to feel the life growing within her, he had fallen completely and irrevocably in love with the most generous, caring woman he'd ever known. She was sweet and naïve one moment, wise and down to earth the next. She was honest to a fault, funny when he least expected it, and sexy enough to drive him wild with desire. How could he have ever thought that what he felt for Zoe was nothing more than his needy libido?

And how could he tell her that now? After the awful, hurtful things he'd said? He couldn't unsay them, and he doubted there was anything he could say now to erase the hurt he'd inflicted. He'd never be able to banish her look of shocked comprehension from his own memory either, but that was a penance he'd have to live with even if she did find the generosity to forgive him.

He didn't know if he had any chance to mend any fences, but if he did, it had to start with an apology. He didn't have a problem with saying he was sorry when he'd been wrong about something. But this was going to be the hardest apology he'd ever had to make.

CHAPTER 23

After another sleepless night, Jake dragged himself out of bed, determined to see Zoe and try to put things right between them again. He and Celia had to be at Safe Haven at one. He had a lot of paperwork to fill out, and he wanted Celia to have a chance to visit the place before it was a done deal. But surely three hours would be enough time to say what needed to be said. If only he knew where to start.

In a fog of exhaustion, he put cereal in front of the twins and downed two cups of black coffee. Celia joined them in the kitchen, but her rambling recollection about events long before Jake's birth fortunately didn't require any answers. After gobbling down their breakfast, the twins mumbled their excuses and disappeared out to their tree house. Then Celia got up and meandered into the den to drink her coffee in front of the television. Jake took himself back upstairs for a much-needed shower.

Finally feeling a little more pulled together, Jake made sure Ava was awake and knew he'd be out for a bit. Then he squared his shoulders and left the house.

Bill Clifford waved briefly before turning his attention back to mowing his lawn, probably trying to get it done before the heat of the day. It was only nine, and the air felt hot and sultry already. Danny sat on his front step intently assembling a balsa wood glider. The twins giggled in their tree house as Jake passed. Everyone's life seemed to be humming along as usual. All except his own. And at least part of his gloom was self-inflicted.

Zoe had burst into his life, bringing laughter, joy, a generous spirit, and her friendship. She had accepted him just as he was, with all the baggage he possessed, giving more than she took. And she had been far more honest than he when that friendship flared into something hotter. She had let him see her desire without pretense and responded eagerly to his. Then she'd opened her heart, and he had turned away.

Jake had made a lot of stupid mistakes in his life. Mistakes he couldn't fix. He just hoped this wasn't going to be the worst one yet.

As he reached to open the gate between their yards, he heard Zoe's old green truck engine crank, then sputter and turn over. He jerked to a disappointed halt at the sound of the truck being put into gear and watched her back out of her driveway. She must have seen him standing with the gate half open, because she pulled up to the curb and let the passenger side window down.

"Did you need something?" Zoe leaned awkwardly across a pile of boxes to peer out at him. "I'm dropping this stuff off for the tag sale at church. But then I'm headed to the grocery store."

Jake shut the gate again and approached the truck. He rested his hands on the open window frame. "Um . . . No. Just . . ." He couldn't explain himself with the truck still in gear and Zoe obviously anxious to be on her way. *I'm sorry* wasn't enough, and anything else needed more time. "I'll catch you later."

Zoe hesitated, her head cocked to one side. Jake thought her eyes looked a little tired, as if she hadn't been sleeping any better than he had. And there was a faintly haunted expression on her face he suspected he was responsible for. But then she smiled, and some of her usual sparkle returned. "See ya, then."

"Yes, ma'am." Jake removed his hands from the truck door, and Zoe pulled back into the circle. A moment later the battered green truck had disappeared around the corner, and Jake was no closer to resolving the mountain of misunderstanding between them.

Zoe hadn't returned from her shopping expedition before Jake had to leave for his appointment at Safe Haven. Feeling a confusing mix of frustration and disappointment, Jake ushered Celia to his van and left for their meeting.

The appointment included a tour of the facilities he hadn't expected, and Celia dawdled the whole way, admiring this or commenting on that. She was especially taken with the posters of Paris and insisted on telling Jake about each. She'd read all about the sights of Paris and was eager to share her fascination. They were at Safe Haven until nearly suppertime.

By the time he got home and got all his girls settled for the evening, he had to leave for his regularly scheduled volunteer training night at the fire station. Reluctantly, Jake changed into jeans and boots and headed out again. Tomorrow he would talk to Zoe.

As Jake followed his family out of St. Michael's into the hot sunshine of the late August morning, he saw Zoe tucking flowers into the bed of her truck. She waved gaily and headed back into the church. Yet another delay, but not exactly a bad one. He'd have time to make sure Celia and the twins were fed and occupied before Zoe got home.

But ten minutes later, as he pulled into Awbrey Circle a stream of four cars followed him. They pulled up one behind the other in front of Zoe's house. Then Zoe's friend Bree climbed out of the lead car. A moment later, at least a dozen women had piled out of the cars and began climbing the stairs to Zoe's porch, laden with pink, beribboned bags and boxes wrapped in baby shower paper. Jake's heart sank.

Bree saw him and came hurrying over to explain. This was a surprise shower for Zoe. Both her sisters were here and several of her friends from work. Surprising Jake even more, Ava, who'd disappeared into the house a moment before, reappeared with a large pink and white box of her own. She'd known about the shower and never mentioned it. Or perhaps she thought he didn't have a need to know given the week that had just passed.

Jake spent the afternoon tinkering with the engine on Zoe's old lawnmower. He didn't intend to let her mow her lawn anytime soon, if ever, but he needed a chore that kept him in the garage where he could keep an eye on Zoe's house and be ready to head over the minute she was alone.

He hustled upstairs several times to check on Celia and make sure she wasn't instigating some new disaster he hadn't thought to guard against. He stopped to see what the twins were up to on each trip through the house, then hurried back to the garage and his vigil.

Finally, as the afternoon turned into evening, the women began to leave. Ava dashed across the yard, frowned at Jake, then slipped into the house without a word. Zoe hugged each of her friends and sisters and then stood at the end of her walk, watching the cars pull away from the curb. She was beaming from ear to ear, but even from his garage, Jake could see the exhaustion in her body.

Perhaps tonight was not a good night to explain what an idiot he was.

Zoe turned and trudged up the stairs to

her house. Jake hovered in the doorway to his garage, uncertain what to do next. As he stood there, torn with indecision, another car turned in past the old gateposts and slowed.

The silver BMW convertible crept around the circle as if the handsome, black-haired driver wasn't sure which of the three houses he was looking for. Then he stopped in front of Zoe's house.

The man sat gazing up at the house for a moment before climbing from the car. He hesitated at the end of Zoe's walk. Jake decided he should go over and find out who the new arrival was, but before he got the oil wiped off his hands, the man strode confidently toward the stairs.

He was tall — at least as tall as Jake, maybe taller. Dressed in sharply-creased trousers and a fine-knit, baby blue sweater with a beige linen jacket, the man looked like a model for a higher class of clothing than Jake had ever owned.

The man knocked on Zoe's door, and a moment later Zoe appeared. A look of total astonishment lit her features. One of Zoe's brothers? The man said something, and in another moment, Zoe pushed the door wider to let him enter. The last thing Jake saw before the door closed again was the man slipping one arm about Zoe's shoulders and then bending to kiss her on the mouth.

Pain sliced into Jake with the force of a blow to the solar plexus. Brothers didn't kiss their sisters on the mouth. But lovers did. This man with the confidant assurance of Zoe's welcome had to be Molly's father. But why, after ignoring her for most of her pregnancy, was he here now?

CHAPTER 24

Zoe shut the front door with more force than she intended and ducked out of Porter Dubois' unwanted embrace. Porter looked as handsome as ever. His raven-black hair had been recently trimmed by a stylist rather than a barber, and the expensive blue sweater matched his eyes to perfection.

But neither the sleek black hair nor the sky blue eyes affected her as they once had. A fleeting vision of overgrown, sun-streaked hair and warm gray eyes flickered through Zoe's mind, making Porter's carefully cultivated appearance seem conceited and too perfect to be real.

"What do you want?" Zoe wished the dogs hadn't been put out in the back yard during the baby shower. She could have used a little moral support. It would have been especially satisfying considering Porter's distaste for animals in the house.

Undaunted by her refusal to return his

kiss or warm to his casual overture, Porter smiled at Zoe with maddeningly arrogant familiarity.

"Nice place you have here. Nice location anyway. House could use a little work, but the view of the Intracoastal is impressive. Does the property include waterfront?"

"What do you want?" Zoe repeated, ignoring his assessment of her home.

"I've come to my senses. That baby" — he glanced briefly at her bulging belly, then back at her face — "is mine, and I've come to offer the proposal I should have made months ago."

"Why?" Zoe was floored by his effrontery.

"I should have thought *why* was a given. We had sex. You got pregnant. I take responsibility."

"Why now?" *What happened to change his mind?*

"Better late than never, wouldn't you say?"

Zoe backed away from his confidant overwhelming closeness. "What did my father offer you?"

Porter raised his perfect eyebrows. "Why do you think your father has anything to do with it?"

"Because a few months ago you were pretty eloquent about what your plans were for your life, and they didn't include a baby.

Or even a wife, if I recall." It had certainly taken her father long enough to accept the fact that she was going to go through with keeping her baby and raise it with or without his support and approval. "I'm sure it's occurred to Dad that if my baby is a bastard it won't do his image any good."

The earnest smile on Porter's face didn't falter. "You can't blame him. He's chairman of the Encourage Abstinence movement in the Wilmington school system, and he's a prominent member of the community with the reputation of a dedicated family man. But what helps your father's reputation or not isn't my concern here. Our child is."

"You told me you would sue me for entrapment if I told everyone you were the father of my baby." Instinctively, Zoe cradled her stomach with both hands. She was having trouble comprehending Porter's about-face. As if Molly also had a problem believing her father's change of heart, she squirmed in Zoe's womb.

"I was wrong." Porter actually managed to look abashed. Zoe had never seen that expression on his face before, and it pierced her carefully constructed defenses.

"Wrong about what, Porter? The abortion or the entrapment?" She struggled to maintain her air of aloof contempt.

"Look, Zoe. We need to talk. Can't we do it somewhere more comfortable than your front hall?"

Reluctantly, Zoe backed into the living room, still littered with pink wrapping paper and piles of tiny baby garments. She pushed aside the new car seat and carrier combo and sank onto the couch. Porter lowered himself gracefully into a slip-covered easy chair and rested his elbows on his stylishly clad knees, paying no apparent attention to the disarray around him.

"I understand why you doubt my sincerity. I gave you good reason for such reservations, but I'm over it now. I just needed some time to work through things. This isn't about your father. It's about doing what's right. I still care about you, and our baby needs a father. I can provide things you can't. Don't you think you owe it to our child to at least consider my proposal?"

"I don't even know what your proposal is yet, do I?"

Appealing to her desire for the best her child could have in life was a smart move. Zoe couldn't tell if it was a calculated one or if Porter really meant it.

"I thought a proposal between a man and a woman, especially with a baby on the way, usually involved marriage." Porter reached into his jacket pocket and produced a small satin-covered jeweler's box. He flipped it open to reveal a stunning princess-cut diamond that sparkled brilliantly in the brightly lit room.

Zoe sucked in her breath in astonishment. She jerked her gaze from the ring to Porter's face and caught him looking at her with a bemused, almost boyish expression.

"Did you want me to go down on one knee? I can do that if you'd like. It's not really my style, and I know how you hate hypocrisy, but . . ." Porter reached for her hand.

Zoe pulled back. So many conflicting emotions raged through her, she couldn't think straight. Maybe she did owe it to Molly to give her legitimacy. Maybe Porter really did care. The ring was gorgeous! But what if her father had twisted Porter's arm? Even more important, could she possibly agree to this, knowing she loved someone else?

"I — I need time to think."

Porter set the box on the table next to his chair and leaned across the gap separating them. "Of course, you do. We've waited this long. Another day or two won't hurt."

Zoe stared at the ring glittering in its box.

She felt trapped and uncertain.

Porter put a bent finger under Zoe's chin and turned her gaze away from the ring and toward his handsome, earnest face. "I'm asking you to marry me and let me take care of you. We were good together, and we can be good again. And our baby . . ." He shot a quick glance around him and then looked back into her eyes. "Our little girl will have two parents to care for her. Take whatever time you need to decide. But think about what you owe our daughter. And me. And your father, of course."

Porter stood with easy grace. Then he bent, cupped her chin in one hand, and lowered his head to hers. Zoe meant to turn her face away, but for some reason, she didn't. Porter's kiss was brief, at first, then swiftly warmer, and suddenly suggestive. Zoe jerked back.

After a moment, Porter straightened, turned, and walked out to the hall.

"I'll call you tomorrow." Then he let himself out.

CHAPTER 25

Jake stood on his porch, gazing toward Zoe's house. He'd showered and changed into a clean pair of cargo shorts, shoved a pizza in the oven for Ava and the twins, and made a salad for Celia. He hadn't felt much like eating anything himself, so he'd come out into the soft evening air to reconsider his options regarding Zoe.

The expensive car still squatted pretentiously in front of Zoe's house. Jake stewed impotently. Was the man planning to stay all night? A streak of hellish jealousy blazed through Jake's veins. Zoe had told Jake quite matter-of-factly, that her baby's father didn't love her. So what was he doing here now? Maybe this guy wasn't her former lover. But the memory of that casual kiss taunted Jake.

It was the kiss of a man totally confident that his embrace would be welcome. The casual kind of greeting a man gives a woman he's been intimate with. A sick mixture of disappointment, loss, and resentment roiled in Jake's gut. He'd finally realized what he'd jeopardized with cutting words and the stubborn refusal to listen to his heart. And now he might never get the opportunity to redeem himself or convince Zoe to give him another chance.

As he stood, his hands clutching the railing, fingernails digging into the old wood, he heard the door to Zoe's house open. He jerked his head up and saw Zoe's visitor shut the door behind him and cross the porch.

He descended the stairs and strode toward his car with the air of a man who'd completed a successful mission. He slid into his car and shut the door. Then the engine purred to life. As Jake watched, the man ran a careful hand over his smartly styled hair and gazed at himself for a brief moment in the rearview mirror before he put the car in gear and pulled away from the curb. As he drove past, Jake heard the faint sound of his radio, a smooth jazz number on a baritone sax.

Jake disliked the man intensely. And he'd never even met him.

Zoe barely heard the door shut or the car

start. She vaguely noticed the deep growl of Porter's engine being revved before he pulled away from the curb. Her emotions were in turmoil.

If she had never met Jake, maybe the decision would be easier. In spite of not being in love with Porter, perhaps over time, they would find a way to create a comfortable partnership. And a stable, two-parent home for her baby would have been paramount. The fact that she'd allowed him to kiss her just now seemed to prove she wasn't completely immune to his charm in spite of the hateful things that had been said months earlier.

Zoe cupped her hands around her belly. Molly was proof that she wasn't immune to Porter's sex appeal either. But charm and sex appeal weren't enough to base a marriage on.

Porter had told her to consider Molly's best interests, but not a single word had been said about what might be best for herself. There hadn't been even a hint of love in Porter's proposal. Not even for the child he suddenly professed to want. What if Porter turned out to be a cold, distant father who never demonstrated any feelings for his child? How would that benefit Molly?

Every day women brought children into

the world without the aid of a spouse and reared them from infancy to college without the input of a father. Zoe had a home and a job. She was financially able to support herself and her baby, maybe not in luxury, but comfortably. She was smart and capable, and she knew she would be a good mother. A great mother. Even without a husband. But still . . .

There was Porter's six-figure income to consider. And the likelihood of a partnership in the near future and the prestige and security that would bring. He had a large beautiful home in the most elegant part of historic downtown Wilmington. Molly would have every advantage and be able to attend any college she desired. Porter might never look at Zoe with the love in his eyes that Bree's husband had once had for Bree before the war had robbed them of the life they'd planned together, but Porter would never abuse her or their child. Life would be comfortable. Their future would be reliable.

Zoe gazed around the tumbled disarray of her living room — the haven she had created for herself and her child. It wasn't elegant or expensive like Porter's home, but it was comfortable and more than adequate. The things that had needed repair had been fixed or replaced. Zoe's father would never let Molly miss out on college, illegitimate or not. Did they really need what Porter was offering?

A week ago, this decision would have been so much easier. A week ago, Jake had still been popping in and out, fixing things, checking on her, sharing tidbits of his life with her. A week ago, she'd still been blindly in love. Still hoping for so much more. But that dream had withered in the face of Jake's harsh honesty. There would never be a future with Jake. Her choices were going it alone, or accepting Porter's loveless offer.

Zoe got off the couch and began to gather up the discarded gift boxes. She felt almost numb. It was all too much to process right now — too much, she suspected, to process in twenty-four hours. She had no idea what she would tell Porter when he called the following day. The only thing she was certain of right now was that she wouldn't tell him flat-out *no*.

Zoe stacked the flattened boxes in a pile and carried them to the kitchen. She heard Jet scratching softly at the door. She'd forgotten all about the dogs. She let them in, apologizing with effusive hugs, and let their tail-wagging acceptance wash through her. When the eager dancing had calmed down, she fixed their dinner and put the bowls down.

At least I know my pooches love me just for being me, she thought as she returned to the living room with a trash bag and began filling it with crumpled paper, bits of ribbon, and big pink bows. After carting all the boxes and the trash bag out to the back porch, she snagged the laundry basket off the washer and returned to the living room. She carefully removed the tags and dropped each miniature garment into the basket, then carried the basket to the kitchen and loaded the washer with baby clothes and baby detergent.

When the living room was tidy again, Zoe began to turn out the lights. The ring box still sat where Porter had left it. The diamond solitaire winked up at her in the light from the table lamp. Zoe snapped the box shut and shoved it into her pocket. She turned off the lamp and headed for the door.

In the hall she paused, took the box from her pocket, and opened it up again. She swallowed hard, struck anew by its beauty and the unexpected offer it represented. Then she headed for the kitchen where she carefully placed the box on the windowsill above the sink, the lid still open. A reminder that she had a decision to make.

CHAPTER 26

Jake lay on his bed with his hands folded behind his head staring into the dark when the phone rang. Realizing he'd left his pager in the kitchen, he grabbed the handset and brought it to his ear, expecting to hear the volunteer fire dispatcher.

"Cameron here!"

"Jake?" Zoe's voice was clipped and totally without the warmth it used to hold whenever she'd said his name before.

"This is Jake. What's up?" He swung his feet over the side of the bed and sat up.

"Celia's here again. She's folding clothes, and she says she can't leave until she's finished."

Jake jammed his fingers through his hair with a sigh. "Sorry about this. I'll be right over."

He punched the *off* button and tossed the phone on the bed, then scrambled back into the shorts he'd dropped on the floor a couple hours earlier. He couldn't find his T-shirt, then remembered he'd chosen to put on a dress shirt after his shower. He hated ironing, and he'd taken the time to hang it up again in spite of his anguish over Zoe and her detested visitor. He dug a T-shirt out of his drawer and pulled it on as he hurried down the hall.

Zoe's porch light wasn't on, but the door was unlocked. He should talk to her about leaving her doors unlocked. Maybe she'd been too distracted to lock it behind her visitor when she'd followed him to the door. Maybe the man had let himself out, and Zoe had forgotten to check it later. A pang of loss shot through Jake, but he shoved it aside and called out.

"Zoe?"

Scotch hurried forward, barked twice, then began to wag his tail. Jet appeared and shoved her head under Jake's hand for a pat.

"We're in the kitchen."

Jake strode into the kitchen and found Zoe seated in a chair in the corner by the dryer with a laundry basket between her feet. Celia, standing on the other side of the open dryer door, looked up at Jake's entrance with surprise. Then pleasure flooded her face.

"Martin! I didn't know you were home." She hurried to Jake and gave him an uncomfortably effusive hug.

Jake glanced at Zoe in apology, then back down at his mother-in-law. "What are you doing here, Mom?"

"I'm folding the baby's clothes. Look, isn't this just the most darling dress?" She held up an impossibly small garment made of soft white material with pink roses and tiny pink bows. "Donna is going to look so pretty in this. Don't you think?"

"I'm sure she will, but you really don't need to finish folding the clothes tonight." He tried to remove the dress from Celia's hand, but she whisked it out of reach and returned to her post by the dryer.

"Of course, I must. You know I can't go to bed before all my chores are done." She placed the folded dress in the basket by Zoe's feet and picked up a one-piece sleeper. "It will only take a few minutes, but if you want to help, you know many hands make light work." She gestured toward the half-full dryer of baby clothes.

"It's okay, Jake. I really don't mind if she helps fold them. And it might be easier if we — if you just let her finish. You don't need to help, though." Zoe set a stack of pink and yellow onesies in the basket and reached back into the dryer. "Just pull up a stool. We'll be done before you know it."

"I'm really sorry about this," Jake apologized again. "I'm sorry about everything. I wish I could . . ." Could what? Take it all back? Take back the unforgiveable words he'd said to her the last time they had been together?

"This isn't your fault, Jake." Zoe's voice had finally found some of the warmth he'd gotten used to, but she was talking about Celia, and he knew it.

He approached the dryer and had to reach past Zoe to grab a handful of baby clothes. He wanted to fall on his knees at her feet and beg her to forgive him. He wanted to pull her into his arms and tell her he'd been dead wrong. But he could do neither with Celia blithely folding baby garments just two feet away, so he carried his share of the clothing back to the island and began folding. "I hope Celia didn't wake you up this time."

"No, not really. I was upstairs, but I got hungry and realized I'd forgotten to have any supper. So, I came down to scrounge for some leftovers and found Celia finishing the chore I'd begun before I headed off to bed."

"Looks like Bree pulled off a very successful shower. You made quite a haul." Jake had forgotten how small newborn clothes were. "Tiny, aren't they?" He held up an undershirt that didn't look big enough for one of the twins' dolls.

Zoe had been thinking the same thing as she'd unwrapped her gifts that afternoon. But the bit of white jersey looked even tinier in Jake's big, sun-browned hands. Her own fingers went still as she watched, fascinated by the deftness of those large hands as he neatly tucked the sleeves under, then folded the undershirt in half and added it to the growing pile on the island counter. He picked up a frilly top next and smoothed the ruffles down, found the matching bottoms, and smoothed them out as well. It was clear Jake had folded little girl clothing before. That he was very familiar with the task, in fact.

Try as she might, Zoe couldn't conjure up an image of Porter ever taking on such a chore. A pang of longing shot through her so sharp and overwhelming it felt like she couldn't breathe for a moment. When she could, she scrambled to think of something to say. Anything to distract herself from the difficult choice she had to make.

"H-how are the twins? I haven't seen them all week." Perhaps Jake had told them to stay away.

"They were at my sister's place for a few days. Her girls are four and six. She had the week off from work, and she figured why not. Jenny and Becca are like oil and water, and the twins keep them from fighting all the time, which makes Kate's life easier."

"It seems odd that I've never met your sister's kids or her husband, for that matter. Come to think of it, I thought most of your family lived around here. How come I've never run into any of them besides Kate and Aunt Catherine?"

Jake made a wry face. "I don't know. Everyone's been unusually busy lately. We usually see each other more often than we have so far this summer. Everyone managed to get over for the Fourth of July, and Philip's been by a bunch of times since he got back to the States in June."

Zoe had been at her brother Michael's house for her sister's engagement party over the fourth. If Zoe had been free, maybe she'd have been invited to Jake's place and gotten to meet the rest of his family instead of spending the day envying her sister Erin and the man she'd brought home to introduce to her family. Ken hadn't been able to keep his eyes off Erin or the smile off his face, and he'd fit right into the boisterous

Callahan clan. Jake would have fit right in too, except . . .

Jake reached into the dryer for the last of the baby things.

The clean, fresh hint of whatever shampoo he used and his own musky, masculine scent filled her nostrils. Her body reacted with its customary jolt of pleasure. Zoe shot out of her chair and retreated to the sink, filled a glass with water, and drank it down as she strove to regain her composure. *I've got to get over him,* she admonished herself sternly.

"How many Camerons are there?" she babbled, trying to ignore the aching sense of loss.

Jake stopped folding a bath towel with a princess crown on one corner and looked over his shoulder at Zoe. "There's quite a crowd when we're all together." He held up one hand and folded down a finger. "There's Kate. Her husband Ethan and their girls." He folded down three more fingers. "My brother Ben, his wife Meg when she's home. She's in Iraq just now. She's a Marine MP. Anyway, they have two boys, Rick and Evan." He started to tuck the towel under his arm and put his other hand up and then shrugged. "Not enough fingers. Philip and Will aren't married yet. And of course, my mom and dad and Aunt

Catherine. That's the usual crowd anyway. Sometimes one or another of my aunts or uncles and their families will show up, too, but when that happens, we're usually all out on the island at my parents' place."

"Sounds a little like my family."

The corner of Jake's mouth tucked in, and he made a soft little sound in his throat before he resumed folding the towel. "If you mean overwhelming, then, yeah!"

"Martin?" Celia's soft voice dragged Zoe's attention back the problem that had brought Jake over to her house in the first place. Celia moved toward the island and added a handful of socks to Jake's neat piles of baby clothes. She put a hand on Jake's wrist and gazed up at him with a look of yearning that almost made Zoe feel like a peeping Tom.

"Martin?" Celia said again. "When are you bringing your wife and the baby home from the hospital?"

"I'm Jake, Mom." Jake took her hand off his arm and held it in both of his own. "Marsha's husband. Remember?"

Celia looked totally confused. "Who's Marsha?"

"Never mind, Mom. Your chores are done. It's time to get you home to bed." He urged her toward the hallway. He looked back at Zoe with a pained expression in his eyes.

"She's moving into Safe Haven on Wednesday. I wish I could promise you won't find her poking about your house again, but it seems to be happening with more frequency, and Wednesday is still three days away."

"Can I help?" Zoe didn't know why she volunteered. Except that the look of unhappiness in Jake's eyes was more than she could bear. She wanted to gather him into her arms and tell him it would all work out, but she couldn't. Not anymore. But she could help get Celia settled into her new surroundings. "I have a doctor's appointment on Wednesday, but not until afternoon, and since my boss gave me the whole day off I'm free until two-ish."

"You shouldn't be moving furniture and heavy stuff. Not seven and a half months pregnant." Jake glanced at Zoe's belly, which she noticed was half-naked now that she'd gotten to her feet.

Embarrassed, Zoe tugged her pajama top down. "But I can make up her bed and help her unpack." *I can help make sure you don't fall apart at the seams. I hope we're still friends, at least, and that's the least a friend would do.*

"I — I can't ask you to —"

"You didn't ask. I offered. Besides, you know you want to borrow my truck. It'll be a lot easier than the van. Right?" Zoe stood in the open doorway while Jake guided Celia toward the stairs.

"I was going to ask my dad if I could borrow his, but that's way out on the island, so if you really don't mind, I'd be grateful for the loan. There's no reason you have to go, though. I know how to drive a stick."

"And I know where things are over at Safe Haven, so stop arguing." Zoe had no idea why she was pushing so hard to tag along on what would certainly be an emotionally difficult move for Jake. It wasn't like she didn't have enough baggage of her own to deal with right now. Or maybe she was trying to avoid her own baggage.

"Thanks," Jake surrendered graciously. "It shouldn't take more than an hour or so to get her stuff moved."

Celia started down the stairs, but Jake hesitated at the top, his hand on the railing, his expression uncertain. A shock of sun-streaked hair had fallen across his forehead. He looked about fifteen years younger. Lost and unhappy. And never more appealing.

"See you Wednesday." Zoe stepped back, ready to shut the door before she lost the battle not to smooth Jake's hair off his face and kiss away his unhappiness.

"Wednesday, then." Jake reached toward

her, but then dropped his hand to his side. "Don't forget to lock your door. Next intruder might be more to worry about than Celia and her friend Martin." Then he turned and loped down the stairs to catch up with Celia.

Zoe shut the door and carefully turned the deadbolt before collapsing against the old oak panel.

How can I possibly marry Porter while I'm still in love with Jake?

CHAPTER 27

Celia puttered about her new room at the Safe Haven Assisted Living Facility looking confused and lost. Jake had already set up the bed, and Zoe was making it up with Celia's familiar bedding when Jake and the handyman from the center brought the matching dresser in.

"Martin?" Celia tapped Jake's arm. "Why am I here?"

"You live here now," Jake answered patiently for the twelfth time.

Celia peered at Jake appraisingly. "What is wrong with the house you grew up in?"

"It's too big for us now. This will be much easier to take care of."

"Oh, that's so good of you to think of. I really don't care for housework very much." Celia ran her hand along the bare surface of her dresser. "Where are my pictures?"

"They're right here." Zoe lifted a canvas tote onto the bed and took out the first newspaper-wrapped frame. She handed it to Celia and reached for a second.

"Are you sure she's going to be okay?" Jake whispered in a worried voice.

He was suddenly so close she could feel the heat of him and sense the tension and worry. Zoe continued unwrapping framed photos and handing them to Celia. If she turned around right now, she knew she'd fling her arms about him and hug him in reassurance. And it would have nothing to do with her overwhelming desire for him to close his arms about her in response. Nothing at all!

Ha! Who was she fooling?

Porter had called on Monday as promised. And she'd listened to his renewed urging to accept his proposal for Molly's sake if not for her own. Zoe had said little but pictured Jake folding baby clothes during the entire conversation. Yesterday hadn't been any better.

Maybe if she didn't see Jake for a few weeks, this aching need to be close to him would fade, and the idea of being married to Porter would seem less daunting. It was what she should do. Time her visits to Celia when Jake was at work or at the fire station. Stop sitting on her porch gazing at Jake's house, hoping he would just happen to see her there and come over to chat. And stop the wishful thinking and get serious about Porter's proposal.

Her father would be pleased if she married Porter. He'd be happy to have her back in Wilmington again, too. Closer to his sphere of influence. Close enough to act as his hostess again whenever he wanted to entertain. Close enough to be used *again,* came the unbidden reaction to that last thought. Zoe ground her teeth.

"What are you thinking about that has you looking so grim?" Jake dropped onto the bed and looked up at Zoe. She made the mistake of looking at him, and the earnest concern in his soft gray eyes lanced right into her heart.

"My father!" Zoe replied, hastily looking away. She handed Celia the last of the photos and folded up the tote.

"You looked like you wanted to hit someone. I'm glad it's not me. What's your father gone and done now?"

Zoe's shoulders slumped. *He really does care. Like Bree cares. Like my brothers care. But it's not enough. I want it all.*

"Nothing. Not really. I was just . . . well, never mind." She pasted a smile on her face and turned to face Jake again. "Is everything in from the truck?"

"It is. What needs doing next?"

"Hang all the things in that suitcase in her closet. The hangers are in a box somewhere."

"Yes, ma'am." Jake got off the bed and started rummaging through the half-unpacked boxes.

Celia had taken the photo of Martin and carried it to her rocker where she sat humming softly to herself as she touched the faded face. Zoe had come to the conclusion that Celia's first love had been the older brother, rather than the younger one whom she'd eventually married. She rarely spoke of Richard anymore, and her entire focus seemed to be on Martin. Perhaps the teenage crush Celia had confessed to had been very much more than that, but Celia had been too young to catch Martin's eye. Only now that both Richard and Martin were long dead, and Celia's mind had returned to the distant past, she was free to express her feelings for the gallant young soldier she'd pined for so futilely.

Zoe considered the strange coincidence that she and Celia had both had fallen irrevocably in love with a man who hadn't even been aware of their feelings. Celia had gone on to marry someone else. She'd had children by him and from what Jake had told Zoe, been happy with Richard. But she'd never forgotten her love for Martin. Zoe wondered if her life would be like Celia's. If she married Porter because he was the father of her child, would she find some level of happiness in life, yet secretly dream of Jake and pine for what might have been for the rest of her days?

Trying to banish her unhappy musings, Zoe grabbed another suitcase and opened it on the bed. Then she pulled out the drawers in Celia's dresser and began arranging her things exactly the same way they'd been before she'd taken them out of the dresser just a couple hours earlier. It was important that as much of Celia's world remain the same as possible, and Zoe had carefully taken note, not just about how her clothing had been arranged, but where each photo had sat on the dresser top.

She glanced over her shoulder and noticed that Jake had apparently taken a similar mental catalog. Celia had a decided preference for lining all her clothes on hangers by order of color, her favorites to the right, the least favorites on the left. Jake had hung all Celia's blue garments together on the right hand side of the closet. Next to them were green things, and now he was putting a yellow blouse on a hanger. She smiled at the thoughtfulness she'd come to know he was capable of. Marsha had been a fool.

Finished with his task, Jake gathered the remaining hangers and dumped them back into the box. Then he changed his mind and put a few of the extras on the rod.

"Done," he announced, sliding the closet door shut.

His timing was perfect. Lunch, Zoe knew, was served at twelve thirty, and a staff member would show up soon to escort Celia to the dining room for her midday meal. It would be a good chance for Jake to take his leave of her. Zoe knew it was going to be hard for him.

Almost as if she'd conjured the young man up with her thoughts, a lanky, dark-haired man wearing a maroon tunic and a winning grin showed up at the door. "Ready for lunch, Mrs. Jolee?"

Celia looked up from the photo of Martin and frowned. "I should go home for my lunch."

"Well, ma'am, today you are invited to dine with us," the young man told her in an upbeat voice. "We are having cheesecake for dessert, and I've heard that's your favorite."

"Did you hear that, Jake? They're having my favorite, and I'm invited."

Jake gaped at Celia in surprise. Then his

face sobered, and Zoe could see the battle he fought with his emotions. He held out his hand to his mother-in-law and helped her from the chair. Gently he removed the photo of Martin and replaced it on the dresser.

"I'll meet you outside," Zoe mumbled and grabbed her purse and a bundle of totes before hustling past the attendant and out the door.

She would give Jake his privacy. She knew if he broke down, she wouldn't be able to resist comforting him. But right now she didn't think she could deal with the feelings that would flood through her if he enveloped her in his embrace. She was way too emotional. So was Jake. What a maudlin pair they made.

She didn't have long to wait. Jake showed up before she'd even had time to buckle her seat belt. He tossed the suitcases into the empty truck bed and hiked himself into the passenger seat. He handed her the keys then stared out the window, his eyes averted from her gaze.

Zoe put the key into the ignition. "She's going to be okay, Jake."

"I know," Jake said in a husky voice. "It's me that's falling apart."

Zoe put the truck in gear and backed out

of the space before she could do something stupid. "You'll be okay, too. You'll be over here as often as you want, and I'm sure you'll find she's busy as a beaver keeping up with her new social life."

"She won't need me."

Zoe was shocked at the raw, bare pain in Jake's voice. She yanked the truck over into the first empty parking space she came to and put it into park. She reached across the cab of the truck and pushed the overlong bangs off Jake's forehead, then touched his averted cheek with the tips of her fingers. "She'll always need you, Jake. Just not in the same way."

"She called me Jake," he said, still struggling to maintain his composure. He stared out the window for another long moment before turning to face her. His eyes swam with tears. "She remembered . . . it was . . . me." His voice broke.

Zoe gently brushed away the tears Jake probably didn't even realize were running down his face.

Jake knew he'd given up his right to find solace and comfort from her, but at the moment, he wanted desperately to pull Zoe into his arms. It was a measure of her generosity that she'd come with him today at all, never mind expecting her to let him cry on her shoulder. He wished she were going home with him, not to fill the void left by Celia, but because there was a huge hole in his life where Zoe belonged. A hole he hadn't known was there until he'd pushed her away.

With effort, Jake pulled himself together. "Sorry." He backhanded the residue of tears out of his eyes and off his face. "It was supposed to be Celia breaking down, not me."

"You know, Jake. I've seen the look in Celia's eyes when she talks about Richard or Martin. She loved them both. Maybe Martin a little more than anyone ever knew. But she loved them both with all her heart. And she loves you just as much. She has the same happy smile in her eyes when she calls you Jake as she does when she thinks you're Martin. So whenever you go to see her, she'll be looking at you with that smile and remembering how good it feels to love and be loved. It won't matter what name she calls you by. And it won't matter that you aren't there every minute. So much of her happiness is in her memories now, and she has those even when you can't be there."

"I never thought of it that way."

But now that Zoe put it into words, he knew what she meant. He knew the bright smile that lit Celia's face when he came in from work, or even just in from working in the yard. And he knew that so long as Celia favored him with that smile when he went to visit her, the connection between them would still be there.

Zoe put the truck back in gear, glanced over her shoulder, and then pulled out into the street. "You're lucky."

"Lucky how?" Jake gazed at Zoe's profile, thinking how much luckier he'd be if he hadn't messed things up between them. If Zoe's mysterious visitor hadn't shown up last Sunday and Jake still had a chance to fix the biggest mistake of his life.

"You have two mothers." Zoe darted a sideways glance at him, then turned back to the road. "I haven't had a mom since I was twelve. I'd give anything in the world if I could jump in the truck and go visit my mom any time I liked. Or call her on the phone. You've got a godmother who loves you, too. Even when she's being difficult."

Jake thought about the mothers in his life. The woman who'd given him life, bandaged skinned knees, and helped him with his homework. Who'd put up with his teenage arrogance, stood by him when he'd gotten into trouble, and applauded every achievement, however small. She was only a twenty-minute drive away on the other side of the bridge.

He thought about Celia and how she'd adopted him into her home and family without ever condemning the reason for it. She'd treated him better than he'd deserved and loved him as if he'd been her own son, rather than her son-in-law. Even Aunt Catherine with her inevitable criticism and endless advice was always there at the other end of the phone whenever he called. And if he had an emergency, she'd respond in an instant. Complaining about it maybe, but she'd be there and always had been.

He glanced across the width of the truck at Zoe's profile and felt overwhelmed with chagrin. He had three mothers, and she had none. And he'd been acting like a spoiled brat just because he couldn't keep things the way he wanted them to be.

"Thanks for giving me a kick in the butt to remind me."

Zoe snickered. "You're welcome. But if I really give you a kick in the butt, it'll be for being stupid. Not because you're going through a difficult time and you just needed a shoulder to cry on a little."

Too bad someone hadn't given him a kick in the butt about his relationship with Zoe before he'd screwed it up beyond redemption. That had been the stupidest thing he'd ever done — even more thoughtless than getting Marsha pregnant, and, as it turned out, with higher stakes.

The memory of that casually confident kiss he'd watched Zoe's fancy visitor bestow on her flashed into his head.

"You had company Sunday. Before Celia, I mean." Curiosity had been eating him up for days. The usually voluble Zoe, who chatted at length about everyone else in her life, had said nothing about the man or what he meant to her.

Zoe jerked her gaze toward Jake then immediately back to the road. She remained silent while she drove the last half-mile and turned the truck into Awbrey Circle. It was another minute before she finally answered. "Bree threw me a shower. I had a ton of company." She turned into her driveway and pulled to a stop. "Didn't Ava tell you all about it? It was fun, and everyone was incredibly generous. You should know. You helped fold it all."

Without lingering, Zoe turned the engine off, then pushed her door open and slid out of the truck. Was she trying to avoid discussing the other visitor who'd come after all the women had gone? Jake was sick with jealousy, and he just couldn't let it go.

He jumped out and turned to face her over the bed of the truck. "I saw a pretty fancy car pull up after all the ladies left. I thought maybe it was one of your brothers?"

Jake rested his forearms on the side of the truck bed and tried to act casual as she reached for her bundle of now-empty totes. He thought she flushed a little, but maybe that was his imagination.

"That was Porter Dubois." Zoe wouldn't meet Jake's gaze. "He's — he's Molly's father."

Jake had been right. The way the man had kissed Zoe in that brief moment before one of them had closed the door had been pretty revealing. Jake's imagination had conjured up a whole lot more in the way of intimacy once they were alone, even though he didn't actually know if Zoe had welcomed Porter's advances. Had she leaned into Porter the way she had when Jake had kissed her? Had she melted at Porter's touch, returning his kiss with fire and sweet abandon?

Jake gripped the side of the truck so hard he half expected the metal to give under the pressure. Carefully, he relaxed his grip. "I realize it's none of my business, but . . ." He'd made sure it was none of his business by crushing her hopes for anything serious between them. ". . . but I thought you said he didn't want to be a father. What's he doing here now?"

"He changed his mind."

A red-hot flood of jealousy filled Jake's head. Images raced through his mind. Setting up Molly's crib while Zoe watched. Holding Zoe in his arms with her pregnant belly pressed hard against his groin. The incredible tenderness he'd experienced as he'd curved his hand around her stomach and felt her baby move. Those moments had been so sweet and so intimate. The idea of this guy Porter sharing anything like them with Zoe made Jake want to smash something. He ground his teeth in frustration, then got himself under control.

Zoe still wouldn't look at him, so he gathered up the empty suitcases and walked around the back of the truck to stand next to her. "Took him long enough. You going to let him back into your life?" Jake did his level best to keep the jealousy out of his voice.

"I — I don't know." Zoe lifted her shoulders as if the weight of the world rested on them, then dropped them again and sighed heavily. "I don't know."

"Do you love him?"

"He's Molly's father." Zoe did look at Jake

then, but she hadn't answered his question. "A girl needs a father, don't you think?"

"Depends on the father," Jake replied evenly.

"He asked me to marry him."

Jake's heart did a nosedive into his boots. "And you said . . . ?"

"I didn't say anything. Yet."

Jake didn't know if he should be on his knees begging for her forgiveness and pleading with her to consider marrying him instead, or if he should stay out of it and let her decide about Porter without complicating her life any more than it already was. It was on the tip of his tongue to say *I love you. Marry me. Marry me, not this jerk Porter who didn't know it when he had a good thing to start with.*

Except Jake hadn't known a good thing any better than Porter. Zoe deserved far better than either of them. And the fact of the matter was Porter was the biological father. If Zoe felt marrying him was the best thing for herself and Molly, she had the right to make that choice without Jake pulling her in a different direction.

"So . . . you're thinking about it?"

"Oh, Jake. I just don't know. I wish I knew why Porter changed his mind. I think I could make it work, if only I was sure about . . ."

"About what? His reasons?" That didn't sound like a woman in love. But Jake wasn't any expert in the arena of love and marriage. "Didn't he tell you why?"

Zoe made a rueful face. "He did and he didn't. I mean, he said all the right things. I just don't know. I need time to think."

"Take as much time as you need."

"That's what Porter said. But he calls every day to see if I've decided yet."

"It won't make any difference to Molly if your wedding anniversary is before or after her birthday in the long run. Just don't jump into anything you aren't totally sure about."

"You really are a good friend, Jake. I'm sorry I lost sight of that." Zoe put her hand against Jake's chest for balance and tiptoed up to kiss him on the cheek. "Thanks for the support and the advice."

Jake forced himself not to drop the suitcases so he could pull her into his arms and turn a friendly kiss into a steamy declaration. He swallowed hard and let her step away. "My pleasure, ma'am."

Zoe turned to walk up across the lawn to her porch steps. Jake watched until she reached the top then he called after her. "Zoe?"

She stopped, hand on the rail, and looked down at him with her brows raised in a wordless question.

Jake strode quickly to the bottom of the stairs. "You need anything. I mean *anything.* You ask me. Got it?"

Zoe smiled, her broad, all-encompassing smile that worked its way into her eyes and lit up her whole face. "Seems like I've already gotten all the favors I should expect from the dad next door. Don't you think?"

CHAPTER 28

Although it was late when the phone rang, Zoe wasn't in bed yet. She wasn't even dressed for bed. She'd started reading a book Bree had loaned her and hadn't been able to put it down, so she was still curled up in her oversized chair with the book on her lap, living a life a long way from Tide's Way, North Carolina.

She jerked into action when the phone trilled a second time and hauled herself out of the chair with some difficulty, given her now tremendous girth. *Should have brought the phone with me,* she thought as she hurried toward the kitchen. *But who knew anyone would be calling so late?*

"Hello?"

"Zoe? Can you give me a ride home?"

"Ava?" *Why is Ava calling me?*

"Please? My — my ride's not in any condition to be driving, and I can't call Dad."

"Why not?" Zoe was still trying to process the request. She stretched over to peer out the kitchen window. "He's home, and all the lights are on, so I know he's up. He's probably waiting up for you." Zoe glanced at the clock and realized it was after midnight. That meant all the lights should not be on at Jake's. Unless something was wrong. Her heart sped up. "Ava? Where are you? What's wrong?"

"I — I'm not where I told Dad I'd be. Everyone's been drinking. And maybe worse. I just want to come home." Ava's voice rose on a note of panic.

"Give me the address." *Thank God for GPS!* "I'll be there as soon as I can."

Ten minutes later, with the address Ava had provided punched into her navigation gadget, and the gadget snapped into the dash mount, Zoe turned onto Jolee Road and headed south. She'd considered calling Jake before she left, but then thought better of it. Besides the fact that he'd have had to wake the twins to go after Ava, Ava might have had some other reason for calling Zoe instead of her father.

So Zoe had waited until she was five minutes away before calling Jake to let him know where she was headed. He'd been worried sick and clearly upset that Ava hadn't called him, but he'd heaved an audible sigh of relief. Zoe prayed that tonight's little episode wouldn't erode the growing trust between father and daughter.

"In five hundred yards, turn left onto Budding Road," the female voice of Zoe's GPS interrupted her thoughts. She turned her high beams on to better illuminate the road she was coming up on. As soon as she made the turn, both sides of the narrow road were lined with cars parked bumper to bumper with the street-side tires on the edge of the pavement and vehicles leaning precariously into the currently dry drainage culverts.

It wasn't hard to pick out the party house. Lights were on everywhere, inside and out, spilling out over the lawn and into the road. Clusters of youngsters clutching cans of beer gathered, some on the lawn and some in the driveway. And here and there, among the shadows, couples kissed with varying degrees of passion and disregard for the lack of privacy. As she slowed, scanning the scene for a sight of Ava, Zoe noticed a girl sprawled backward across the trunk of a car. Her blond hair was spread across the dark painted surface, and her wisp of a skirt was hiked up to her waist. A vaguely familiar teenager stood between her thighs with his hands braced on the trunk lid while his naked buttocks bunched and plunged with unmistakable intent. Neither noticed Zoe's noisy truck passing less than ten feet away.

Zoe jerked the truck to a stop, praying out loud that the blond hair didn't belong to Ava. Then the passenger door opened, and Ava slid onto the seat beside her.

"Thanks for coming," Ava said, falling back against the seat with obvious relief. "This party is way crazier than I thought it would be."

Zoe glanced back at the shameless pair by the car, but the girl was already smoothing her skirt back into place. The boy had zipped up his shorts and was lighting a cigarette. He offered it to the girl who took a long drag before pressing herself against him and raising her face for another kiss. As distressed as their parents would be if they knew what their children had been up to, the act appeared to have been consensual. It was none of Zoe's business and too late to put a stop to anyway. She was just glad it hadn't been Ava and Travis.

"That's Andrea," Ava said as the blond girl sauntered past the truck with one arm draped around the boy's neck. "And Travis," she added with a sharp note of bitterness in her voice.

"Oh!" Zoe couldn't think of a thing to say to that announcement. She put the truck in gear and began a three-point turn. No wonder the boy had looked familiar. She'd met him before — after dinner that first night at Jake's house.

"I called your dad. Just to let him know you were okay. Why didn't you tell him where you were going?"

"I did tell him where I was going. To start with, anyway. We went to my friend's house. We were going to watch movies and stuff. But Travis —" Ava gulped back a sudden sob. "Travis said he was totally bored, and he wanted to come here instead."

Zoe shot a look in Ava's direction, but then had to pay attention to navigating around the cars crowding the edges of the street. Why was it that every heavy-duty conversation she got into lately happened while she was trying to concentrate on driving safely?

"Then what happened?" Zoe turned back onto Jolee, glad to leave the congested side street behind.

Ava stared out the window and didn't speak for a few minutes.

"Ava?"

"I think Travis is into grass. Or maybe something worse. There was a lot of stuff

304

around."

"Did he ask you to try anything?"

Ava nodded. "He said blowing a little smoke would make me less uptight." Her voice broke. "He said — he said it would get me in the mood."

Zoe had no trouble figuring out what kind of mood Travis had in mind. The image of Andrea and Travis going at it with shameless abandon on the trunk of a car within sight of at least a dozen people replayed itself in her mind. They had certainly been in the mood. Jake would have a fit if he ever found out.

"I told him I didn't want to get in the mood, and I asked him to bring me home. But he ditched me instead." Tears streamed down Ava's face, but Zoe had to concentrate on the road. Even though it was late, the streets weren't deserted. Not on a Saturday night. She took one hand off the wheel to reach across and tuck a long strand of silky blond hair behind Ava's ear, then gave the shoulder a squeeze.

"He just walked away and left me there." Ava's tears turned noisy. "He knew I had no way to get home, and he didn't even care. Next thing I know, Andrea is sitting on his lap. He had one hand clamped around her breast and the other shoved up her skirt. His tongue had to be clear down to her tonsils."

Considering how quickly Ava had slipped into the passenger seat of the truck, she had to have been close enough to watch the entire encounter play out in all its intimate details. The betrayal couldn't have been more graphic or hurtful.

Ava gulped. "Daddy was right."

"Fathers often are," Zoe agreed soothingly. They were nearly home, and she knew Jake would be waiting at the door, ready to pounce. The last thing Ava needed right now was a lecture. She'd clearly learned a painful lesson, and Jake wouldn't improve his relationship with his daughter by shouting at her.

Zoe turned the truck around and headed back the way she'd come. With summer still in full gear, the ice cream and miniature golf place had been teeming with business when they'd passed it just moments ago. Zoe announced a sudden and unquenchable craving for a waffle cone filled with chocolate ice cream and topped with a cherry.

She patted Ava's shoulder one more time and asked her what her favorite flavor was. As soon as they pulled into the brightly lit area around the busy ice cream stand, Ava excused herself and dashed to the ladies' room. Zoe guessed she wanted to splash cold water on her face and remove the evidence of her tears. Zoe took out her phone and called Jake.

Jake sat on the swing just beyond the reach of the porch light, waiting for Zoe and his daughter to return. He hadn't been very happy when Zoe called a second time to advise him they were stopping for an ice cream, but he could see the wisdom of her decision now. He'd had time to calm down and think about the bare-bones report Zoe had given him while Ava was out of earshot. The only thing Ava was guilty of was trusting Travis and not remembering to call home to tell Jake about the change of venue. She hadn't experimented with anything, and she had stuck to her guns when Travis tried to embarrass her into giving in. Then she'd had the wisdom to call Zoe for a ride home. All things considered, Ava had behaved with remarkable maturity and good sense.

He recalled Zoe's words of advice, given all those months ago after the two had gone shopping together. *Ava has a good head on her shoulders. You need to trust her to make some decisions on her own. And let her know*

307

you're there for her anytime she needs backup.

Jake had a lot to thank Zoe for. Not just her willingness to listen to his problems and wade in to help whenever she could. And not just for heading out to pick Ava up in the middle of the night, either. But for thinking ahead and realizing he'd need to cool off before he confronted Ava about tonight's fiasco.

He heard the truck before he saw it. It really needed a tune-up. Perhaps he'd find time this week to drag his toolbox over to her driveway and give the old heap a thorough check up.

Instead of pulling up out front, Zoe passed the house and turned into her own driveway before stopping. Neither Zoe nor Ava got out of the truck right away, so Jake waited, trying to be patient. Finally the doors opened, and Zoe slid awkwardly to the ground. Ava came around the truck and gave Zoe a hug, then turned and started slowly across the lawn. Zoe stood in her driveway, watching until Ava got to the bottom of the stairs and waved good night. Then she climbed her own stairs and disappeared into her house.

When Ava reached the porch and started

across it to the front door, Jake spoke. "Hey, Ava."

She jerked to a stop. Clearly, she hadn't seen him sitting on the swing in the shadowy corner of the porch. "Hey, Daddy." She turned and walked hesitantly toward him, then leaned back against the porch railing. "I guess Zoe told you everything."

"Probably not everything, but enough. I'm proud of you."

Jake wished he could see her face, but the sudden tightening of her posture seemed to indicate he'd taken her by surprise.

"You're not mad?"

"I was worried when you missed your curfew. So I called Bethany's house, and she told me you'd already left. Hours ago. Then I was really worried, and the longer you were gone, the more worried I got. You should have called."

"I know, and I'm sorry." Ava sounded chastened, but there was a hint of some deeper emotion she was keeping inside. Jake wondered what Zoe had not told him about the break up with Travis.

"Are you okay, Ava? Travis didn't do anything to you, did he?" *I'll kill him if he did!*

Jake saw her shake her head in the dim light.

"So, what's the matter, kitten? I get the

feeling there's something more bothering you than a wild party you weren't enjoying."

Ava sniffed, shook her head, then sniffed harder. "You were right, Daddy. You were so right about Travis."

"I hesitate to ask, but I'm not right all that often —"

"All he wanted was sex!" Her voice rose to a squeak. "He said he loved me, and I believed him. But he lied. He couldn't possibly love me. Otherwise he wouldn't have hooked up with Andrea less than ten minutes after I told him I didn't want to smoke a joint and get in the mood. Daddy, why do boys have to act like that?"

Jake swallowed uncomfortably. How was a father supposed to answer that kind of question? He'd been a randy teenager eager to get laid, and not so long ago that he didn't remember what it felt like. He knew how boys worked. If he had a son, he'd have told the kid in no uncertain terms to keep his pants zipped. But what was he supposed to tell Ava? He had to say something.

"It's the way we're wired, I'm afraid. When a boy gets into his teens, his body goes nuts. His voice drops an octave or two, he sprouts whiskers, and there's a whole lot of testosterone pumping through his system.

310

He wakes up one morning and realizes that the girls he despised just the day before are developing too. And they are looking pretty darned great, in fact. Then he gets brave, or desperate, and he tries kissing one. When he discovers how soft the girl is and how exciting it is to touch her, he just wants more. And if she's willing, one thing leads to another, and suddenly they're both doing things they never intended to do."

"Is that what happened with you and Mom?" Ava's tone was carefully neutral.

Jake cleared his throat and decided on honesty. "Pretty much."

Ava gasped as if she hadn't expected the unvarnished truth. "And you regret it. I bet you wish I'd never been born."

"I regret a lot of things, Ava, but you aren't one of them. Not for a minute." Jake reached across the space that separated them and found Ava's hand. He tugged gently until she yielded and came away from the railing. He pulled her down onto his lap and wrapped his arms about her as if he could shield her from the harsh realities of life and growing up.

"Sometimes," he began softly, then kissed her forehead. "Sometimes people ask, if I knew then what I know now, would I make different choices? But it's not always that

311

simple. Perhaps if I'd been wiser or better informed, I'd not have urged your mother to do something neither of us was really ready for. But the trouble is, the moment I held you in my arms I knew there was no way on earth I'd change a single thing."

Jake felt Ava's sobs begin, small at first, then growing until she trembled in his arms. He pulled her closer, kissing the top of her head and smoothing the silken tumble of hair that fell past her shoulders. When the crying subsided into a few ragged hiccoughs, Jake dug into his pocket to retrieve his handkerchief but discovered he didn't have one. Instead, he yanked the bottom of his jersey free, lifted Ava's chin, and wiped her eyes. She tried to smile, but the smile slid, and tears welled up again.

"I bet Mom would do it different."

It felt like someone had stabbed Jake in the heart. Marsha most definitely would have chosen not to have Ava if she had it to do over again. Ava was too smart to fool with half-truths and platitudes.

"Maybe she would have," he agreed, pulling Ava close again. "But I wouldn't. Not in a million years."

"I love you, Daddy."

"I love you, too, kitten. More than you will ever know." Now his eyes were filling with tears. Sweet Jesus! All this estrogen was turning him into a wuss.

Jake sat in the swing a long time after Ava had hugged him for the last time and taken herself to bed. He stared across the shadowy lawn to Zoe's now totally dark house and thought about all the things he *would* change if he could.

"I love you, too, Zoe. I should have told you so when I still had the chance," he whispered into the quiet night.

CHAPTER 29

Zoe expected to feel a little nervous as she approached Jake's house with a bowl of cornbread salad in one hand and a pie-taker in the other. She hadn't expected the mad scramble of butterflies currently churning in her gut. Her footsteps slowed as she shut the gate behind her and crossed the lawn.

Jake's driveway overflowed with vehicles: three pickup trucks, his aunt's late-model Buick, two minivans, and one low-slung, expensive-looking, sports car. Jake had asked her if she was serious about meeting the rest of his family when he invited her to his end-of-summer barbecue, but it wasn't like this was an important job interview or meeting prospective in-laws for the first time. It was just Jake's family, and she and Jake were just friends.

He wasn't a talker, and she'd had to pry information out of him. His brief comments had made it clear he admired all three of his brothers, thought his sister was smart, pretty, and a lot of fun, and his parents were the best. What would they think of their son's new neighbor? The unwed mother-to-be, who had claimed so much of Jake's time of late and insinuated herself into every aspect of his family?

Two boys dashed past her with Taffy chasing after them. Must be the nephews Jake had mentioned. Zoe glanced back at the tree house and wondered if the twins and their girl cousins were up there hiding from the boys. A hum of voices came from the back yard, punctuated by an occasional shout of laughter. Zoe's nervousness increased.

"Are you going to stand down there all afternoon, or are you coming up?"

Zoe's gaze jerked toward Jake's front porch. His Aunt Catherine stood at the top of the stairs, as elegant as ever, her eyebrows arched in question.

"I guess I better bring these in the house where it's cool until it's time to eat." Zoe lifted the cornbread salad slightly, then began to climb the stairs, not an easy or graceful task with both hands full and her ungainly girth making the stairs seem endless.

"Here, let me." Catherine reached for the salad as Zoe reached the top. Her gaze flicked down over Zoe's swollen belly, then back to her face with an unreadable expression. "Y'all might as well come in and meet everyone."

"Yes, ma'am." Zoe handed the woman the salad bowl. She would have extended her hand in greeting, but Catherine had already turned to open the door. Rather than holding it open, though, Jake's godmother sailed on ahead down the hall toward the kitchen.

"This is Zoe. From next door," Catherine announced as she deposited Zoe's cornbread salad on the table.

Ava looked up from a platter of vegetables she was arranging and grinned. Kate waved a greeting and smiled around a half-eaten stalk of celery clamped between her teeth. The other occupant of the kitchen dried her hands on a towel and bustled in Zoe's direction.

"I'm so glad to finally meet you. Jake talks about you all the time. I'm Sandy Cameron. Jake's mom."

Sandy didn't look old enough to have a son Jake's age. She barely looked old enough to be Ava's mom. With her straight blond hair in a swinging ponytail and her brown eyes twinkling with youthful merriment, Zoe would have guessed her to be closer to forty had she not known better. *Good genes,* she thought. *I hope I look half that great when I'm her age.*

Snatching the pie-taker out of Zoe's grasp, Sandy plopped it onto the counter. Then she enveloped Zoe in a welcoming hug. Zoe felt momentarily awkward with her big belly pressed between them, but Sandy's casual friendliness melted her embarrassment, and Zoe returned the woman's embrace.

Sandy backed off, holding Zoe by the shoulders. "Jake was so right. You are just as pretty as can be."

Zoe gaped. Jake had told his mother she was pretty? A jumble of things caromed through her startled brain. The echo of Jake's voice, telling her that she had more sex appeal than any woman he'd ever known. The idea that Jake, the untalkative one, apparently talked about her all the time, to his mother, at least! Was there a chance that he cared more for her than he was willing to admit, even to himself? Could there really be more than just friendship between them after all?

"Isn't your baby due soon?" Sandy asked as she lifted the lid of the pie-taker and sniffed.

"Yes, ma'am. In another month," Zoe confirmed. Her brain still scrambled with the new revelations about Jake. "I hope you like peach pie."

"It's one of my favorites. But come, you need to be sitting outside in one of those comfy chairs with folk waiting on you." Sandy gave Zoe's protruding belly a gentle pat and then urged her toward the back door.

Sandy moved with the athletic energy of a much younger woman as she hustled Zoe down to the back yard and dragged a big Adirondack chair into the shade a short distance from the cluster of men standing around the grill. Then she grabbed one of the boys Zoe had seen racing past her out front and sent him off to bring Zoe a glass of sweet tea before trotting back up the stairs to the kitchen. Just as the boy returned and handed Zoe the glass, the tallest of the men around the grill turned and noticed her.

He shoved the bottle of beer he'd been drinking into Jake's hand and came toward Zoe. "Guess I'm going to have to introduce myself."

Zoe struggled to get up.

"No, no, no. You stay sat. I'll come down to you." He grabbed a folding beach chair and dropped into it. "You must be Zoe." His smile was broad and contagious.

"And you must be Jake's father." Zoe

couldn't help grinning back at the hand-some blond man with touches of gray at his temples and twinkling blue eyes. He might be several inches taller than Jake, but she'd have guessed the relationship even without seeing them side by side. Jake's eyes were gray, and his hair a little darker, but they had the same square chin, the same peaked eyebrows and high cheekbones, and the same dimple punctuating their left cheek when they smiled.

"Nathan Cameron. Jake's daddy," he confirmed. Zoe's hand disappeared into his big, warm grip. "But call me Cam. Please. Jake tells me you bought the old Jolee house, and he's been helping you fix it up."

"That's me. The lady with the grand plan, but a lot short on experience." Zoe snickered at herself. "It if weren't for Jake, I think the place would still be falling down around me. I owe him a lot."

"Nah. Keeps him out of trouble. Besides, he's —"

"C'mon, Dad," Jake cut his father off, snagged another free lawn chair, and plunked it down between Zoe and his father.

Another obviously Cameron male appeared behind Cam. "I'm Ben, and that's Will over there." He pointed to the man who had taken over the grilling duties. He could have been a clone. "Pleased to finally meet ya."

"I guess twins run in the family, huh?" Zoe made note of the fact that Ben wore a blue shirt, and Will's was a loud Hawaiian print. Blue for Ben. Wild for Will. It was the only way she was going to be able to keep them straight.

"They do at that, ma'am," Ben chuckled. "The two wild Indians running around are my boys, Evan and Rick. Lucky for me, they're *not* twins."

Then the last of Jake's brothers stepped into the circle of tall men towering above her. In spite of Jake's father's insistence on her staying seated, Zoe felt totally overwhelmed and couldn't resist the need to drag herself back onto her feet. Cam and Jake leapt to their feet as well.

"Philip. My biggest big brother," Jake made the introduction.

The only differences between Jake and this brother were a few years and a much tidier haircut. This had to be the brother who was still in the Marines and temporarily stationed at Camp Lejeune.

"Ma'am." Philip took Zoe's proffered hand in a friendly greeting. He squinted slightly with an openly assessing gaze. Then his face broke into a grin that rivaled his father's. "Jake didn't do you justice."

Unused to such admiration and not knowing how to respond, Zoe looked toward Jake for salvation.

"Well, I tried. But I'm not so good with words," Jake answered his brother's charge. A flush crept into Jake's cheeks, and the pink grew bright under his tan, astonishing Zoe even more.

"I think you're very good with words," she blurted, then realized how that might be interpreted and felt an answering flush blossom in her own face.

As the brothers traded knowing looks and lifted brows, Zoe muttered some inanity about needing to refill her barely sampled glass. She shot one last look at Jake and fled.

Philip jabbed Jake in the ribs. "When are you planning to propose?"

"I don't know if she'll have me — now."

"Now?" Philip's brows rose. "What have you done to spoil your pitch?"

Ben turned from watching Zoe's retreat. "Maybe Jake doesn't want another kid. Especially one that's not his."

"That's not it!" Jake defended himself in a rush. "I don't have a problem with the baby. But I — I maybe gave Zoe that impression." Jake closed his eyes, trying to block out the memory of the expression in Zoe's eyes when he'd made that outrageous statement. It didn't help, so he opened them again. Philip studied him with a furrowed brow. Ben bit his lip as if he was wondering if he should say something or not. His father's expression didn't give anything away, but he was clearly thoughtful.

"Maybe you need to correct that impression then," Ben finally suggested. "I would, if I were you." He glanced pointedly toward Zoe, then back at Jake. "I definitely would," he repeated as he turned away and returned to help his twin at the grill.

Philip gave Jake a brotherly cuff on the side of his head. "And do it before it's too late." Then he sauntered back to the cooler and grabbed another beer.

"Brothers can be a pain sometimes, but they only want the best for you. Even when they don't see the whole picture," Cam offered gently.

Jake had two uncles living and one who'd been killed in Vietnam. He guessed his dad had probably gotten a lot of unsolicited advice himself when he was younger.

"Maybe they don't know everything, but they aren't really wrong. I had my chance weeks ago, but I panicked. I said things I didn't mean and I hurt her. And now . . ."

"Apologies aren't easy. I should know.

Some of the shit I put your mother through —" Cam shook his head and made a disgusted little sound in his throat. "She forgave me for all of it once I found the courage to admit I was wrong and told her so."

"It's not that simple, Dad."

"Doesn't get much simpler than I'm sorry. Or I love you. Or both."

"But her baby's father is back in the picture."

Cam's blond brows pinched together above his blue eyes.

"He showed up a couple weeks ago and gave her an enormous diamond."

Cam glanced toward the table where Zoe was moving plates around to make room for a basket of rolls. "How come she's not wearing it, then?"

"She's not sure why he really proposed, and she's trying to decide what's best for the baby." Jake hesitated. Then he told his father everything.

". . . so I backed off. I thought she should have the space to consider her options for her and her baby without me and Porter circling around, trying to mark our territory like a couple of alpha dogs peeing on everything."

"Well, there's a reason dogs pee on things.

It's a calling card to let all the other dogs know who's around and who's interested in staking a claim. If you don't tell Zoe you love her *and* her baby, she's got no way of knowing you're one of her options. What has she got left to choose from?"

Jake felt like his father had jabbed him in the solar plexus. The simplicity of his father's observation left him breathless. Jake hadn't given Zoe a choice between Porter and himself, only the space to make a choice between Porter and nothing. What an idiot he'd been. Again!

"Your mom had a lot more to forgive me for than you've given Zoe. She deserves your honesty, if nothing else." Cam grabbed Jake's shoulder and gave it a squeeze. "Talk to her. Apologize. Tell her how you feel. Then trust her to make the right decision."

Jake blinked hard, trying to keep the stinging in his eyes from becoming an embarrassing display. "Thanks, Dad. I will. Tonight."

"Good," was all his father said as he gave Jake's shoulder another squeeze before moving away to sneak up on Jake's mother and surprise her with an unexpected hug. His mother squeaked with pleasure as she turned in her husband's arms and snaked her arms about his neck.

Jake watched the tender scene that had always been such a central part of his parents' lives. He wondered if he still had any chance to make something similar possible between himself and Zoe. Not once since that disastrous night on her front porch had Zoe leaned toward him in invitation or given him any encouragement to think she might still welcome his touch. But, she'd helped him settle Celia into Safe Haven and given him the emotional support he needed to cope with the change. She hadn't hesitated to go out in the middle of the night when Ava called needing a ride home, and she'd helped Jake make smart choices about how to handle the crisis. She'd pretty much invited herself to today's party, so she could finally meet the rest of his family.

Jake studied Zoe's bare fingers splayed across the swollen stretch of her abdomen. He pictured Porter's ring where he'd last seen it. After Jake had replaced a blown fuse, he'd gone to the sink to wash the dust off his hands. Late afternoon sun, slanting through the window, had glinted brightly off the polished facets of the big stone. It had been impossible to miss.

It was a beautiful ring. Expensive. A testament to every advantage Porter Dubois could offer Zoe. Jake, on the other hand, although a construction engineer with a decent salary, was a volunteer fireman on the side, had a family to support, three girls to put through college, and an eight-year-old van.

But he loved her, and he'd never told her so.

Tonight, he promised himself. Tonight he'd tell her. Jake's heart lurched a little at the silent promise. As soon as this shindig was over, he would walk her home and find a way to tell her all the things he'd just told his father.

"Are the ribs done?" Ava called out as she slid a tray of watermelon onto the table. Kate pushed through the screen door with one hip and let the door slap shut behind her. She headed down the stairs with a giant bowl of potato salad in one hand and a basket of chips in the other.

"Done and ready to eat," Will called back. He grabbed a spatula and began shoveling the spicy, vinegary ribs onto a platter. Jake went to help with the hot dogs, but as he reached for the fork, Zoe beat him to it.

He wanted to close his hand over hers. He wanted to wrap his other arm about her and give her a hug like the one his father had just given his mother. He clenched his hands at his sides and did neither.

As she speared hot dogs, Jake got distracted by the slow, deliberate arc of an elbow or perhaps a knee moving across Zoe's distended stomach. Without stopping to think if it would be acceptable or not, he covered the little knob with his hand. "She's a busy little bee, isn't she?"

"I think she's going to be a gymnast." Zoe pressed her free hand to the other side of her stomach.

Jake felt the knob jerk in response. "Or a basketball player." He wanted to kiss Zoe so badly that it hurt.

"You guys coming or not?" Will passed the platter of ribs under their noses on his way to the table.

Later, Jake promised himself. *We'll talk later.*

Conversation over dinner revolved around Hurricane Gertie churning its way toward the Atlantic coast and school, which had started just a few days earlier. The storm track looked to bring the storm ashore somewhere north of Hatteras sometime Tuesday night or Wednesday morning. Only time would tell how bad it might get. Jake asked Kate if his girls could stay with her family when Jake got the call to report in at the firehouse. Ava was more concerned with having cheerleading tryouts cancelled. And the twins were just worried that school would be closed just as their year had gotten under way.

Lynn and Lori loved their new teacher and were thrilled with the whole idea of kindergarten. They couldn't stop chattering animatedly about it. Jake's youngest niece Becca pouted because she was still in preschool, and Jenny, the older one, puffed out her flat little chest in a superior attitude because she was in first grade.

Jake was acutely aware of Zoe sitting next to him on the picnic bench — aware of the continued movement in her belly and the intoxicating scent of her perfume. He wanted to touch her, to put his hand over the baby squirming inside her and an arm about her shoulders. He wanted to claim her as his and make sure all the other dogs knew it.

He'd given Porter two weeks to win her over, and that was long enough. Besides, his father was right. Zoe deserved a choice. When this party broke up, he was going to tell her the things he should have said weeks ago. He'd offer her a sincere apology first, then bare his heart and let her choose between the man who'd only fathered her child and the man who wanted to be there when that baby was born and love it like his own. Between the man who was just doing the right thing and the man who'd finally come to his senses and wanted to give her a Cinderella ending after all.

When everyone's attention had moved on to a discussion over the possibility of spending Christmas at Disney World, Jake leaned down to whisper in Zoe's ear. "We need to talk. Can I walk you home after?"

CHAPTER 30

"Hello, Zoe." A deep, urbane voice Jake didn't recognize cut through the general hubbub of family conversation. "I drove all the way over to this backwater to take you out to dinner, but I see you've already eaten."

The man Jake had last seen driving away in a silver BMW approached. He totally ignored everyone else at the table as he bent toward Zoe's surprised face. Jake felt a rush of resentment and jealousy. Even though Zoe turned away to avoid the man's kiss, Jake seethed.

Philip and Ben looked from Jake to the newcomer with questioning expressions. Ava and Kate gawked. As well they might. Even Jake had to admit the man was extraordinarily handsome. Everyone else had on shorts and jerseys, but the interloper was decked out like Mr. GQ in dressy gray slacks and a linen shirt that probably cost more than Jake's entire firefighting turnout gear.

Zoe jumped to her feet and would have lost her balance had Jake not grabbed her elbow to steady her.

The man put a proprietary arm about Zoe and drew her against his side. "Are you going to introduce me to your friends?"

Zoe pushed herself free of his arm and made the introductions.

Her introduction of Porter Dubois as a lawyer who worked for her father, rather than as the father of her baby, and her resistance to the man's possessive familiarity gave Jake a spurt of smug satisfaction.

Then Porter bent to speak to Zoe in a voice pitched too low for anyone to hear, and Zoe blushed, ruining the momentary triumph. Jake fumed, but there was nothing he could do about it without making a scene.

"Sorry to eat and run." Zoe flushed again and looked at Jake with apology in her eyes. She nodded toward Jake's parents, then his brothers and Kate's husband. "It was nice to meet everyone. I hope . . . I hope I'll see y'all again right soon."

Then she turned to Porter. He held his hand out to take hers, but Zoe ignored it and walked off ahead of him toward the corner of the house. Porter turned back, smiled as if he were a politician running for office, and then followed Zoe.

"That's the competition?" Philip asked, his brows lifted.

"That's the father of Zoe's baby," Jake answered, not bothering to keep the angry resentment out of his voice. Unwilling to meet his parents' concerned looks or his brothers' told-you-so expressions, he feigned a sudden interest in Zoe's corn-bread salad.

Silence fell over the group, but only for a moment before the little girls returned to the subject of Disney World.

"You should have called," Zoe told Porter as they crossed the lawn toward her house.

"I did. You didn't answer."

"Must have been pretty last minute because I was home all day until a couple hours ago."

"I decided talking on the phone wasn't getting us anywhere. I figured if I came to plead my case in person, you'd see reason. I called on my way up here."

"See reason? You make it sound like I'm being *un*reasonable."

"Well, you are."

"What's unreasonable about wanting time

332

to make such an important decision?" They reached the stairs, and Zoe paused to glare at Porter before starting up. "Marriage is a big step."

"And parenthood is a big responsibility," Porter shot back. He tried to put a hand under Zoe's elbow, but she jerked away.

Porter had caught her off-guard on his first visit. She'd been unbelievably complacent letting him kiss her. Twice! Now the thought of him even touching her was repellent. There was no way she could marry this man and submit to a lifetime of his arrogantly possessive touching and kissing.

"Yeah, well, I'm willing to take that responsibility, and I've decided I don't need your help." Zoe hurried up the stairs as fast as her bulk would allow. She was going to make this break as swift and painless as possible. She wanted Porter Dubois out of her life. And she wanted him out now.

She'd argued the case from both sides. Three sides if you counted Molly's. And the cons outweighed the pros about a dozen to one. The only thing Porter could offer her was financial security, but she was doing okay, and money never meant that much to her anyway. Her father might be upset with her now, but he would come around once his granddaughter became part of his life.

Stacked against that was a lifetime of regrets. A home that held no loving warmth. A social life that meant nothing to her and would only take time away from being the kind of mother she wanted to be. And a coffin nail in any hope of finding the kind of love she craved.

Besides, Molly wouldn't benefit from a father so focused on his work that he was never around. Zoe knew that much from her own growing up years. And it wasn't like she planned to cut Molly off from any kind of relationship with her father.

"It's still my kid. I can insist on my rights."

"I won't . . . stop you." Zoe had to pause at the top of the stairs to catch her breath. "Molly has a right . . . to know her father, and . . . I wouldn't take that away from her."

"You've already named our child? And you didn't consult me?"

"You weren't around when I was thinking of names for *my* baby." Zoe yanked the screen door open and charged into the hall. Porter strode in behind her with maddening persistence.

Jet hurried over to welcome Zoe home, while Scotch barked at the intruder with all the hair on his back straight up in alarm. Hoover looked from Zoe to Porter as if trying to decide if this man was a threat or not.

"Good God, Zoe! Three dogs? Wouldn't one have been more than enough?"

Zoe recalled Porter's opinion of dogs, once expressed after a visit to Bree's house. Bree's big, shaggy, English sheepdog had slobbered happily all over Zoe's skirt and left dog hair thoroughly embedded in Porter's charcoal trousers. Porter had made it clear that in his opinion dogs didn't belong in the house. Another reason she couldn't marry this man.

"Hush, Scotch!"

The terrier stopped barking immediately but continued to murmur threats low in his throat as Porter followed Zoe into the kitchen.

Zoe crossed to the sink and reached for the ring box. She didn't feel even a sliver of regret as she flipped the lid shut over the pretty ring. Then she turned to face Porter.

"I can't marry you." She thrust the box in his direction, but he didn't take it.

"Now you *are* being unreasonable."

"Look, Porter. I don't know why you suddenly changed your mind, and frankly, at this point, I don't care. If you'd asked me back when I first discovered I was pregnant, I would have said yes. But you didn't, and

I've grown up since then."

Porter raised his eyebrows with condescending arrogance. "Grown up?"

"And wiser. You don't love me, and you never did. I was just a convenience. And I'll be honest. I didn't love you either. I wanted to, but . . ." Zoe shrugged. She stepped close enough to tuck the box into Porter's shirt pocket. He grabbed her wrist.

"Think about our — think about Molly. We don't have to be in love to give her a two-parent home. Think about all I can give her."

"Take your hand off me." Now all three dogs growled.

Porter dropped Zoe's wrist and darted a nervous glance toward the dogs. "They don't bite, I hope?"

Zoe moved to the far side of the kitchen island and hiked her butt onto a stool. She wasn't afraid of Porter and didn't believe for a minute that he would hurt her physically. But she liked having the barrier between them, and they did need to talk. "They won't hurt you so long as you don't threaten me."

Porter scoffed. "So now I'm a threat? I come here with good intentions, offering you my name and all my worldly possessions, and I'm a threat?"

This time it was Zoe's turn to scoff. "I have no doubt there would have been a lengthy and detailed prenup for me to sign had I accepted your offer. But I've told you *no.* So from here on out, the discussion is about your paternal rights. I'd rather you weren't with me when Molly is born, but you can visit as often as you like. I won't stop you."

"Perhaps you should return to Wilmington and live with your father."

"Why? So Dad can badger me into changing my mind about marrying you?"

"So you won't be alone."

"I'm not alone here. I've got my dog squad for protection. And my cats to keep me company in bed. And I'll have Molly."

"And the redneck next door."

"He's not a redneck," Zoe shot back in Jake's defense.

Porter's face took on an arrogant sneer. "He's not the kind of man you're used to."

"If you mean, he's the kind of man who cares about other people before he worries about himself, then yes, he's definitely not the kind of man I'm used to, but —"

"And you're in love with him."

Zoe considered denying it, but then decided there was no point in lying. "Yes, I'm in love with him. But that's the end of it.

He's been married and got burnt. He doesn't want another wife. But, he's a wonderful neighbor, and he's been there to help me out these last few months far more than you or my father ever were. He's become a very good friend."

Porter looked as if he wanted to say more, but decided to let it go while he hunted for a better argument. "When is your due date?"

"The end of the month."

Porter stood up. He pulled the box from his pocket and placed it on the counter. "Having a husband does have its advantages. You might want to change your mind. Call me when you go into labor so I won't be the last to know I'm a father."

He turned and stalked out. Scotch followed him with all the officiousness of a starched-up butler. Zoe heard the front door shut, then Scotch returned and sat at her feet waiting for praise.

Zoe bent to pat the dog, and pain stabbed sharply in her groin. She gasped and straightened again. The contraction weakened after a brief moment and disappeared.

"It's too soon," Zoe murmured. She got up and went to the sink. She reached for a glass, filled it with water, and drank. Then waited. Nothing. Not sure what to do next, she headed to the living room, then changed her mind and went out onto the porch. Carefully, she lowered herself into a rocker and relaxed.

She spent the next few minutes wondering if there would be another contraction or if that was a random Braxton Hicks. She'd begun to have some of the early contractions about a week ago, but they had felt different. And they'd gone away when she walked around. If another one started, she'd get up and walk around the porch or go sweep the kitchen floor.

Jake's family gathering seemed to be breaking up. Aunt Catherine's Buick pulled out first, followed by the sporty little car that turned out to belong to Philip. Jake's parents appeared next and climbed into one of the pickup trucks. As it backed into the road, Jake's mother turned and waved to Zoe.

Another five minutes passed before Ben and his two boys came around the corner of the house followed closely by Will. The boys clambered into the back of the stretch-cab pickup truck, and Will got into the passenger seat. In another moment, they were gone as well.

The last to leave were Kate and her family. Zoe watched the two little girls scramble into their seats while Kate and Ethan climbed in front. Jake stood beside the mini-van with one hand on each of his twins' shoulders. Then he bent, probably to say goodbye to Ethan through the open window. As the van pulled away the twins waved and kept waving until the van had turned the corner and disappeared.

Jake glanced across the span of lawn and noticed Zoe sitting on her porch. He waved, pointed to the twins, then in the general direction of his upstairs, and finally, at her. He must be trying to tell her he'd come over after he put the twins to bed. Whatever he wanted to talk about must be urgent. He turned the twins toward the house and gave their butts a soft pat, then followed them up the walk.

Molly was going to miss out on so much. Zoe would have felt bad about turning Porter down, except she couldn't feature Porter ever being that casually loving with his children. She couldn't imagine him giving them baths or putting them to bed, either. Reading to them, maybe, but overseeing the brushing of teeth and tucking them in didn't seem like Porter's thing.

Her own father had never even been home at bedtime. He came home for supper but would be off again before the dishes had been cleared. Even when Zoe's mother was still alive, he'd seemed to always have one meeting or another every night.

Zoe grunted and doubled over as another contraction hit her. She struggled out of the chair and walked to the end of the porch and back. It seemed better, so she continued walking until it went away again. *Might as well sweep the floor,* she thought, and headed inside.

When she got to the kitchen the dogs were standing at the back door, so she let them out, then grabbed the broom and began sweeping. By the time the floor was clean, she'd had two more contractions, but they were weaker. More false labor.

She'd picked up the dog bowls before she started on the floor, so she fixed their suppers before putting the bowls back down. Then she went to the door and called them in. Scotch and Hoover headed directly to their bowls. Jet stopped for a pat, then joined the rest of the crew. Zoe grinned. Her Dog Squad! Porter had been appalled!

Admittedly, she'd been a little appalled herself after returning from the rescue shelter. She'd gone with the idea of getting a dog to keep her company and at the same time, ward off unwelcome guests once she'd moved out of her father's house and into her own. The shelter had just hosted an

341

open house fundraiser, and nearly all the dogs currently at the shelter had been adopted. All except her three. They'd been sharing a cage and hung together as if finding comfort in numbers. With three pairs of pleading brown eyes gazing hopefully up at her, she simply couldn't take just one and leave the other two behind.

Her compassion had paid off. The trio had run off her unwelcome guest, and Scotch, at least, had vocalized all the displeasure Zoe didn't feel free to express. Zoe grinned and gave them all another round of hugs.

As she sank onto a stool, she noticed the ring box still sitting on the counter where Porter had left it. She wasn't going to change her mind. She should have made him take it with him. She got up to put it back on the windowsill, and another sharp stab of pain shot across her back and into her gut.

The phone rang. After a moment of holding her breath, willing the contraction to go away, Zoe reached for the phone. "Hello?"

"It's Jake."

Like he had to tell her who was on the other end of the line. She'd know his voice anywhere.

"I don't think I'll be able to get over there tonight after all. I just got a page, and I'm

342

headed to the fire station."

"Stay . . . safe." She tried to keep the catch from her voice, but the ache in her gut hadn't let up yet.

"Are you okay?" He sounded rushed.

"I'm fine." At least she hoped she was fine. She would have been happier knowing he was right next door if this turned out to be the real deal, but with Bree only a couple miles away, she wouldn't be alone. Not if she didn't want to be.

"You're sure?" Worry laced his words in spite of his need to be gone.

"I'm sure. Take care of yourself, Jake."

"I always do. Look, I'll catch up with you later if this turns out to be a nothing." Then the line went dead.

Zoe reached to put the phone back on the hook and stood clutching the sink for support. *Please God, this has got to be just a false alarm. I still have a month to go.*

CHAPTER 31

Zoe awoke in the morning surprised to find herself still at home and still pregnant. In spite of erratic timing, the contractions had seemed pretty persistent when she'd finally gone to bed. She'd been seriously worried and had fully expected to be lying awake with an eye on the clock until it was time to call someone for a ride to the hospital.

But it hadn't been the real deal after all. And now it was time to get up and get dressed for work. She wallowed her way to the edge of the bed and slid her feet to the floor. Man, but she felt huge. She was so ready to be done with this pregnancy. Waddling to the bathroom a dozen times a night, feeling like a beached whale any time she wanted to get up out of a chair or off her bed. Even her maternity clothes had grown snug. How was she going to endure another month?

Showered and dressed, Zoe's attitude

improved. She headed down to the kitchen to fix herself some breakfast. Halfway there, the phone began to ring. Hurrying just wasn't an option any longer, so she hoped whoever was calling would let it ring awhile. But the ringing stopped before she got to the phone.

"Rats."

Zoe let the dogs out into the back yard and turned the kettle on for her insipid morning brew of herbal tea. Real coffee was another thing she was looking forward to as soon as Molly was born.

The phone began to ring a second time. This time she had only two steps to reach it. "Hello?"

"Good morning, Zoe. I tried you a moment ago but didn't get an answer. Did I wake you up?"

"No, Daddy. I was halfway down the stairs. I'm not moving all that fast these days." What on earth could her father be calling about first thing in the morning?

"I wanted to catch you before you headed out for work. Got a few minutes?"

"Sure. What's up?" The kettle screeched, and Zoe reached to pour the steaming water into her mug.

"I just talked with Porter."

Zoe's heart lurched unpleasantly. Now she

knew the reason behind the early morning call. Porter must have arrived at the office and gone straight to her father to whine about his spurned offer. "Lucky you." She couldn't keep the sarcasm out of her voice.

"I'm not the lucky one, but you don't seem to have a grasp on what's in your own best interests. Porter told me he asked you to marry him, but you turned him down. Care to tell me why?"

"Six months ago Porter demanded I get an abortion. He was very straightforward in his rationale for not wanting to become a parent or to get married. Now he comes here with a flashy ring and tells me he's changed his mind, but he didn't give me a single believable reason for such a dramatic reversal."

"What do you call a believable reason? Isn't the fact that he's the father of your baby motivation enough?" her father sputtered.

Zoe could imagine his face getting red and knew he was winding up to deliver a lecture. She took a sip of herbal tea and settled in to endure it until he'd said his piece.

"I brought you up in a decent God-fearing home. Bringing a bastard into the family isn't exactly how I expected you to conduct your life."

"You didn't seem to mind me sleeping with him." Zoe couldn't help arguing back. Her father had done everything but turn down the sheets to encourage her affair with Porter.

"I thought you would eventually get married. The current social custom of sleeping together before marriage is deplorable enough, but you were careless and got yourself pregnant which is another thing entirely. Porter just happens to be willing to set things straight."

Willing? Now she *knew* her father had been behind Porter's about-face. "What did you do? Bribe him with a partnership?"

"I might have mentioned that as my son-in-law, he would certainly be offered a partnership. Same as any of my own sons. But I did *not* bribe him."

"Well, I'm sorry to disappoint you, Daddy, but that's not a good enough reason to get married. You might not call it bribery, but I doubt Porter would have had anything more to do with me if you hadn't dangled that carrot in front of him."

"Porter will be a good provider. He'll see that you want for nothing, and he'll give the kid his name. Isn't that worth considering?"

"I have considered it. Very carefully. And it's not enough. The *kid* needs more than just her father's name and the benefits of his wallet. She needs love and acceptance. She needs to grow up with parents who love and respect each other. But Porter doesn't love or respect me, and I don't love him."

Zoe heard her father's snort of derision. "Love is a very poor value to base a marriage on. The two of you have a lot in common, similar upbringings, similar tastes in music and entertainment, same religion, the same values. People fall out of love after the *I do's* all the time. It's the other things that hold a marriage together. Look at your mother and me."

"Mom died. How do I know you two would still be married?"

"Then look at your grandparents. They had an arranged marriage. They barely even knew each other before their wedding day, and they were married for sixty-seven years."

"Arranged marriages are as dead as Abraham Lincoln."

Zoe's father hadn't become a good lawyer without perseverance or without taking the time to marshal all his arguments beforehand. And he knew when to abandon a losing argument and try a new tack. "What about my grandchild? Marriage would allow you to be a stay-at-home mom. You would be there twenty-four-seven until she's old enough for school. And see that she has the chance to participate in whatever activities she wants as she grows up. How are you going to pay for piano lessons and ballet, or maybe she'll turn out to be an athlete? Do you have any idea how much private clubs cost? And what about her college education? Have you considered any of that?"

Zoe sighed. She wasn't going to win her father over to her way of thinking, but she didn't want to create a rift they'd never get past either. "I have considered all of that. I would love not to have to put Molly into day care and —"

"You're naming her after my mother?"

"Molly Ann. After your mother and mine."

Zoe heard her father breathing. Apparently she'd said the one thing that could derail his sermon.

"Molly," he murmured softly, obviously touched. "Molly Callahan."

"I'm glad you approve." She'd finally done something right. "Will you come to see her when she's born, Daddy?"

When her father didn't answer right off, Zoe wondered what was going on in his head. Had he finally given up trying to change her mind? Or was he just mustering his resources for another attack?

"Of course, I'll come to see her. And you. I wish things were different, but you're more like your mother than you know. She had a mind of her own, too."

"I'll take that as a compliment."

"Your mother could be the most stubborn woman in creation when she got a bee in her bonnet. But she was a fine woman. You're very like her."

Zoe knew that was likely to be as close to telling her he loved her that her father might ever get. The one thing she knew without doubt about her parents' marriage was how much her father had loved her mother even though he'd never known how to show it. He'd been devastated by Ann's death, and in his grief he'd buried himself in work, leaving his children to fend for themselves much of the time. Zoe hadn't planned it that way, but perhaps naming her daughter for her father's mother and wife was the single best way she could have ensured he'd come around to accepting the reality of an illegitimate grandchild.

"I love you, too, Daddy."

"Ah." Her father cleared his throat. "It's going to be a busy day. I better get to work."

"Yeah, me, too."

"Call me when it's time. Okay?"

"I will. Bye, Daddy."

After she hung up, Zoe drank her now cold tea, thinking about her father. He blustered and argued. He seemed aloof and cold even with his children, but how much of that was just because he didn't know how to be any different?

She'd always thought Porter and Daddy were a lot alike. They had the same work ethic. The drive to excel. An obsession with appearances. And the need to win. Maybe Porter didn't know how to be loving any more than her father did. She felt sorry for him. But not sorry enough to pledge the rest of her life to him.

If she ever married, she wanted to feel treasured. She didn't want to have to go looking for proof that her husband cared about her. Not the way her mother had. Like Jake had said, she wanted the fairy tale.

The thought of Jake brought back all she'd learned about him yesterday. And about his family. Jake's dad and her own couldn't have been more different. Where Patrick Callahan, whose black hair was still unmarked by gray, was rarely seen out of a suit and tie, Jake's dad's sun-bleached fair hair and tawny skin attested to a man who lived his life working out of doors in short sleeves and a hard hat. His tanned hands were rough and calloused rather than soft and pale. Cam had laugh lines at the corners of his eyes instead of worry lines between his brows, and he offered up his free time as a qualified EMT, on call at all hours of the day and night instead of heading up prestigious non-profit boards and arranging meetings to suit his own convenience. Yet, in spite of these vast differences in lifestyle, they had raised very similar families — big families, with children grown into friendly, responsible adults who stuck together, watched out for one another, and enjoyed each other's company.

Her mind flashed to the image of pretty, petite Kate, surrounded by four tall brothers in a group hug while their mother snapped a photo of them. Then one with Kate's husband Ethan and all the grandchildren. And finally one with the timer set and everyone in it, even Zoe who wasn't family at all, but Sandy had insisted. It was just like when her family managed to gather under the same roof at the same time. Zoe had a whole album of photos documenting the years. Friends came and went. Spouses and grandchildren got added. Some family members disappeared. Like her mother. And Ava's.

Jake and Zoe had a lot more in common

than Zoe and Porter. Why couldn't Jake be the one with the ring offering marriage?

CHAPTER 32

Jake spent all day battening down the work site in preparation for the coming hurricane and thinking about Zoe and missed opportunities. His father's warning echoed over and over in his head along with images of Porter possessively leading Zoe away from the table, symbolically peeing on every bush along the way. Marking his territory the way Jake had misguidedly recoiled from doing. He'd been a damned fool.

The fact that he still hadn't made time to talk to Zoe tormented him as he pushed his crew and himself. The eye was following the predicted path, and the storm had grown in size. Even though landfall was expected to come well north of Hatteras, the possibilities for disaster loomed on both fronts. Even the fringes of a storm the size of Gertie could wreak havoc on a construction site, picking up sheets of plywood and tossing them around like playing cards, tumbling unsecured piles of lumber, tearing at loose tarps, dumping containers of supplies, and spreading litter for miles. Marrying Porter for all the wrong reasons. Marrying Porter because Jake hadn't offered her an alternative.

With the construction site taken care of and the crew sent home for the duration, Jake locked his mobile office and climbed into his van. Twenty minutes later, he pulled into his driveway, determined to head directly over to Zoe's and talk to her without further delay.

But her truck wasn't in the driveway. He checked on his girls, then policed up his own yard, putting away bikes and lawn furniture while keeping an eye out for the battered green truck. His own yard secure, he headed over to Zoe's where he hauled her rubbish barrels into the garage and tied the old rocking chairs to the porch railings. When he was satisfied that he'd done all he could and Zoe still hadn't returned from work, he headed home to take a shower and get cleaned up.

He was toweling himself dry when his pager went off. He called in, hoping it was just a fire, but as he'd feared, they wanted anyone who could get there at the firehouse as backup for the regular crew. He hustled into clean jeans and tossed a change of clothes into a duffle. Then he headed for the twins' room to pack a bag for them.

Ava rushed up to him in the hall. "Is there a fire, Daddy?"

"No. I've just got to spend the night at the firehouse, so I'll be dropping you off at Aunt Kate's. Pack up whatever you need for an overnight. Okay, kitten?"

Ava didn't question him because they'd been through this drill before. Even when Celia was still living at home, Jake hadn't felt comfortable leaving his mother-in-law and the girls alone during a hurricane.

After a fairly organized scramble, the twins and Ava had collected all the things they needed and were piling into the van. Zoe's truck had appeared in her driveway, but there was no sign of her. Jake hesitated.

The storm was already howling. If he'd been watching the television, he was sure he'd have seen the usual windbreaker-clad reporter leaning at an impossible angle against the wind with rain splattering in his face as he shouted out a status report on what anyone watching could already see outside their own windows.

Jake needed to get his girls settled. He'd call Zoe and check on her when he left Kate's.

The enormous oak tree by the old brick gatepost tossed wildly in the teeth of the wind as Jake pulled onto the main road. That tree had seen storms bigger than this one and would probably see a lot more, but already the ground was littered with leaves and branches torn off that tree and others.

At the next intersection Jake had to wait for a gap in the long line of cars retreating from the outer banks. The sound was a froth of whitecaps and churning waves. Jake didn't want to think what the ocean looked like on the other side of the barrier island. His mother would be at Aunt Catherine's in the relative safety of Wilmington and his dad at the ambulance station, hoping to do nothing more than play cards all night.

Finally, Jake got a break and pulled out. Rain slashed at the windshield, and he clutched the steering wheel a little tighter as a gust rocked the van. It was going to be a wild night.

"Will we have another blanket house?" Lynn piped up from her seat in the rear of the van.

"A blanket house?" Jake shot a glance at Ava.

"Aunt Kate draped blankets over the Ping Pong table in the playroom last time we stayed over during a hurricane. She made them a picnic supper to eat in their cave, and then they got to sleep there."

Now that Ava explained it, Jake remembered hearing about the cave. Leave it to his sister to turn a hurricane scare into an adventure.

"Maybe you will," Jake told his daughter. "Maybe your Aunt Kate will have a different adventure. But you'll have fun with Becca and Jenny, whatever you do."

"Is Becca a baby?" Lori asked.

"Jenny says Becca's just a baby," Lynn added.

"Becca is not a baby, and I'd better not hear that you called her that. Be nice to her," Jake admonished.

"I'm always nice to her." Jake saw Lynn nodding her head vigorously in the rearview mirror. "But Jenny isn't."

"Jenny's bossy," Lori stated with a touch of irritation in her voice.

Lynn and Lori began a low-voiced discussion that Jake couldn't quite make out. He let their chatter float along in the back of his mind. The realization had just hit him that Zoe would be alone in the midst of the coming storm. Perhaps he should have asked her if she wanted to stay with Kate as well. Kate wouldn't have thought twice about an extra guest.

He fumbled at his belt for his cell to give Zoe a call but then dropped the phone on the console. He needed two hands on the wheel. Ten minutes later, he pulled the van into his sister's driveway. He'd call Zoe after he got the kids settled.

Jenny and Becca tumbled out the front door with shiny slickers flapping in the wind and ran for the van.

"Mom said we can have another cave house," they called excitedly in unison as rain spit in their faces.

The twins scrambled out to join their cousins while Ava and Jake gathered up their bags and made a dash for the house.

Another ten minutes, and Jake was back in the car wiping water out of his eyes. He grabbed his cell and punched in the speed dial he'd assigned to Zoe's home number. He listened to it ring. And ring. And ring.

Where was she? He knew she was home. Her truck hadn't gotten home by itself. Why didn't her machine pick up, at least? He hung up and tried her cell.

"C'mon, Zoe. Answer the phone," he urged as concern mounted. Maybe she was just in the shower. He'd call from the station.

Jake backed out of the driveway and headed toward the firehouse. Traffic had let up finally. Apparently everyone had gotten to wherever they planned to sit out the storm and hunkered down for the duration. After another harrowing fifteen minutes of white-knuckle driving, he pulled into the parking lot in front of Joel's. The shiny New York-style diner glimmered wetly in the driving rain. Security lights glowed weakly from the darkened interior. Joel had closed early. Jake tried calling Zoe again. Same result.

With rain driving relentlessly against the windshield, Jake tried to decide if he should continue on to the station or detour back to check on Zoe. Darkness had come down like the curtain at the end of a play. Jake couldn't see the tossing trees anymore, only flashes of light as branches danced between him and lights around the condo complex across the street. Flooding was inevitable, and the fire department would be called out to help with emergencies, but concern for Zoe nagged uncomfortably.

She was probably fine.

But what if she wasn't?

Jake tried both phones again. No answer at either number.

The station would have to wait. He dialed the station number and told the dispatcher where he was headed. Then he pulled out and turned back toward home.

The first sign of trouble loomed across the entrance to Awbrey Circle. The old tree that he'd thought would weather a hundred more storms had lost the fight in the forty-five minutes since he'd left to take the girls over to Kate's. It completely blocked access to the cul-de-sac and had taken down a pole and the power and phone lines with it.

They'd had too much rain, and the ground had been too wet. The entire root system had given way. Jake inched past the branches that extended into the main road and pulled the van into the entrance of a new subdivision that had never been built. He reached into the glove box and found his flashlight, then got out of the van.

Before he'd gone ten feet, his jeans were soaked. It felt like he was climbing a mountain just battling his way back up the road to the cul-de-sac, but eventually he reached the downed tree. Branches creaked in the wind as he picked his way under and over and through the tangled mess. The tree had toppled the old brick gatepost as well, and he had to take care not to trip over jumbled chunks of brick and mortar. A tossing branch snatched his hat off. Jake made a futile grab for it before it disappeared into the dark.

Stepping free of the tree at last, Jake broke into a run. He cut across the grassy island in the center of Awbrey Circle and dashed up Zoe's walk. Taking the steps three at a time, he almost crashed into her door before he slid to a stop on the rain-slick porch.

"Zoe!" Jake pounded on the door. The house was completely dark without power. Zoe hadn't even lit a candle. "Zoe!"

No answer.

Jake tried the door. It opened. He should have known! Dripping all over her polished floor, he yanked the door shut and called again. "Zoe?"

"I'm . . . in the . . . kitchen." Her voice sounded strained and frightened.

Jake hurried to the kitchen. His wet boots slipped and skidded as he went. He flashed his light around the kitchen. Zoe crouched beside the back door. His heart jumped into his throat. He scrambled to her side.

"What happened? Are you hurt?"

She lifted her head to look at him. Her eyes were huge and dark with fright. "The baby is coming."

CHAPTER 33

Panic lanced into Jake.

"But it's too soon! Almost a month too soon."

Zoe clutched at his rain-soaked slicker. "I know —" She broke off with a gasp and doubled up.

Please, God! Not here. Not now. Not like this. Jake prayed frantically. Cold sweat sprang out on his brow. Not another premature baby. He couldn't bear it. Not again. Not Zoe. This couldn't be happening.

Zoe's face crunched in pain, then slowly cleared. Her fingers loosened their death grip on his slicker. Jake tried to gather his wits while his brain scrambled to deny Zoe's announcement. She couldn't be in labor. She had another month to go.

"I tried to call you," Zoe whispered raggedly. "But there was no dial tone."

"Lines are down," Jake responded automatically. His heart and mind didn't want

363

to accept the disaster facing him.

"The dogs, Jake." Suddenly, Zoe doubled over again, clutching her belly. "Got to . . . let . . . the dogs . . . in."

Ignoring the dogs, Jake held on to Zoe until the contraction passed. His mind raced. He needed to get Zoe to the hospital. But an ambulance couldn't get to the house. Neither could his van. No way she could make her way through that downed tree either. Even with help.

"The dogs," Zoe reminded him as she straightened again.

Reluctantly, Jake left her and moved toward the door. The moment the door cracked open, a dripping-wet canine trio bolted into the room. They immediately went to Zoe and began nosing her thighs.

"Sorry, guys." Zoe bent to pat each sopping head. "I keep doggy towels in the bottom drawer." She pointed in the general direction of the corner cabinet.

Jake yanked the drawer open and grabbed a towel. Before he'd finished giving the dogs a quick rubdown, Zoe was huffing and puffing and clutching the counter for support.

"You'll do," he told the dogs as he dropped the sodden towel on the floor and hurried back to Zoe's side. He steadied her until the puffing stopped.

"How long has this been going on?"

"I don't know." Zoe looked up at him, her eyes wide. "Jake. I'm scared."

She's scared? I'm terrified! I have to call someone. I have to get help. I can't do this again.

Jake pulled Zoe into his arms and hugged her hard. "Don't worry, babe. Everything's going to be okay." While he was reassuring her, another contraction hit and she tensed. He rocked her gently, waiting for it to pass and tried desperately to get a grip on his escalating panic.

"Let's get you into the living room where you can get comfortable."

Zoe took a shuddering breath and nodded.

Jake shrugged out of his slicker and tossed it into the corner with the sodden towel. He put a supporting arm around Zoe and guided her toward the living room. As soon as he could get her settled he'd start calling for help. Starting with the fire station. Or his father. Dad would know what to do.

He eased her into her favorite chair. Then he fumbled for the holster on his belt. But when he pressed the *on* button there were no bars. He dialed anyway. Nothing happened.

Fear sliced into his heart. Jake forced

himself to breath slowly. And think. What should he do first? What did he need to do until he could get a signal and get help?

Some light. They needed light.

"Where are your candles? You do have candles around, don't you?" They needed to be able to see, and his flashlight wasn't enough.

Zoe nodded. "In the cabinet over the fridge."

"Hang tight. I'll be right back."

"Jake!" Zoe grabbed for his hand and clung, her eyes shut tight.

Jake waited the contraction out, his mind frantic with disjointed thoughts. As soon as Zoe relaxed again, he dashed back to the kitchen, flashed his light into the cabinet, and found the jumble of candles and holders. He grabbed the hem of his T-shirt and pulled it away from his body to form a pocket, then shoveled the candles into it along with the box of kitchen matches he'd found sitting on the counter.

Back in the living room, Zoe was huffing and puffing again. Jake dumped his load onto the ottoman and reached to hold her hands while she worked her way through the contraction. He still fought to keep fear at bay, but now that he was doing something, he'd begun to gain a semblance of control. In a minute he'd try the cell again and call his dad. He had to stay calm. Panic wouldn't help Zoe or Molly.

He glanced at his watch. Eight twenty. Quickly, he began lighting candles and setting them in places they wouldn't be likely to get knocked over.

"You got any blankets down here or anything?"

"In the dryer." Zoe pointed back in the direction of the kitchen.

Jake made a second dash to the kitchen, yanked open the dryer, and scooped out a freshly laundered pile of sheets.

"Jake, what am I going to do?" Zoe asked when he returned to her side.

He dropped the sheets beside the chair and knelt next to her.

"I promised I'd . . . call when it . . . started," Zoe whispered with tears in her eyes.

"I don't think Bree will be able to get here. The big tree is down across our road. I'm just praying we can get an EMT in here."

"I promised my dad. And —" Zoe looked up at him with desperation in her eyes. "And Porter."

CHAPTER 34

Porter's name, uttered with such urgency, dumped a pail of ice water over Jake's pounding heart. In the last crazy half hour since he'd found Zoe in labor, he'd forgotten all about Porter Dubois and his claim on Zoe and her baby.

He'd been so busy trying to calm his own terror and hers that he'd forgotten to wonder what else Zoe needed. Beyond the obvious. Beyond the physical needs of a woman in labor.

But, I'm here, babe. And I love you. "We'll call your dad as soon as I get a signal. And" — Jake hesitated, hating Porter, resenting Zoe's promise to call him — "and Porter."

"Oh, God —" Zoe began panting again.

Jake held her hands. He had to go for help. He had no idea what he should be doing. It was too soon. Way too soon. Zoe needed someone qualified to do all the right things. Jake wasn't it. He glanced at his watch again. It had been less than two minutes.

"I need to go get help," he told Zoe as soon as she was breathing normally again.

"No!" Zoe clutched at his hands, her eyes dark with distress. "Please. Can't you just call for help on your cell?"

"There's no signal. And even when I do get through, the ambulance won't be able to get in here. The oak tree on the corner is down. Someone needs to clear a way, and I've got a chain saw."

"I'm scared." Her voice trembled.

So am I, babe! You have no idea how scared!

"It's going to be okay." *Please God, let that be true.*

Jake grabbed his phone off the floor where he'd dropped it and punched in 911 again. Still no bars up. He put it to his ear and listened anyway. Nothing.

If only he knew how much longer she had. Maybe he could calm her down enough so she'd let him get back to his van and drive to the station to get someone better qualified than he was. He tried to think of the questions he'd be asked when he did get through to someone. The fire department had brought in a doctor to discuss a number of scenarios a Good Samaritan might run into and how to handle them until qualified help arrived. One of the topics was untimely childbirth. At the time, Jake had been so busy denying it could ever happen to him again that now he had to scramble to recall what the doctor had told them.

"Has your water broken?"

Zoe nodded, but didn't say anything as her face contorted with another effort.

"Any blood or anything?"

Zoe shook her head side to side, still panting hard.

"Do you feel like you need to push?"

Again she shook her head. Then her face began to relax, and her panting slowed to a stop.

Jake desperately wished he could talk to his father. Dad would know what to do. How much time did she have? He tried punching in his father's cell number but got the same dead air result. He closed his eyes and tried to recall everything he'd learned in that session at the fire station about how labor progressed.

The first thing that came back to him now was a disconcerting discussion about the stages of dilation. The idea of looking to find out just how advanced Zoe's labor was made him squirm with embarrassment. But what if the baby's head was already showing? *Oh God! What if it's just like Karen?*

370

Jake didn't want to think about that night with Karen. "Mind if I . . . kind of take a look and see . . . see if I can . . . see anything?" What would he do if he could see Molly's head? His gut tightened and his heart raced.

When he'd happened upon Karen Ostringer's car at the side of the road, he'd thought he was stopping to help a motorist in distress. What he'd found was Karen sprawled across the back seat, her knees spread and a baby's head already emerging. He hadn't had time to be either embarrassed or afraid before the tiny mite slipped into his shaking hands.

"I don't mean to embarrass you, but —"

Zoe nodded, looking equally uncomfortable with the request. "Good thing I didn't get upstairs to get clean panties when my water broke." She giggled nervously. A hot rush of mortification surged into Jake's face in spite of the urgency and fear.

"We're going to get through this, Zoe. Try to relax between contractions. I'm going to get a couple of those towels. I'll be right back. I promise." He was delaying, and he knew it. But he had to get out of there for a minute. He had to get a grip on himself.

He snatched up his flashlight and hurried to the kitchen. He grabbed two more towels

371

from the drawer by the door, then stopped at the sink to get one of them wet. He noticed the little blue box sitting on the windowsill. Closed now, but still there. He wondered if the ring was still inside. Then he heard Zoe call out. He forgot about the box and dashed back to the living room.

Zoe was panting hard again. Man, but the contractions were close together. *Please, God,* he prayed, not sure what he was praying for.

"Do you want to lie down or stay where you are?" he asked when the contraction had passed.

"Lie down, I think," she answered in an uncertain voice.

Jake grabbed one of the clean sheets he'd dumped earlier and spread it out over the carpet. Then he helped Zoe from the chair and eased her down onto the floor. Pillows! She needed pillows. He checked the couch but there were only two tiny decorative ones there.

He started for the stairs, but Zoe grabbed his hand. Another contraction was starting. While he waited for it to pass, he remembered the little rabbit Marsha had used to help her concentrate when they'd gone through childbirth classes. Did Zoe have a talisman? He ran through other things he

should collect when he made a dash upstairs. Baby things. Receiving blankets at
least. But first he needed to look and see if
the baby's head was showing. He couldn't
avoid it any longer. There might still be time
to go for help.

"Zoe?" Jake pushed her damp curls off
her face. "First I'm going to take a look . . .
down there. Then, I'm going upstairs to get
some pillows and stuff for the baby. Do you
have a talisman? Something you practiced
with, I mean?"

Zoe smiled weakly. "In a blue overnight
bag, beside my closet door. There's a — just
bring the whole bag down."

Jake gave her hands a reassuring squeeze
and then let go. As he slid the hem of her
skirt up past her knees, embarrassment
made his skin prickle. He took a quick look,
then sucked in a lungful of air. He'd been
holding his breath and hadn't realized it.
Nothing showing. Nothing except the parts
of Zoe he had no business looking at.
Intimate places. His face felt beet red.

"Look, Zoe. I can't see Molly's head or
anything. So there's probably still time for
me to get out to my van and go after medi-
cal help. You should be —"

"Noooo!" Zoe's panicked voice rose to a
squeak as she shot up and grabbed for him.

Jake pulled her into his embrace, burying her face against his chest. "Okay, babe. Okay. I won't go. Just — take it easy." He was so far from taking it easy it amazed him his own voice didn't squeak.

Get a grip, he admonished himself. So maybe he wasn't a trained EMT, but he *had* been trained to keep his head in an emergency. He just needed to focus on Zoe and stay cool. Lots of preemies made it just fine without any special help.

He felt her body clench with tension. He rocked her gently, waiting for the spasm to pass. "It'll be okay, babe. I promise," he whispered into her hair.

"Bree told me you delivered a baby once," Zoe said as soon as the contraction let up.

Jake didn't want to think about it. "Yeah, once. But I didn't have a choice that time."

"So, maybe you don't have a choice this time either."

"But —"

"Please, Jake. I'm afraid to do this alone. What if you go, and then you can't get back again?"

That possibility hadn't occurred to Jake. He knew he could get back to the van, and he'd been focused on that as his only alternative to get help with his cell phone not working. But there could be flooding.

There could be more trees down. The idea of Zoe delivering her baby alone and terrified sent a shock wave of horror through his system that successfully overrode his own desire to turn this whole mess over to someone else. If only he could talk to his father. Reluctantly, Jake gave up the idea of going for reinforcements. "Okay. We'll do this together. But I have to run upstairs and get those things."

Jake took the stairs two at a time. He found the bag right where she'd said it would be. Then he tucked all four pillows from her bed under his arm. On the way across to the nursery, he pulled his cell out and tried again, hoping against hope that he might get a signal up here. Still nothing. Must be a tower down or something.

In the nursery, he opened a drawer and shined his flashlight into it. Tiny socks and lots of little pink outfits. He yanked open the second drawer and found blankets, T-shirts and onesies. He scooped up a fistful of blankets and one shirt. A stack of diapers sat right on top, so he grabbed a couple of those as well. He took a quick look around, but nothing else leapt out at him as necessary, so he hurried back downstairs with his haul.

When he got to the living room Zoe had

her eyes closed and her mouth pursed as she blew out short little puffs of air. He waited until she was done, then put the overnight bag next to her. He lifted her shoulders and shoved the pillows behind her. "Better?"

"Much!" Zoe shuddered gratefully and shifted her weight against the pillows. "Jake?" She swallowed convulsively. "Thank you. For coming back to check on me. And for not leaving me alone."

He reached out to push a tangle of sweaty curls behind her ear. He hoped his own fear and inadequacy didn't show. She was already calmer now that she had extracted his promise to stick with her.

Zoe rummaged in her little bag and finally drew out a little blue Smurf. She seemed a little self-conscious as she set it down on the edge of the ottoman. Jake glanced at it and snorted, temporarily surprised out of his fear.

The little blue Smurf was rigged out in a yellow fire jacket with a fire hose in its hand.

"Anyone you know?" His heart skipped a few beats.

"I named him Jake. I hope you don't mind."

Confusion and hope warred in Jake's chest. The jeweler's box still sat on her windowsill, and Zoe had wanted to call Porter. But she'd named her talisman Jake. And it was a fireman, not a lawyer.

"Tell me about the other baby." Zoe cut into his thoughts.

"What other baby?"

"The other . . . one you . . . delivered." Zoe gasped and began panting.

Jake reached for the Smurf fireman and held it where she could see it. "Focus, babe. Focus." She held his free hand in a punishing grip but kept her eyes on the little fireman as directed.

When the contraction was over, Zoe prompted, "Tell me about the other baby."

"That was a long time ago." The less she knew about that outcome, the better.

"But not likely something you'd forget."

Like he could forget how tiny the little mite had been. Or how still. Or how helpless Jake had felt trying to breathe life into its premature lungs.

"But you don't want to tell me about it?" Zoe urged, her eyes calmer now and bright with interest.

"I'd rather not."

"Why?"

"The story doesn't have a happy ending."

Zoe frowned. "Bree said you were like a Good Samaritan, or something."

Jake closed his eyes, trying to think of a good reason not to tell her the whole sorry story. He heard her gasp and start breathing hard and kept his eyes shut. Maybe she'd just drop it.

Zoe whimpered, and Jake's eyes flew open. She had hers pinched shut, and a look of pain radiated across her face. Already he was failing her.

He touched her cheek. "Open your eyes, babe. Look at Little Jake. You can do this."

She opened her eyes and focused on the Smurf. Of course she could do it. The question was, could he? That other woman had meant nothing to him.

Zoe sagged against the pillows and relaxed her grip again. "You're not going to tell me, are you?"

How could she be so determinedly focused on this in the midst of her own crisis? "I'll tell you later. Right now I need to focus on you." And he needed to get visions of Karen and her doomed infant out of his head.

Jake leaned down to kiss Zoe's forehead. She began to pant again. Jake snuck another peek under her skirt. Still no head showing. At least this time, he didn't blush, and he took long enough to assess what he was looking at. He held the little Smurf fireman for her to focus on. It felt like it might have been longer since the last contraction. He checked his watch. It had been. Should he be worried about that? He wished he could at least talk to his father.

Jake settled Zoe back onto her pillows. Then he checked his cell again. Still no signal. "Relax, babe, I think it's going to be a while. You need to save your energy."

Zoe squirmed with mortification. Five minutes ago . . . a half an hour ago, or however long it had been since Jake had found her squatting by the kitchen door overcome with pain, she'd been too terrified to feel embarrassed. But suddenly the intensity had faded, and the reality of her situation hit home.

Maybe there *was* time for Jake to go for help. Maybe even time to get to the hospital. Should she let him try?

A bolt of panic shot through her all over again. Her mother had been alone when Zoe's baby brother was born. By the time someone found her, she was unconscious. Bobby had lived, but her mother hadn't. Zoe had been told her mother's uterus had just worn out. Too many babies had robbed it of the resilience needed to contract and stop the bleeding. Zoe was younger, and this was her first baby, but the thought of being alone still terrified her. Alone was far worse than the indignity of Jake seeing her like this. If she couldn't have Bree, Jake was the next best friend she had.

Hurricane Gertie howled outside. Zoe's windows whistled under the onslaught, and bits of debris and broken branches rattled against the sides of the house. It would have been scary enough even if she hadn't been in labor.

"Please, don't leave me." She sounded like a coward, but she couldn't help it.

"I'm not going anywhere." Jake leaned down to wipe her face with the corner of a damp towel. "I promised. Besides, I need to keep my little buddy here company." Jake set the Smurf on the floor beside her. "You want to try lying on your side? I could rub your back a little. It might help you feel more comfortable."

Zoe eased over onto her side and pulled her knees up under her swollen belly. Jake's warm hands began to work their way down her spine. Zoe groaned in pleasure.

Jake popped his head over her shoulder and looked into her face. "You okay?"

She nodded. His head disappeared again, and the massage resumed. It felt good. His hands were strong and comforting. They eased her taut muscles between contractions and helped her relax. As long as Jake was here, and she wasn't alone, she'd get through this.

Zoe floated in a strange kind of limbo. She had no idea how much time went by. Contractions came and went, but she was tired and didn't try to keep up with the panting routine. Instead, she concentrated on going with the flow as each wave of pain came and went, envisioning the process, knowing that each contraction brought her closer to the birth of her daughter. In between contractions she focused on Jake's hands tirelessly kneading her aching back. Each time a spasm would begin to peak, he reached across her to remind her to focus on the little Smurf who sat in a pool of candlelight on the floor just inches from her face. Jake held her hand and let her squeeze as hard as she needed. When it was over, he wiped her brow and resumed his massage.

No one could actually sleep at a time like this, but Jake was helping her achieve the next best thing. As she drifted from one peak to another, she thought she heard Jake whisper *I love you,* and her heartbeat quickened with hope. But maybe that had only been a dream, a figment created out of her desire to hear him say it. If it weren't for the increasing discomfort, she could almost wish this time would go on indefinitely. Just her and Jake, isolated from the craziness outside in a cocoon of warmth and candlelight. His touch was so comforting. So reassuring. So welcome. She wanted him to go on touching her forever.

"What time is it?" she asked in a dreamy haze.

"Just after midnight." He continued rubbing her lower back.

"What happened to the dogs?"

"I shut them up in the kitchen. They were getting too nosey."

"Jet especially, right?"

"Right," he agreed.

"Is the chief going to be upset that you never showed up at the fire station?"

"I called to let them know I was coming back to check on you before I came in. I think they've probably guessed I'm still here. I was hoping someone might jump to conclusions and send an EMT out to help, but — but they didn't."

Zoe cried out as a sudden sharp pain lanced through her. Fear blossomed instantly.

"It's okay, babe. It's just another contraction. Maybe we're getting closer." He sounded so calm and reassuring.

Zoe let go of her panic reluctantly, then

realized that in talking about the dogs and Jake's job, she'd lost her focus. She stared at her little Smurf and forced herself to relax, but the intensity of the contraction spiked anyway.

Jake eased her over onto her back again and held her hands, huffing and puffing along with her as the spasm clutched at her. It felt like her body was turning inside out.

The idyll was over.

Again and again pain ripped through Zoe with appalling force as she fought to stay in control.

"Jake! It hurts!"

"I know, babe. I know. Let go of my hands for a minute."

Zoe let go and clutched at fistfuls of bunched up sheet instead. "Oh, God!"

As the vice-like grip of the contraction tightened, an overwhelming need to push slammed into her. Vaguely she heard Jake's voice telling her he saw Molly's head. Vaguely, she noted that he'd shoved her clothing all the way up to her waist and was now hunched on his knees between her feet.

"Push, babe. Push."

She pushed. The wave crested in a shower of pain and urgency. Then it slowly gave way to intense discomfort.

Zoe lifted her head off the nest of pillows

to see the top of Jake's sun-streaked head bent low between her knees.

"She's almost here," he told her, his voice hushed and a little shaky.

Zoe felt the wave coming again. This time she rode with it, bearing down hard. Grunting with the effort. Feeling Molly slip free. Continuing to push even when Jake gasped in surprise and began praying. Then she heard Molly's first faint squall.

CHAPTER 35

Jake knelt on the floor between Zoe's feet, clutching a slippery, bawling infant. No problem with her lungs. Relief washed over him, and his heart burst with love for this tiny scrap of humanity he'd just helped into life. He wanted to cradle her against his chest and protect her forever.

Molly let out another robust cry of protest. It was the sweetest sound he'd ever heard. His eyes filled with tears as he bent his head and pressed his lips to the tiny forehead.

"Welcome to the world, Molly."

Jake laid Molly across Zoe's stomach, then reached for Zoe's hand and guided it to the infant's back. He scrambled for the pile of receiving blankets he'd brought downstairs. He wrapped Molly in one of the blankets. Then he helped Zoe bring her just-born daughter to her breast.

Zoe, flushed and grinning, gazed at her baby. She touched the tiny cheek with a shaking finger. "Oh, Jake!" Zoe glanced up for a moment, then back to the baby. "She's beautiful."

Jake watched, amazed all over again, as Molly rooted instinctively for Zoe's nipple and found it. "You're both beautiful."

He kissed Zoe's forehead. *Thank you, God. Thank you, God. Thank you, God.* The refrain filled his head and his heart as relief poured through him. He'd been praying so hard for nothing to go wrong. And his prayers had been answered. He wanted to hug them both.

The lights flickered and then died again.

Suddenly, Jake noticed that the wind had weakened. He'd been so intent on the birth, he hadn't realized that Gertie had moved on. He wiped his hands on his still damp jeans and reached for his cell phone.

He had a signal. *Praise the Lord!* He dialed nine-one-one. When the dispatcher answered, he explained the situation, unable to keep the joy and pride from his voice. The dispatcher congratulated him and called him Dad. His chest squeezed in pain. If only he was Molly's daddy. He swallowed and went on to explain about the tree and the need for men with chain saws, before breaking the connection.

"I knew you could do it." Zoe reached for

his hand and closed her fingers around his.

"You did all the work, babe." This time Jake kissed Zoe's mouth. With Molly cradled between them, Zoe returned his kiss with warmth. When he drew back, her wonderful hazel eyes were awash with unshed tears. "You're a champ," he muttered huskily, then backed hastily away.

He found another clean sheet and covered Zoe. He draped a second little blanket over Molly and slumped back against the ottoman. He'd felt less tired after fighting a nasty fire for twice as many hours. But never had he felt so elated with the results of his efforts. The cloud of Karen and her little boy faded in the light of Zoe and Molly and this magical moment of triumph.

In a minute, he'd give her his cell phone and let her call Porter. It was almost two o'clock in the morning, but that shouldn't matter to a new father eager to hear the news. In another minute, Jake would let her make the call. But he wanted to pretend, for a few moments longer, that it was just him and Zoe and Molly.

Zoe hugged her sleeping newborn as she gazed at Jake's beloved face. He looked so peaceful and pleased as he slumped tiredly against the ottoman. She'd known nothing truly awful would happen so long as she wasn't alone. And Jake had been there for her. In spite of everything, he'd been there. Maybe he had said he loved her all those hours ago, while he rubbed her back. Maybe he'd tell her again. As soon as she told him her decision regarding Porter.

Porter!

Zoe gasped in disbelief. She hadn't given a moment's thought to Porter since that first aborted attempt to call him. She didn't want to think about him now, but she'd promised he wouldn't be the last to know he was a father.

He didn't have to know right this minute, though. For just a little while longer, it could be just her and Jake and Molly in this little bubble of candlelit solitude, like it had been through the long, hard night. Candle-light flickered across Jake's face. His gray eyes were dark in the wavering yellow light, his expression soft. A faint smile curved his lips.

"Have I said thank you, yet?" Zoe put a hand on Jake's knee. He covered it with his own.

"I wouldn't have missed it for anything," Jake whispered.

Then Zoe heard the unmistakable sound of chain saws in the distance. Jake scrambled to his feet.

Their bubble in time had burst.

Jake hurried to the window and saw a half dozen lights piercing the darkness at the corner of their street. Two of the lights separated themselves and bobbed across the circle toward Zoe's house. Men at a run. The EMTs were on their way at last.

CHAPTER 36

Her very first visitors were Jake, Ava, and the twins. Zoe heard Lynn and Lori chattering excitedly outside her door, and she had only a moment to button her robe before they dashed into the hospital room. Instantly hushed, the twins stared at Zoe and Molly with solemn gray eyes.

"Hey, Molly!" Jake touched Molly's contented little face with one big calloused finger. He looked at Zoe with a question in his eyes. She nodded, and he scooped Molly into his arms and nuzzled his face into her blankets. "I've brought you a fan club."

Ava peered over her father's arm. "Oh, Zoe! She's beautiful. She's so tiny!"

"Five pounds, one ounce," Zoe announced. "Just big enough to stay with me instead of being shut up in the preemie nursery. Just imagine how big she would have been if she'd waited to be born when she was supposed to be."

"What an adventure you and Dad had." Ava turned toward Zoe and hugged her hard.

"Your father was a rock. I don't know how I'd have managed if he hadn't come back to check on me."

Ava laughed, then whispered, "What'd he think of your little fireman?"

Zoe had forgotten that Ava knew about the talisman. "He didn't say." Jake had snorted in surprise when he'd seen it, but the spurt of hope she'd seen in his eyes had caused her heart rate to soar.

Ava glanced from her father to Zoe, then shrugged with a smug little smile tugging at her mouth. "I'm sure he noticed, even if he didn't say anything. And, in case you were worried about the menagerie — don't. Dad's taking care of the lot. Oh, and this is for you and Molly." Ava handed Zoe a shiny red bag.

Ava's smile, Jake's reaction to the Smurf, and a dozen other little things suddenly began to fill Zoe with a queer sense of anticipation. Then she gave herself a mental shake. *Don't start imagining things that aren't there.*

Jake had settled into a chair so the twins could get a better look at the baby. Zoe watched the heartwarming tableau for a moment and then returned her attention to the red bag.

She pulled out a tiny shirt with the legend, *I arrived in a hurricane!* on the front and *Molly* scrawled across the back. "Oh, Ava! When did you have time to make this?"

"There's more." Ava gestured toward the bag.

Zoe fished out another tissue-wrapped package and opened it to reveal a jersey her own size. This one had a photo of her very pregnant self, taken in profile just a couple weeks ago. Below it, with the same carefree scrawl as Molly's shirt, *Molly & Me* was written in hot pink.

Zoe held her arms out to hug Ava again. "I love them."

Ava blushed happily. "I added the part about the hurricane this morning. Dad was so anxious to get over here and check on you, it just barely dried in time to wrap."

Zoe glanced back at Jake. The twins hung over the arms of the chair on either side of him. He looked up at her and grinned. For a moment, Zoe tried to pretend they were all one family. But it was just an illusion. The closeness of the night before had been banished the moment the EMTs and their cases full of gear had arrived in her living room.

Zoe smiled back at him, wishing things were different. Wishing the intense closeness they'd shared through the night had meant more than just friendship. That she hadn't imagined those words of endearment.

She reminded herself she was lucky to have such a good friend. And she had Molly.

Then Bree sailed into the room with Sam close behind her bearing a big pink stuffed elephant and a mischievous grin.

Zoe heard a knock on her door and pushed herself up straighter in the hospital bed. She smoothed down the standard issue hospital johnny and the flowered robe she'd brought with her, then did her best to finger comb her tangled curls. She looked awful, but there was nothing she could do about the tear stains on her face.

The doctor's visit and his report about Molly had been heartbreaking.

"Sorry it took me so long to get here," Porter said as he strode into the room. He wore a dark gray suit with a blue shirt and red power tie. His court attire.

The nurse who'd been making notes on Molly's chart looked up and gaped. Porter had that effect on women. He'd once had that effect on Zoe. At the moment, however, he felt like an unwelcome intruder.

But Zoe had promised Porter free access in Molly's life. Today could be no exception. The nurse looked from Porter to Zoe and back.

She's probably wondering what this Adonis could possibly see in me.

"Would you please bring me my baby?" Zoe asked the still-gaping nurse.

"Of course." The nurse tore her gaze away from Porter and lifted Molly from the bassinet. She settled Molly into the crook of Zoe's arm. "Buzz if you need anything." Then she left, shooting one last glance of appreciation in Porter's direction.

"So, this is my daughter?" Porter approached the bed and bent slightly to peer into Molly's sleeping face. "She's got your red hair. Isn't she a little small?"

"Would you like to hold her?" Zoe made a motion to lift Molly in Porter's direction.

"Ah, no. Not . . . I've never held a baby before," Porter admitted, backing up a step and looking a little anxious.

"She won't break," Zoe assured him. "Even if she is small."

"Is everything there?"

Zoe's chest squeezed tight in distress. "What do you mean, is everything there?"

"She's got ten toes and all the requisite

things?" Porter hovered uncomfortably. Zoe had never seen him so ill at ease, but her own anguish trumped any uneasiness he was feeling.

"She's got everything except —" Zoe hesitated. It had just been a screening. Maybe there was nothing wrong with Molly, and more tests would prove that, but . . . Porter was her father. He had a right to know. "She failed the hearing test."

Porter took another hasty step back as if hearing loss might be contagious. "I didn't know there was any deafness in your family."

Zoe cuddled Molly closer but wasn't sure just why. "Maybe she got it from your side?"

"Never!" Porter took another step toward the door.

"You can't catch it. She was born that way. If it turns out she *is* deaf, that is." Zoe was beginning to feel angry. This was not the reaction she'd expected. Especially not from Molly's father.

"There have never been any retards on my family tree." Porter took yet another step toward the door. "Even a partnership isn't worth giving my name to a handicapped halfwit."

Zoe felt the shock of his words clear down to her toes. She gasped for a breath and felt herself hyperventilating. She gazed down at her daughter and got herself under control. "Deafness has nothing to do with intelligence."

"Yeah? But there's no way to tell until it's too late to do anything about it."

"Do anything about it?" Zoe felt her lungs struggling for air again. What did he think one did about a handicapped child except love it all that much more and work a lot harder to make its life as easy as you could?

"I made a mistake listening to your father. I should never have come here."

"No, you shouldn't have."

Porter had his hand on the door.

"Wait!"

He hesitated but was clearly in a hurry to make his escape before she could force him to acknowledge his flawed child.

"Could you please hand me the plastic hospital bag in the closet?" Zoe shifted Molly to her other arm and pointed toward the closet. The bag held the clothes she'd been wearing when she arrived at the hospital.

Porter approached the closet, opened the door, and picked up the bag as if it, too, might be contagious. He dropped it on the bed next to Zoe and appeared about to wipe his hands on his trousers until he thought better of it.

Zoe had never seen this side of the man, and it disgusted her. Jake had knelt in the midst of all her mess, ignoring the condition of his own clothing while he held Molly with the reverence of a holy relic. He'd kissed her damp, cheesy little forehead with tears running down his cheeks and whispered words of love and thanksgiving. Porter didn't even want to touch his daughter all cleaned up and smelling sweet like only new babies can.

"You are a pretentious, self-important ass. I can't imagine what I ever saw in you." Zoe dug angrily through the plastic sack one-handed, hunting for the jeweler's box she'd asked the EMT to grab for her at the last minute when they were wheeling her out of the house.

"There!" She slammed the box into his hand. "If either Molly or I ever see you again, it will be too soon."

Porter jammed the ring into his trouser pocket and backed toward the door. "You won't," he bit out with angry disdain. "Have a nice life." Then he was gone.

Zoe drew Molly into a tight embrace. She should have felt some remorse for banishing Molly's father from her baby's life, but she didn't. They would be happier without him.

Molly was better off never knowing what a jerk her father was.

Even though Molly couldn't hear her, Zoe rocked both of them back and forth as she hummed "You Are My Sunshine" to her little girl, all the while realizing in the back of her mind, how close she'd come to making a horrible mistake.

When she'd calmed down enough to write without her hand shaking, Zoe settled the sleeping infant between her thigh and the bedrail. Then she reached for the folder the hospital lady had left with the birth certificate form to be filled out.

Molly Ann Callahan, Zoe began in careful block letters. Under father she wrote, *unknown.*

CHAPTER 37

Zoe's father arrived long after visiting hours were over, but in his usual persuasive style, had charmed his way past the head nurse anyway. He bent over the bassinet with a look on his face Zoe had never seen before. He gently touched Molly's soft baby cheek with one big finger and then stood gazing at her for a very long time. When he straightened and looked at Zoe over the expanse of room that separated them, he smiled awkwardly, then skirted the bassinet and lowered himself into the chair by Zoe's bed.

"I was wrong. I'm sorry."

Zoe gaped at her father in astonishment. Patrick Callahan never apologized for anything. Nor had Zoe ever heard her father admit that he had made a mistake.

"I was wrong about Porter Dubois. He's a better than average lawyer, and I'll give him a good reference, but I've asked him to look for another firm."

"You didn't have to do that for me." She wondered what Porter had said to excuse himself over the failed attempt to win Zoe's agreement to his marriage proposal. Or if he'd mentioned anything about his visit to the hospital earlier in the day.

"I didn't do it for you." Patrick harrumphed, then pursed his lips. "Well, maybe a little. But mostly, I did it for her." He pointed at the sleeping infant.

"What did Porter tell you?"

"It wasn't what he told me. It was what I overheard him telling someone else. He's woefully ignorant about the subject."

Zoe's father gazed across the room at the little bassinet for a long time, then finally back to Zoe. "How much do you know about my brother Sean?"

"Not a lot. I know he was killed riding his bicycle when he was just eighteen." Zoe wondered why they were discussing her long-deceased uncle.

"My brother was born deaf."

"Uncle Sean was deaf? How come I never heard about that before?"

Zoe was stunned by the information. Her father rarely talked about his only brother, but somehow his being deaf seemed like a detail that would have been mentioned at some point. Zoe knew only that Sean had been on his way to Stanford when he was killed by a drunk driver who'd lost control of his car.

"Sean had a little hearing, but not much," her father admitted. "He wore hearing aids when he was little, but learned to lip-read so well he didn't like to wear them most of the time. He was a straight-A student and an amazing athlete. He was never a *halfwit.*" Patrick spit out the last word in disgust. Then he leaned closer, resting his palms on the edge of Zoe's bed. "Is that precious little mite really going to be deaf?"

"We don't know for sure. She failed the screening, and I'll have to take her for a follow up in a month." Zoe felt tears build behind her eyes.

The doctor had assured her that one of the best Early Hearing Detection and Intervention programs in the country was just a few hours' drive away. Zoe had been given a whole packet of information to read, but the thought that her little girl might have to fight for equal treatment her whole life cut deep.

Porter's reaction had shocked Zoe completely, but she knew there would be prejudice to be overcome, even from people who meant well. She had envisioned a child who repeated everything she heard, chattered like Jake's twins, and loved music as much as Ava. She'd imagined lying on the beach at night holding hands with Molly while they pointed out stars and talked about anything that came to mind.

But Molly might never even hear Zoe's voice. Or the sound of the ocean. Or wind rushing through the trees, crowds cheering at a parade, the laughter of her best friends, or a lover whispering in her ear. It just seemed so overwhelmingly unfair.

"You see she gets the best doctors. Whatever it costs. You just have them send the bills to me." Zoe's father reached out to cover Zoe's hand with his own.

"I love you, Daddy." Zoe struggled to keep her tears in check.

"Yeah, well . . . She's my granddaughter." Patrick pushed himself out of the chair and returned to the bassinet. "She's my granddaughter," he repeated in a husky bluster. Then he picked the tiny infant up awkwardly, blankets trailing, and pressed her against his suit jacket with his cheek against her downy red head. "My little Molly."

Bree and Zoe's youngest sister Kelly showed up on the appointed day to take Zoe and Molly home from the hospital. Bree had remembered to stop by Zoe's house to get the car seat which she and Kelly had struggled to get installed in Bree's back seat, and that had made them late arriving. But eventually all the documents were signed, Molly was strapped into the carrier, and the carrier base checked out by hospital staff. Then they were on their way home.

As Bree turned into Awbrey Circle, Zoe gaped in stunned silence at the huge space where the big old tree had once stood. Only half of the original brick gatepost had been left standing, and even that tilted at a rakish angle. Bree pulled into Zoe's driveway and turned off the engine. Zoe climbed out of the car and turned to view the wreckage. Deep gouges marked where the tree had fallen, but the bulk of the massive trunk had been cut up and hauled away. A new pole had replaced the one the tree had taken down with it when it fell, and the electric wires and phone lines had all been re-attached, but the ground was still littered with twigs, splinters of branches, and leaves.

Zoe shuddered at the thought of Jake fighting his way through that mass of tossing broken foliage and downed power lines to get to her. He could have been seriously hurt, but he hadn't given a thought to his own safety. *He was more worried about me.* As the realization hit her, a surge of renewed hope flowed into her heart. Jake had said nothing about their relationship since the night he'd retreated in haste after telling her she wanted a fairy tale he couldn't give her.

But maybe it wasn't about her. Maybe he was just afraid of getting his heart trashed a second time. What if he had said *I love you* the night Molly was born in spite of his determination not to be vulnerable to the whims of a woman ever again?

If he didn't love her, why had he come back to check on her when he should have been reporting to the fire station? Why had he cried when Molly was born? And where had the tenderness come from when he'd kissed her afterward?

Maybe it was time to stop waiting for Jake to make the next move.

Then she remembered Porter's visit to the hospital. Although she couldn't imagine Jake ever reacting to Molly's disability the way Porter had, the whole scene had shaken her faith. What if the idea of dealing with a deaf child was too much for Jake to accept?

"Looks like a war went on here!" Bree commented, bringing Zoe's attention back to the surrounding scene.

In addition to the missing oak tree, a half-broken gatepost, and the piles of sawdust and wood chips on the ground, bits and pieces of broken toys, a fractured trash can, and other debris lay scattered around the cul-de-sac. Puddles of water still saturated the lawns, and the culvert was full to the brim.

The Cliffords had obviously not returned home yet, as the roof of their storage shed had been caved in by a big branch that still lay half-on and half-off the small building. A piece of their gutter hung at a crazy angle from the corner of the house, and the door under the porch where Danny kept his bike had been ripped off its hinges.

Two of Zoe's garage windows must have shattered, because they were now boarded up with pieces of plywood. Jake's doing, Zoe suspected. The flowers she'd planted around the mailbox were totally flattened, and the shrubs around the house needed serious pruning.

Jake's place appeared to have survived intact, but the twins' tree house would need shoring up before they could play in it again. A section of railing had been splintered off, and the struts supporting the platform looked precariously uneven.

"It sounded even worse than it looks," Zoe admitted as she gazed around in awe.

Leaving in the pitch dark on an ambulance stretcher with Molly cuddled in the crook of her arm and three big men trundling along at her side, Zoe hadn't been aware of the destruction. It had all passed in a blur. But now, looking at it in the daylight brought back memories of the tumultuous heaving of trees, pelting rain, and the thunder of the wind. And that had been after the worst of the storm had passed.

"I'll bet," Bree agreed. "Sam and I were down in Wilmington with my mom. There were branches down, but we never lost power."

Turning her back on the damage, Zoe bent to release Molly's carrier and lift her out of the car. Bree ducked into the car after her to wrestle with the car seat's base.

"It was nothing like the last hurricane, thank God." Kelly gathered up a clutch of shopping bags and butted the door shut with her hip. "Daddy sent his man over to clean up our yard, but it wasn't really that bad. He should have sent the guy up here."

"I still know how to use a rake," Zoe assured her sister as she carried her sleeping baby up the stairs.

As soon as she opened the door, the issue of her debris-strewn lawn was forgotten. All three dogs bolted free, then doubled back. They were torn between greeting Zoe and checking out the slumbering bundle in the carrier. Jet prodded Molly's blankets with an inquisitive nose, then glanced up at Zoe as if looking for an explanation. Hoover sniffed Molly cautiously, but thoroughly, then sat down to see what would happen next. Scotch *whuffled* softly as if aware that his usual loud barking might wake whatever it was. Zoe scratched each of the dogs behind their ears, then picked her way between them and into the house.

"Nothing like a welcoming committee," Kelly said, stopping to pat each furry head before following Zoe into the hall.

In spite of the enthusiastic canine welcome, Zoe felt the emptiness where Jake might have been if things were different. She parked Molly, still in her carrier, in a corner of the sofa to sleep undisturbed and offered Kelly and Bree something to eat. Ava had called the hospital before catching the school bus that morning to assure Zoe that there was food in the fridge and a coffee cake on the counter.

As they sat on stools around the kitchen island enjoying a hot cup of coffee and a slice of Ava's coffee cake, Zoe kept a smile on her face and tried to dismiss the fears that hovered just below the surface. Their father had apparently told Kelly about the hearing test and Porter's defection because neither woman mentioned either. But they were agog with interest about Molly's untimely arrival in the middle of the storm and Zoe's engaging neighbor's involvement in it.

"He's a fireman. At least he's a part-time volunteer fireman. And you told me he delivered a baby once before." Zoe directed that last bit at Bree. She still hadn't heard the whole of that story and curiosity was killing her.

"And it was just the two of you here together?" Bree ignored the hint. "How cozy."

"Gertie was howling outside, and the tree had come down, cutting off the electricity and my phone." Zoe felt a catch in her chest at the remembered panic when she realized she was going into labor and had only her dogs for company.

Kelly's face took on a suitably horrified expression. "Weren't you terrified?"

"I was scared out of my mind," Zoe admitted.

"But then came the hero from next door to the rescue," Bree said with satisfied relish.

"Bree, please," Zoe begged her friend to leave the issue of Jake alone.

Bree's grin faded, and she studied Zoe

with a serious expression. "Sorry. It just seemed kind of romantic. I didn't mean to embarrass you."

Kelly came to Zoe's rescue. "Being in labor hardly seems very romantic to me. Especially with the power out and no doctor at hand. I'd have been a basket case."

"I pretty much was," Zoe confessed. "I was lucky Jake thought to check up on me before reporting to the fire station. He wanted to go for help, but I kind of panicked and pleaded with him not to abandon me. So he stayed." Zoe deliberately turned away from the probing look in Bree's eyes. "As soon as he got a signal, Jake called nine-one-one, but by then Molly was already born. Once they managed to cut through the big tree, the EMTs arrived to take us to the hospital. The rest is all kind of a blur."

Except for the memory of Jake's tireless hands rubbing her back and the tenderness in his voice as he coached her through the contractions. Or how the word *babe* kept dropping into his encouraging patter. None of that had been lost in the shadowy memories of that stormy night.

Nor had the look in Jake's eyes just before he'd kissed her with Molly still suckling at her breast moments before the lights flickered back on, then off again. When Zoe closed her eyes, she could still remember what the pressure of his mouth had felt like on hers. And the feeling of utter connection they'd shared in that magical moment.

Zoe studied her plate, carefully loaded a bite of cake onto her fork, and brought it to her mouth.

"I guess Daddy turned into a marshmallow at the hospital." Kelly cut another sliver of cake and slipped it onto her plate. "This cake is delicious. You have to get the recipe for me."

Zoe mumbled in agreement as the memory of her father cooing and babbling nonsense to Molly at the hospital flashed into her head, pushing the images of Jake out, at least temporarily. Her father had still been there, comfortably ensconced in the rocker with Molly asleep in his arms when the night nurse came on duty at eleven and reminded him that visiting hours had been long since over. Zoe had never seen that aspect of her father before. Maybe he was mellowing, and he'd be a whole lot different as a grandfather.

"What are you grinning about now?" Bree helped herself to a second slice of cake as well.

"I was thinking about Daddy with Molly. He's going to spoil her rotten."

"All those bags in the living room?" Kelly gestured in the general direction. "They're all from Daddy. And believe it or not, he did his own shopping."

CHAPTER 38

Jake climbed the stairs to Zoe's porch with a crazy mix of hope, anticipation, and dread churning in his gut.

He'd seen the stunning ring in the box on Zoe's windowsill that promised a life of security and ease, and he'd backed off to give her time to consider it. But he'd never seen the ring on her finger. Nor had Porter brought Molly and Zoe home from the hospital. Jake didn't know if Porter had even visited *at* the hospital, but there'd been no sign of him at the house.

You've had your chance, Porter Dubois. And you blew it!

The ring in Jake's pocket wasn't nearly as impressive as the one Porter had offered her, but Jake hoped it would mean a whole lot more. He and Zoe had been through a lot together in the short time he'd known her. They'd shared more in five months than most people do in five years. Maybe in a lifetime. And he wanted to share the rest of that lifetime with her.

In spite of his conviction that friends with benefits never worked out, he'd come to realize he and Zoe complemented each other. She filled the holes in his life and in his heart, and he wanted desperately to fill the empty spaces in hers. He was pretty sure she'd already forgiven him for the pain he'd caused her. He was pretty sure she loved him even though she'd never told him so. The signs had been there for Jake to read all along, if only he'd been paying attention.

Quite aside from her willing response to his physical overtures, there had been her interest in his family right from the start. She'd helped him to see his daughter as a young woman instead of his little girl. And, even after he'd hurt Zoe with his careless words, she'd been there for him while he came to terms with Celia's move.

And what about the little Smurf fireman named Jake? Didn't that make some kind of statement about where her heart belonged?

Zoe's utter faith in him the night Molly was born was humbling. But it was also empowering. It had given him the courage to overcome his demons. And it gave him the courage to come here tonight to tell her he'd been wrong and ask her to marry him.

It gave him the hope that Zoe loved him as much as he loved her.

Jake took a deep breath and knocked.

And waited. And knocked a second time.

He knew she was home. Perhaps she was sleeping. He tried the door, which, as usual, was unlocked. He let himself into an empty hall and wondered where the dogs were. Out in the yard, maybe?

The sound of Molly crying came from the nursery upstairs. Then Jake noticed the muted sound of a shower running, which explained why Zoe had neither answered the door nor gone to check on her baby.

With quick, light steps, Jake took the stairs in an eager rush and walked into the dimly lit nursery. Molly lay on her back, her tiny mouth wide with angry cries. She waved her arms with impatient jerks, and she'd kicked off her blanket and pumped her feet in unison with the flailing arms.

"Hey there, kitten. Life's not that bad." Jake scooped her up and cradled her head against his shoulder. He patted her tiny bottom, and the loud cries diminished to hiccoughing sniffs as her mouth rooted around for the source of something to eat. Incredible how a baby so tiny and seemingly fragile could be so vibrant and full of the drive to survive.

"Sorry, can't help you there." Her wet little mouth connected with the bare skin of his neck and it tickled. He chuckled and bobbed up and down, hoping the movement would distract her.

It occurred to him that she might need changing, so he laid her on the padded dresser top and began unsnapping the little pink shirt she was wearing. Her eyes were wide as she gazed up at him with that solemn look only a newborn can manage. The diaper did need changing.

Jake murmured the nonsensical stuff people always tell babies while he tidied her up. She continued to stare at him with wide blue eyes. At least she'd stopped crying. When he finished his task, Jake dropped the diaper in the bucket beside the dresser, found a clean receiving blanket, and wrapped her up again.

As soon as he lifted her back into his arms, she began rooting again, and when she didn't find what she wanted, she began to whimper impatiently. The sound of the shower had stopped, so presumably Zoe would be out soon to take care of Molly's empty tummy. In the meantime . . . Jake moved Molly to his shoulder again and began singing to her.

■ ■ ■ ■

Toweling herself off, Zoe heard Molly begin to fuss and hurried to pull on her robe. Her hair needed brushing, but that would wait. Molly wouldn't mind if her mother looked like a wild woman. Zoe rushed toward the nursery.

The sight that greeted her made her heart jump into her throat. Jake, head bent against the top of Molly's downy red curls, was singing softly as he bobbed her up and down in his embrace. For a moment, Zoe just stood there, absorbing the sight of this big, wonderful man, his eyes shut, singing to her daughter as if it were something he did every day and thoroughly enjoyed.

Then he must have sensed Zoe's presence, and he looked up.

"She can't hear you." Zoe almost whispered the words, afraid of Jake's reaction.

He frowned. "She can't?"

Zoe shook her head and fought the tears that still threatened to flow whenever she thought about Molly's disability.

Jake pulled the baby closer, as if he could protect her from the bad news. The bobbing stopped, and Molly whimpered. Carefully, Jake lowered Molly away from his

416

shoulder and looked into her unhappy little face.

"Are you sure?" Jake asked, still looking at Molly with his big hands cradling her head and her squirming feet punching at his chest.

"Almost sure. They'll test her again in a month."

Jake tucked Molly's head beneath his chin and rocked her back and forth. When his gaze finally lifted to meet Zoe's, his eyes were filled with distress. "I'm so sorry."

Zoe fought even harder to keep her own tears in check when she saw the sheen in Jake's eyes.

"Poor wee Molly." Jake pressed his lips to Molly's temple, but she ignored his kiss in favor of hunting for milk.

"I think she needs you," Jake said, still seeming reluctant to give Molly up.

"It's past time, but she was sleeping so soundly, I thought I could sneak in a shower." Zoe held out her arms, and Jake transferred Molly over, stopping to wrap the blanket more snugly about her as he did so.

He stood, looking awkward and uncertain as Zoe lowered herself into the rocker.

Zoe began to pull her robe aside and then realized Jake was still watching her. In spite

417

of everything that had gone on the night Molly was born, despite the fact that Jake had already watched Molly nursing at her breast when she was just moments old, Zoe suddenly felt self-conscious. She looked up at him wordlessly.

"I'm sorry. I should . . . I'll go." Then he turned on his heel and left the room.

CHAPTER 39

Jake's footsteps quickly receded down the stairs. Then the front door opened and clicked softly closed again. Zoe wondered what Jake had come over for before she'd found him in Molly's nursery. He hadn't said. Or maybe she hadn't given him a chance to say. Zoe wished she hadn't been so squeamish about nursing Molly with him watching. They might never have been lovers, but there wasn't much of her he hadn't already seen. And she'd missed him.

Until his unexpected, heart-stopping appearance just moments ago, Zoe hadn't seen Jake since his visit to the hospital with all his girls the morning after Molly had been born. And he'd gone without a murmur of protest.

Zoe lifted Molly to her shoulder and patted her back until she got the desired burp. Then she settled her into the other arm to finish feeding her.

If only Jake had ignored Zoe's sudden shyness and stayed. She missed him. Missed watching him work as he puttered around her house fixing things. Missed conversing with him about everything from current events to the girls and their problems. Mostly, she missed the way he made her feel when he was close by.

Zoe closed her eyes and let her head drop back against the rocker. Seeing Jake standing in her nursery, calming her baby, had felt so right — so much the way she wished life could be. A tear dribbled down her cheek, and she brushed it away impatiently.

Now I'm just being a weepy new mother. If I want Jake in my life, I've got to talk to him. I've got to tell him how I feel and stop expecting him to be a mind reader. He doesn't even know I turned Porter down.

Molly's mouth let go of Zoe's nipple with a little pop, and her head lolled in a sated, contented sleep. Carefully, Zoe got to her feet and settled Molly into the crib. She turned on the little nightlight and left the room, planning to head downstairs and find something to eat herself. Then she remembered she'd never even combed her hair after stepping out of the shower, so she crossed the hall to her bedroom instead.

While Zoe dragged a brush through her

tangled, half-dry locks, the growing determination to talk to Jake returned. As she pulled on a clean pair of maternity jeans and one of the new blouses she'd bought to wear post baby, she debated calling Jake and asking him to come back. Then she made up her mind to just do it and returned to the bathroom to put on a touch of makeup. Just because he'd seen her at her worst, didn't mean she shouldn't take the time to look her best now.

Filling her lungs with a big breath of resolution, Zoe headed for the stairs.

Jake hadn't gone home after all. He was sitting on the bottom step with his forehead pressed into his palms.

Zoe hurried down the stairs and sank down next to him.

"I thought you went home. I heard the door." She wanted to reach out and touch him, but the taut set of his hunched shoulders made her hesitate.

"I started to go, but I changed my mind," he answered, his voice oddly strained. He clenched his teeth, and the muscles jumped in his temple.

"What's wrong, Jake?"

"Is it my fault?" Jake didn't look at her. He was afraid to hear her answer, but he had to know.

"Is what your fault?" Zoe laid a hand on his knee. The heat of it seeped through his jeans and into his skin, making him excruciatingly aware of how close she sat and how much he wanted to pull her into his arms.

"Molly's not being able to hear. Did I do something wrong when she was born?"

Zoe jerked her hand off his knee, and Jake's fears were confirmed. It *was* his fault. He should have gone for help. Qualified help. Zoe would eventually have forgiven him for leaving, but Molly would always be deaf. He was never going to forgive himself. The groan working its way up his windpipe turned his attempt to apologize into a whimper of denial. He wanted to swear, but he refused to allow himself even that avenue of release.

"Jake! Listen to me!" Zoe dropped onto her knees in front of him. She grabbed his wrists and pulled his hands away from his face. "It's not your fault. I don't know where you got that idea, but it's not."

"How do you know? I might have missed something. She was so perfect." Another cry of anguished denial filled Jake's chest with an ache he didn't think he could bear.

"My uncle was born deaf. It's something in her genes. It's not anything you did or didn't do." Zoe let go of Jake's wrists and wiped his face with her fingers.

Jake blinked, suddenly aware that he was crying. Again. What was it about this woman that wreaked such havoc with his self-control?

"Oh, Jake." Zoe stumbled to her feet and reached out to him. "It's not your fault. Whatever made you think it was?"

"I don't know. I just thought —" Jake's chest felt like it might implode. His heart rate shot into the red, and breathing seemed impossible. Pushing himself off the step, he pulled Zoe into his arms. He pressed his cheek against the top of her head and held on tight as the weight of guilt fell away. "I thought it might have been. And if it was you'd never forgive me. For that. Or anything else. Oh, God, Zoe. I've been such an ass."

Zoe slid her arms about Jake's waist and melted into him. Within her embrace, he felt the tension leave his body slowly.

"What am I supposed to forgive you for? And why should I think you're an ass?"

"I said some pretty stupid things. I should have apologized right off, but stuff kept getting in the way. Or maybe I've just been making excuses."

Zoe released her grip and pushed away to look up at him. "Apologize for what?"

423

"For hurting you. For all the awful things I said. I was wrong. And I'm sorry. And I love you."

Zoe gaped at Jake, her eyes wide and uncertain.

"I love you," he repeated. "I think I've loved you from the first moment I saw you. Only I thought it was something else. I thought I just wanted your body. Then we got to be friends, and I was afraid sex would just mess everything up. Please say you'll marry me."

Zoe remained wide-eyed and silent, but it looked like her mind was racing with thoughts.

"I hope you're not trying to think of a way to let me down easy." Jake held his breath waiting for her to respond. *Say something.* He'd made a mess of this proposal for sure. Instead of the carefully rehearsed apology and the romantic proposal he'd worked out on his way over here, he'd blurted out the first thing that came into his head. It hadn't been a proper apology. And it hadn't been a proper proposal either.

Abruptly, he dropped his arms and jammed his hand into his pocket. He sank onto one knee. Somehow he managed to pluck the ring free without dropping it in his anxious haste.

He swallowed hard. "I want to give you the fairy tale. Please marry me?" He reached for her hand and found her ring finger. "Please say you love me. At least a little. Enough to give me another chance."

Zoe gazed down at Jake into the warm gray eyes that had become so important in her life and realized she was gazing into the future she'd always dreamed of, but never quite believed would happen to her.

"Yes."

"Yes, what? I get another chance? You forgive me? Yes, you'll marry me? Or yes, you love me?"

"Yes to everything."

Jake's ring was still warm from his pocket as he it slipped onto her finger. And he gazed up at her with so much love in his eyes that it felt like she was falling.

"Catch me, Jake. Catch me and kiss me proper."

Jake surged to his feet again and hauled her into his arms. His kiss went far beyond anything proper, but as the fireworks exploded and a flood of emotions swept through her, Zoe decided falling was the most wonderful feeling in the world.

Epilogue

What's that big machine, Daddy? three-year-old Molly signed with agitated hands. Her huge blue eyes darted between Jake and the ultrasound equipment. A worried frown creased her little forehead.

Jake dropped to one knee beside Molly and signed back. *It's the funny camera I told you about. The one that will let us see the babies inside Mommy's tummy.*

"We forgot to tell her it was a really *big* camera," Jake told Zoe, as she settled herself onto the padded table in her obstetrician's sonogram room.

Where do we see the pictures? Molly asked, the frown turning more inquisitive than worried. *Will we get one to take home with us? I want to show it to Lynn and Lori. Can we take a picture to show Grandma Celia? And Daddy, we need one to send to Ava, too. She will be so excited she will want to come home right away. How can the cam-*

era see the babies? Will it hurt Mommy? Her little hands flew fluently through the questions, even as her gaze zipped about the room, taking in all the intriguing paraphernalia.

Jake answered all her questions just as fluently. Molly was such a bright little girl. Full of questions. Full of a zest for life and every adventure it brought her way. Deafness hadn't seemed to slow her down one bit. Jake thought she was way smarter than the average three-year-old, and a lot braver, too. Of course, he could be prejudiced. He felt that way about all his daughters, but Molly was special.

Every once in a while he remembered the incredibly stupid remark he'd once made to Zoe about Molly not being his. He'd been so wrong. Molly had been his from the moment he'd held her, bawling and wet and beautiful.

He'd been wrong about a lot of things in his life, but he had Zoe to keep him from blundering into dumb mistakes now. She was the wisest, most loving woman he'd ever known.

Zoe had been right about how Celia would flourish in the assisted living facility. Celia no longer remembered Jake's name or where he fit into her life, but she never failed to greet him with the same loving smile and fierce hug. She didn't remember the girls' names, or Zoe's either, but it never seemed to matter to any of them. Visiting Celia and the rest of the crew at Safe Haven was just a part of their lives, one that everyone had adjusted to, even himself.

Zoe had been pretty smart about teenage girls, too. Smart about what Ava needed from her father, anyway. Travis was a distant memory, and Ava was a bright, confident young woman with a healthy attitude toward boyfriends and life. She was in her first year of college and had met a new young man who seemed pretty special. Jake had liked him when Ava brought him home for a weekend visit, but as she'd gotten ready to return to school, she'd hugged her dad and told him he was still her best boyfriend. At least for now.

Jake simply couldn't imagine his life without Zoe in it. He didn't want to imagine life without her. His father had been right, too. A man could be married to his best friend. Jake bent to kiss his guiding star, then pulled a chair close to her side.

Come sit with me, he signed to his youngest daughter as he sat down so Molly could scramble into his lap.

"Want to place any bets?" Zoe reached

out to slip her hand into Jake's. "I hope you aren't going to be disappointed if we get two more girls."

Jake leaned forward to plant a kiss on Zoe's brow. "Never," he promised. "If they're as pretty as their mother and as clever as Molly, what's not to love?"

But in spite of his glib assurances, he felt the tightening of longing in his gut. It would be nice to have a son. Not that he would love a son more than his girls, but still . . .

"Good morning!" The technician pushed her way into the room carrying an open laptop. "You ready to check out the twins?" Then she noticed Molly sitting on her father's lap. "And who is this young lady?" She extended her hand toward Molly.

"This is my daughter, Molly," Zoe began. "She can't —"

"Oh, that's right. Doctor Whalen told me." The woman squatted to Molly's level and began signing, *I'm Cathy. What's your name?*

Molly grinned and told Cathy in a sturdy, confident voice. "I am Molly Ann Cameron." Saying it out loud was something she practiced regularly.

Cathy smiled and signed again. *That's a lovely name for a very smart little girl.* Then she straightened.

"You know American Sign Language," Zoe asked, sounding surprised.

The technician busied herself connecting the laptop to the machine. "We had a deaf patient my first year on the job. Learning the basics turned out to be the easiest way to converse with her."

Cathy seated herself on a chair at Zoe's other side and began applying jelly to the transducer. "Do you want to know the sex?" Cathy paused to look at Zoe then glanced at Jake with her eyebrows raised in question.

"I was never any good at waiting to open my presents at Christmas. I don't think I could last until April not knowing," Zoe answered.

"Me either," Cathy chuckled as she pushed Zoe's jersey up to bare her belly and began moving the transducer over Zoe's distended stomach.

Jake leaned closer, clutching Molly against his chest and squeezing Zoe's hand.

Two heads appeared, facing each other as if whispering together. He realized he was holding his breath and let it out slowly. *As long as they're healthy,* he reminded himself. *It will be fine if they're girls. I love my girls.* He hugged Molly closer.

"Well?" Zoe asked.

"One of them is sucking its thumb." Cathy pointed to the screen.

"Amazing," Jake breathed in awe. More than amazing. His heart swelled as he gazed at the two little lives created by the love he and Zoe shared.

The technician moved the transducer, and the view changed. Cathy pointed to a spot on the large monitor. "Hard to tell about either one from this angle."

Jake had no idea what he was looking at. The technician adjusted the view again, prodded Zoe's belly, moved the transducer, and wiggled it tight against Zoe's skin. She told Zoe to roll over and face Jake.

"Gotta be boys!" Zoe heaved herself onto her side. "Men never tell you anything unless you drag it out of them." She winked at Jake and blew him a kiss.

Molly's head swiveled from Jake to Zoe to Cathy and back. The worried frown had returned.

Nothing to worry about, Cathy signed. *We just want to take a look from the other side.*

Everything's okay, sweetie, Jake added, giving Molly a quick squeeze. Then he reached out to reclaim Zoe's hand.

Zoe held her other hand up, fingers crossed.

"Aha! Now that's better." Cathy pointed

431

at the screen again and then looked at Jake with a grin stretched across her face. "I hope you know what you're getting yourself into. Twin boys can be a handful!"

HONEY SPICE SNAPS

Jake's favorite cookies from the kitchen of his mother, Sandy Marshall Cameron

Cream together: 1 cup firmly packed brown sugar and 3/4 cup shortening

Blend in: 1 unbeaten egg and 1/4 cup honey

Add and stir well: 2 1/4 cups flour, 1-1/2 tsp baking soda, 1/2 tsp salt, 1 tsp ginger, 1 tsp cinnamon and 1/4 tsp cloves.

Chill, then roll into walnut size balls, dip first in water, then in sugar. Place on cookie sheet sugar side up.

Bake 12–15 minutes at 350°

ACKNOWLEDGMENTS

Although he will never know it, I owe a great deal of gratitude to my high school English teacher, Fred Keyes, who spent two years teaching me the joy of creative writing, and the magic of words.

Sincere thanks to my editor Deborah Smith for her patience and care with this book, but even more for reaching out and taking the time to find out what I was working on at a time when my life had been so shattered by tragedy that I couldn't pull myself together to make a pitch. Thank you also to Deb Dixon for seeing promise in me and for designing the perfect cover in spite of my dithering.

Thanks also to my wonderful circle of writing friends: Elizabeth Sinclair for painstaking critique, Nancy Quatrano for helping me to keep the conflict in sight and cheering when I got it right, and Dolores Wilson and Vickie King for their unselfish interest

435

and encouragement.

And to my children with love: Lori, Alex, Rebecca, Bobbi, Noel and Jeff — my biggest cheerleaders.

ABOUT THE AUTHOR

Skye Taylor has been a member of Romance Writers of America since 1995 and of the Ancient City chapter in St. Augustine, Florida, for the last four and a half years, where she has served as secretary, conference chair and treasurer. Her publishing credits to date include several nonfiction essays about life as a Peace Corps Volunteer and one mainstream political intrigue, *Whatever It Takes,* published in June 2012. Although she has received several queries about a possible sequel, most of her writing has been romance and women's fiction and it is in those genres she wants to concentrate her future efforts.